THE

OF

THERE ARE NO HEROES
LEFT IN NEVERLAND

JULIET
LOCKWOOD

Also by the author

FATES

Fatewoken

VILLAINS

The Legacy of Villains
The Ruin of Starlight

For Ms. Darby, who might not remember me.
And for my mum. Happy birthday.

Contents

Chapter 1

"Never step aboard the Jolly Roger unless it's to pledge allegiance to the fearsome Captain Hook."
- THE MOSTLY ACCURATE TRAVELER'S GUIDE TO THE ANCIENT WORLD OF NEVERLAND

The men hiding in her bedroom had been sent by her father to kidnap her. She should have realized it had been too long—a full week by her count—without an attempt on her life. She'd clearly grown sloppy.

Sloppier still when they managed to wrestle her to the ground, wrap thick rope around her wrists, and march her above deck. She hadn't even had time to reach for the knife that she always kept in her boot.

All the while, there was something crawling under her skin.

Her father had always told her that she had star-stuff in her veins, but this felt more like...anticipation. Nerves, maybe. It clawed at her first with tiny pincers of fear, and then with shame at the fact that she'd even deign to feel fear in the first place.

The daughter of Captain Hook did not feel fear.

Not even when she stood with her toes hanging off the edge of the gangplank. Jo steeled her emotions into fierce points and faced the dark, unyielding water below as it lapped at the ship's belly like a starving dog. She knew that when it got its hands on her it would be with icy fingers, and wished they were nearer to the lagoons where the water was always warm and inviting—although dealing with the Merfolk would not be a very even trade off.

Behind her, jeers from the pirate crew who had tied the rope on her wrists so tight that they had begun to lose circulation. She wanted to look back, catch any of their eyes and show them her fiery determination, but she was afraid she'd lose her balance on the wobbling plank. And falling was worse than jumping. She'd always been told a move made with purpose was a hundred times better than one made by accident.

So, with an intake of air that filled her lungs to the brim, she leapt, her elegant dive captivating her audience for only a moment before she disappeared beneath the waves.

Dust that's cold! Jo thought, pumping her legs to keep from sinking like a stone into the sea. No one knew what manner of beasts slumbered on the ocean floor, and she wasn't eager to find out any time soon.

Jo swung her arms beneath her legs, fighting both the current trying to drag her down and the pain in her shoulders, so that her wrists were in front of her. She set her teeth into one of the rope's frayed edges and pulled until it gave way, freeing her arms at the final moment before she ran out of air.

She kicked upwards towards the beckoning sun and broke her head over the waves with a tremendous gasp. She reached blindly for a net she knew was floating nearby.

Shaking, cold fingers latched onto the ropes and she was hauled up. Then: strong hands at her arms pulling her back onto the ship.

"You did it, Jo!"

"Heck of a performance kid! Sorry for tying the rope so tight, Capn's orders."

"You might have even beat your Pa's time!"

She grinned at her crew—pirates all, and more loyal than anyone else in Neverland by far. Some short, some tall, some fair, and some weathered. Grizzled men and hardened women who had worked for the captain for ages, though she never knew quite how long. Time worked differently in Neverland.

She did know that some had been with her father since the beginning, since before the Merfolk War, which could've been five, ten, or one hundred years past. They had all aged slowly and carefully, like rum in a barrel. Those under 18, such as Jo herself, always aged at what seemed to be a normal pace until they reached adulthood; it was then that Neverland's magic would leach into them and slow everything down.

There was only one group on the island that didn't age at all, and they sure as dust weren't on her ship.

"Move aside!" barked a familiar voice as the thump of leather boots on wooden steps cut through the excited chatter. "Let me see her!"

The crowd parted without question for Captain Hook.

Tall, broad of shoulder, with dark curls looped into a ponytail at the nape of his neck, the captain was always as put together as one could be while living at sea. His greatcoat and feathered hat set him apart from his crew, with their simple trousers and tunics, but it was his hand that truly gave him the most ferocious, well-known appearance in all of Neverland.

Or, really, his lack of hand.

He swung his silver hook wide as he approached.

"So, you got free."

"Of course," she answered, tilting her chin up.

"But they caught you unaware, they managed to tie you up in the first place."

She grimaced. "A minor error. It won't happen again."

He hummed, looking over her sopping wet form and taking in the straight posture of her back, the unflinching look in her eye.

"Well done, Jolie," he said finally, lips quirking ever so slightly upwards.

"I passed your test?"

He nodded, "Like any good Hook should. I'll have to think of something more challenging for your next one."

She rolled her eyes at that. Of course there would be a next one. There always was with him. "You'll miss the retirement boat if you dally any longer on naming me your successor," she murmured, too quiet for the crew to hear, though most had gone back to their duties. These tests happened often enough that they'd become a part of everyone's daily schedule. "You're not getting any younger, and Neverland's not getting any safer."

He patted the top of her head with his human hand and looked away.

They'd had this conversation more and more over the years, each new wrinkle by her father's eye a testament to his waning strength. On the surface he appeared somewhere just north of 50 years old, but time did what it liked in Neverland. He had been captaining the ship for the last 200 years, and Jo had only joined him for the past 17, most of which he had spent training and testing her for the day that she would take up his mantle.

And now, that time approached. It wouldn't do to have the captain of the ship be seen as weak, and Jolie wanted her father to be safe, above all else.

"Smee!" he barked to his second in command, the bumbling man always waiting just beyond his eyeline. "Get Jolie a towel, and then get my study ready." He looked down, burning eyes no longer glinting with pride but instead drawn back in secrecy. "There's something we need to discuss."

Chapter 2

"Sea legs are non-transferable between the various bodies of water."
- THE MOSTLY ACCURATE TRAVELER'S
GUIDE TO THE ANCIENT WORLD OF NEVERLAND

The way down into the bowels of the ship was a familiar one.

The Jolly Roger was made up of wooden planks that hid secrets behind every door, and Jo knew them all.

They passed by a teal one that opened up directly onto a puffy cloud that liked to follow the ship's passage through the water. They took a left turn at a pale yellow door with no knob—which held either a wylde-beast or a bouquet of daisies, depending on the day.

Of course, there were the crew bunks, which Jolie hardly ever slept in, preferring the gentle rocking of her hammock above deck to the raucous shouts and laughs of her mates below. Plus, she always liked to keep a small amount of distance between her and the other pirates.

She would, after all, be their captain one day, and while they treated her like family now it wouldn't be the case when it was her decisions that lined their coffers with coin and their bellies with fish.

If that eventuality ever came. Jo side-eyed her father as he strode down the halls, the ship's ceilings lengthening for him as he walked and shrinking back down to normal size again as they rounded corner after corner, until finally they stopped by another door.

Her favorite door.

Once it had been white but, thanks to Jo's incessant need for stimulus coupled with a box of enchanted crayons she had bartered from a seagull, it had been decorated in colorful designs over the years: the Jolly Roger sailing the high seas; Jolie and her father holding up a massive catfish that they'd caught, with the tiny mousefish that *it* had caught still in its mouth; Jo's favorite sword, rendered in brilliant gold and silver crayon.

There were miniatures of fairies too, annoying remnants of the past that she could never scrub off, the door just plain wouldn't let her.

Across the top, emblazoned in metallic red ink that shone even in the darkened underbelly of the ship:

Captain's Quarters.

She watched as her father stuck his hook into the lock and turned it once to the left and twice to the right, before it popped open and beckoned them inside.

It was one of Jolie's favorite places in the entirety of Neverland.

Her father's room was a veritable treasure trove, a museum of his adventures and exploits.

There were stacks of coins on most surfaces and glittering jewels spilling out of open treasure chests they'd rescued from the bottom of the sea. The jewels usually disappeared after a month or two and the crew had to go haul it from the ocean floor again, but they made for nice decorations while they lasted. Stuffed birds and magical animal heads bore tribute to the many hunts Hook had taken, and weathered maps with X's marked the spot for hunts yet to come. There were bottled potions and mugs of amber liquid that Jo was never allowed to sniff.

She resisted the urge to go straight to his weapons rack as she followed her father inside, happy instead to stare at the collection of sabers and daggers, of katanas and scythes. Some went back to the before ages, some he'd rescued from battlefields during the Merfolk Wars, and some still had been bought from the traveling merchants who'd once roamed the lands.

Jo's favorite was a slender saber with a gold pommel that she knew from experience fit perfectly in her hand and was quick and deadly when raised towards an enemy—though she had yet to put it into practice against anything more terrifying than a practice dummy or Smee, and even then only when her father was generous enough to let her borrow it.

He was proud of his accumulated wealth and often joked about wanting to drift out to sea with it upon his death bed, though Jo knew the gold-grubbing crew would never let that happen.

A door to the left led to his private chambers, where a plush four poster bed laid in wait for its sole nighttime companion.

And, even though it felt like they were below deck, the wide window located just behind the captain's desk opened up to the beautiful Sea of Skulls. She could even see Skull Rock staring at her just beyond the crest of the horizon, its dark eyes always following the Jolly Roger's trail.

Jolie stared back as she took a seat opposite her Hook, who rummaged through his desk drawers before pulling out a tattered piece of folded up paper with a small "Aha!"

Jo held her breath. Could it be the deed to the Jolly Roger? Was he finally about to pass his legacy on?

Before she could ask, Smee toddled into the room with a plate balanced in one hand, a stack of cups in another, and a worn leather skein of wine between his lips. "Arrgh orr vyye?" he mumbled.

"Fairy's dust Smee, we can't understand a thing you're saying!" Captain Hook snapped. "Set it down here, good fellow."

Smee nodded, bits of wine sloshing out from the skein as he did, and set down the plate—which Jo saw had smoked fish, crackers, hunks of bread, and a sliced apple—and the cups. "Thank you sir. Uh–wine, sir?"

Hook nodded as Smee poured the dark red liquid into the glass.

"I'll take some–"

"Just water for her," her father interrupted, giving her a sharp look. "You've got half a year to go before your 18th, Jolie. Don't waste away your youth pining for wine of all things."

She frowned and crossed her arms. "Am I to believe that you never had a drop of wine before your 18th birthday?"

He laughed and raised his glass, a motion that Jo begrudgingly copied with the glass of tepid water Smee shoved into her hands. "What are we cheersing for?" she asked.

Hook took a long, deep pull from his glass, sopping up the spilled wine from his curled mustache with his breast pocket handkerchief, before saying: "I've had a brilliant idea."

Jo's eyes lit up. She leaned forward in anticipation as her father opened the folded piece of parchment far slower than Jolie liked.

His smile was wide and bold as he finally spread out the paper—which was, in fact, a charcoal portrait—on the desk, and said:
"Peter Pan has called for a truce, and I am going to agree."

Chapter 3

"If you find yourself caught between the conflict of Pan vs Hook, climb the nearest soulfruit tree and hope they don't see you."
- THE MOSTLY ACCURATE TRAVELER'S GUIDE TO THE ANCIENT WORLD OF NEVERLAND

Jo wasn't sure whether her father would pick up more on the shock, the disappointment, or the confusion on her face, but she hoped it was at least one of the three. Dust forbid he thought he saw agreement in her eyes.

He sat in smiling silence as Jo pulled the portrait closer, frowning.

Peter Pan.

Ageless, magical, wicked Peter Pan. His hair, wild as a thorn bush and the color of bright golden sand, sat atop of a charming boyish face that the artist had nearly rendered in all of its beauty. A sly smile.

Slightly pointed ears. A smattering of freckles across a sun bronzed face. On the surface, he looked not a day older than herself.

But the artist hadn't gotten his eyes right.

Jo had never seen Pan in the flesh, but she'd heard plenty of stories, and they all told of the cold wickedness in his eyes. He would weave impossible, deadly magic around you and not feel a lick of remorse, as long as the results entertained him.

She'd even heard stories of him kidnapping people from other worlds, tempting them with glitter and starlight and candy and games, only to trap them within the forest of his frightening imagination outside of his castle. Illusions of one's greatest fears come to life, reality and nightmares mixing so that you didn't know which was which.

Him and his damnable Lost Boys were the reason that they had lost half of the crew over the years, later finding that their bodies had been tossed to the mermaids for feasting, or worse...

She stole a look at her father's hooked hand.

No. This would be a very bad idea, and she told him as such.

"It's been too long that we've fought a tireless war against each other," her father sighed, tapping on the parchment. "And while I grow old, albeit slowly, Pan has never aged. He is strong and cunning and bursting to the brim with magic, and he always will be. It's time to end this."

"So let's destroy him!" Jo shot up from her seat. "We can't just bend over and bow down to his tyranny. How many pirates have died because of the traps in the forest? How many bodies?"

He made to interrupt but Jo continued. "Or if not bodies, how many have lost their minds to his illusions? Him and that dust-for-saken *fairy*," she sneered the word. Puffs of rage blew from her cheeks. "What about mother?"

"Don't speak to me of your mother," he snapped. "She would have agreed with me."

She was momentarily cowed at his tone. Her father was nearly always brusque, always to the point, always wanting something. But he was hardly ever mad, not with her. Bringing up her mother—his wife—was a low blow, she knew, but her filter had never been great when it came to the things she disagreed with. And Jolie Hook tended to disagree with a lot that her father did.

"You really think he wants peace?" she said after a pause. "That he's not lying? No, I won't have any part in this lunacy."

Her father gave her a calm sort of look that one might give a child throwing a temper tantrum, and Jolie withered under its intensity. She could stand up to a raging battalion of Lost Boys, but her father? Not a chance.

"You don't have to take part in it. You just need to watch the ship while I'm gone."

"While you–you're leaving? When?"

"We'll set out in the morning. I've already sent Pan a message to meet us at the Hangman's Tree."

"Could you have picked a more foreboding setting?"

"Jolie," he said, voice stern. "You are right that we have lost many people to this futile never-ending feud. And so has Pan. He will want a truce."

"He's a trickster, father," she hissed, not understanding where this bleeding heart of his was coming from. "He will say anything he can to catch you off guard!"

He smiled. "You are mistaken if you think my guard won't be up. If he tries to pull anything..." He flashed his silver hooked hand so that it glinted in the light.

Pan had been the reason her father wore the hook in the first place, having lost his hand during one of the early battles in the war. He was the reason her mother was gone.

"This is a fool's errand," she said finally.

"As your father, I understand that you're scared," he sighed, gently brushing a thumb over her outstretched hand. "But as your captain," he continued, his face turning to stone, "you best lock that fear into a chest and watch it sink to the bottom of the sea. Hook's are not afraid."

"But I–"

"End of discussion," he snarled, banging his hook on the desk between them. "I will hear no more from you until after I return."

Jo's face flushed with anger and embarrassment at the swift dismissal.

She wanted to reach out and hold Pan's portrait above one of Hook's candles, watch the flames greedily eat at his charcoal picture. Or maybe she would knock over her father's wine and smile when the red liquid spilled across her enemy's face like blood. She wanted to say and do many things that were unbecoming for a woman raised to be a leader, a ruler, a stoic face of determination and strength.

So instead she sneered a "Yes, *captain*," turned on her heels, and slammed the door shut behind her. The ship groaned its discontent and she muttered an apology, patting one of the wooden beams as she walked by.

If Peter Pan laid a single finger on her father, she'd put an end to him, his Lost Boys, and his psychotic fairy sidekick once and for all.

Chapter 4

*"Neverland is not the only world, but it is perhaps one
of the most magical."*

J olie was halfway through trying to convince the moon to toss her
down some constellation-cake when Damien found her.

"Which Lost Boy took a knife to your pie?" he asked, nudging her
over in her hammock so that he could slide in beside her. "And where
can I get a slice?"

Jo rolled her eyes as she made room. "I think we're getting too big
to share this bed much longer Damien."

"I am, anyways," he grinned, flexing one of his ever-growing biceps
and giving it a kiss. "Pretty soon I'll be able to lift an entire whale and
toss it clear out of the sea."

Jo suppressed a snort, aware that night had fallen across the deck of
the Jolly Roger and most everyone was asleep now, content to let the

ship steer itself for a while. "And then you'd rescue the whale, give it a nice pat on the head, and apologize for bothering it."

Damien shrugged, his shoulders rustling against the canvas fabric. "We can't all be the next ruthless pirate queen."

"Yes, well it looks like my father is going to get himself killed any day now so that title might be up for grabs sooner than we think," she chewed out, a cloud darkening her features.

She had to find a way to convince him that his idea was flimsy at best, and dangerous at worst. Tie him to a tree? No, he'd free himself in mere seconds. Ask to attend the meeting? Not unless she wanted to find *herself* tied to a tree. She looked back to the stars for help, but the shining buggers did nothing but twinkle at her.

"I heard," Damien said with a twist of his lips. "He's trying to form a truce with Pan? Even after he–"

"Does everyone know about this hairbrained scheme now?"

Damien shrugged. "Dad told me. Said I need to be the first to know about any ship happenings if I want to be a good boatswain one day."

Jo wasn't the only one with a paternal legacy to follow. Damien was meant to take up Smee's position as soon as Captain Hook stepped down. A boatswain always followed their captain, even into retirement, so once Jo put on that feathered hat for the first time, the Jolly Roger would also see itself with a new second in command.

And truly she could do much worse than Damien. He was kind, as kind as one could be while still being part of the crew at least, and he was mostly brave, except when it came to fighting.

He'd also been her only friend since childhood—ever since a particularly bad incident with stink sap had stuck them together for two days.

"You'll be the best second-in-command Neverland's ever seen," she nodded. "Better even than the infamous no-armed boatswain Ashwar who helped steer his ship using only his legs."

"I'll be a better second-in-command than that trollop Tinkerbell!"

"Yes, you—" Her words faded mid-sentence. Tinkerbell was Peter Pan's right-hand woman. She was as ferocious as she was beautiful, and her name was often spoken with the hushed reverie of fearful respect. Tinkerbell was known as the best assassin across the land—Jo knew that better than anyone. I swear on the Jolly Roger itself that if that winged snake lifts a finger against father I'll feed her to an angry spine-fish."

For a moment she pictured it: the brute tumbling head over feet into the lagoon below, where a 15-foot fish with razor sharp fins was waiting to impale her. She'd have to clip her wings first, to ensure that they wouldn't help her do anything except for leave a pretty corpse.

"Sorry Jo, poor choice of words," Damien winced, patting her lightly on the back of the hand. "But your father wouldn't be having this meeting without a backup plan, would he? You don't think he's not going to have a dagger up each sleeve, and another in his boot for good measure?"

"I think we can't underestimate any of the enemies that live in the Neverwoods."

"If you're afraid—"

"Don't say that word," she interrupted with a glare. "It's not fear, it's reality. We've been fighting with the Lost Boys since the Merfolk War." She gave him a pointed look. "Don't forget that he was the reason we got swept up into that conflict in the first place." For a moment, a fuzzy, hazy memory flashed across her mind.

"Mother? Mother!"

She blinked it away.

It had been a decade, but she'd never allowed that wound to heal. She'd let it fester, let it rot, until the day came when she could kill Peter Pan and move on. Now that day looked like it might never arrive.

"He's sneaky," she continued, "and he's somehow wrangled the forest's magic under his thumb. I wouldn't be surprised if that slippery shadow of his sneaks off during the meeting to come slaughter us all while we wait."

"No shadow is infiltrating our ship," Damien replied. "Magical or not."

Jo sighed and craned her neck back up towards the stars. She scanned the sparkling canopy, looking for one in particular.

Unlike the rest of the stars, which liked to spin and swirl and move about the universe at their leisure, the second star to the left was always in its proper place. Dependable, loyal, and forever there to guide her out of dark places. Much like Damien, though without the constant need to sing sea shanties and complain about the lack of vegetarian food on board.

Her mother had once told her that the stars listened to wishes, and if you wished hard enough they just might grant them.

I wish that this all turns out fine, in the end.

Jolie waited. She wasn't sure what exactly for, but she hoped that the star would give her some sort of sign that things would be okay, that her anxieties and cynicisms were nothing more than the by-product of a life earned through survival and strategy.

After all, agreeing to a meeting in the name of peace only to lull her enemies into putting down their guard? It sounded exactly like something she would do. The star maintained its steady brilliance, though, giving her neither a good sign nor a bad.

"I hope you're right, Damien," she said finally, reaching up and tweaking his big nose playfully. "I'd hate to have to murder Peter Pan."

He snorted. "Don't lie, you'd love the opportunity."

Jo's vicious, toothy grin was her only reply.

Chapter 5

"Rum is half the cost of water, and twice as tasty."
- THE MOSTLY ACCURATE TRAVELER'S
GUIDE TO THE ANCIENT WORLD OF NEV-
ERLAND

"Y ou're really doing this then."

Not a question, there was no doubt that her father was preparing for a trip to shore. On his back, his most luxurious coat, the one with the split tail and the ruffled hem—the coat he only wore to meet with important people. At his side, his saber, polished and freshly sharpened, and tucked into its holster.

But it was the condescending pat on her head as she watched him drain the last dregs of his morning rum that sold it to her.

"You'll understand later, my dear, that peace is a far greater thing than war."

She rolled her eyes, pushing his hand away. "I understand that, father. What I don't understand is why you think Pan wants peace in the first place? He thrives on chaos, his dark magic demands it."

He looked at her with eyes that had seen more things than she'd ever dream of. More things than were in the history books. "Come," he said. "Come sit with your old man before he heads off."

"You're hardly old," she chewed, but followed him to the settee nonetheless.

"I'm hardly young, either. Otherwise you'd be calling me a Lost Boy," he chuckled, then stopped when he saw her blank face. "Alright, poor joke. But what I mean is that I've been in this world a long, long time. Long enough that I still remember what peace felt like, how Neverland glowed when things were at their most comfortable."

He paused, continued. "How the double rainbows quadrupled in size until the entire sky was washed in color. There used to be berries so golden that the animals who ate them shone in the dark. And the sea...she was always kind, never a storm in her skies when we sailed." He put his hand—his real hand—on her knee. "I miss those times. Perhaps this liaison with Pan is a trap, you could be right. Or perhaps it is the beginning of something new. And what a fool I'd be to not try and grab that."

Jolie frowned. She was too young to have experienced what her father was telling her. Too young to remember nearly anything except for fighting and battles and death. She'd had a few good years, when she was younger, but those memories were misted over now. Was it really worth such a gamble?

"A real captain doesn't surrender to the enemy," she said, finally, dragging her eyes back to meet her father's. They were clouded over in disappointment. "Not when the enemy has already stolen so much."

"This is not a surrender. When you are ready to be a captain yourself, you'll see that."

***

Jo hadn't been able to mutter more than a stoic goodbye to her father as he descended into the longboat bound for the nearby shoreline. Hook still didn't seem to understand her disapproval of the meeting, but the tender pat on the head as he passed by almost hinted at an apology, or at least a smidgen of care.

"I will see you for dinner, Jolie," he said. "Have the cook prepare a wild boar, I suspect we will be celebrating a new era of peace."

"Go get 'im Captain!"

"Make Pan back off!"

"Yeah!"

Jo rolled her eyes. Clearly the crew all had his back. But why wouldn't they? Their captain had never steered them wrong. It was a special thing, the trust between the crew and Captain Hook.

"When you are ready to be a captain yourself, you'll see that."

Her father didn't think she was ready yet. Did the crew? The fact that some of them had helped change her diapers or had wiped away her tears after a childhood nightmare could either reinforce their approval of her or remind them that, all in all, she was nothing more than a kid in pirate's clothing.

She watched from the main deck, along with the rest of the crew, as Hook, Smee, and a handful of their best pirates loaded into the boat. The captain drew his sword, thrust it into the sky, and roared "To a new age!"

Everyone copied except for Jo. She merely stared and tried not to grind her teeth as the boat was lowered in the water below. It was bound for the beach some two kilometers away and, beyond that, a short jaunt to the Hangman's Tree where the meeting was to be held.

The irony of the location was not lost on her.

Whether it was Hook or Pan, she couldn't shake the feeling that someone was going to be swinging from its branches by the day's end.

Jolie stayed in her spot, leaning against the Jolly Roger's mast, for the better part of twenty minutes as the crowd around her dispersed. Even though the ship's captain was off-deck, there were still sails to rig, ropes to tie, and fat, gluttonous stowaway mice to chase down.

She nodded to Damien as he ambled off to go check the ledgers. His father was one of the participants in the suicide meeting, but it didn't seem to faze her workaholic friend. If anything, Damien loved it when he left, because it was the only time that he could really shine and show his worth without his dad breathing down his neck correcting him.

Once, Jo had caught Damien with puffy red eyes after he'd been berated about his lack of precision when rolling up a set of newly acquired maps. She'd taken him downstairs, to where she knew the crew stored their rum, and they'd toasted to their legacies until the Jolly Roger unceremoniously dumped them out of the liquor room and into their beds.

Damien had been terrified that his father would find out, but Jolie had taken the brunt of the punishment for both of them, claiming that Damien had found her drinking and had only been trying to get her back to her bunk safely.

A tongue lashing and two weeks of latrine duty had been worth it to spare him the disappointing look, and consequent beating over the head with a slipper, of Smee.

She'd taken the consequences then, and she'd take them now too. But only if she was discovered.

With the hustle and bustle of daily life, no one noticed when Jo peeled herself from the mast and slipped quietly to the stern. It was an ill-trod part of the ship, mostly used to store fish barrels and lobster traps, so she knew no one would stumble upon what she was about to do.

She made sure that her maroon blouse was tucked into her trousers and that her shoes were tied tightly on her feet; it wouldn't do to lose those to the ocean. Jolie reached into a nearby barrel and pulled out the sword that she had stolen—right from under Hook's nose—the night before.

"When you are ready to be a captain yourself, you'll see that."

This is what a captain did. They didn't take no for an answer. They made their own fate.

If she was fast, she should make it to Hangman's Tree right as the meeting started, where she'd either prove that her hunch was right...or she'd be dragged red-eared by her father back to the ship and denied shore leave for a month.

If she was caught.

Jolie knew how to stay hidden, and she knew that the forest around the Hangman's Tree had ample foliage to disguise herself. She could watch over her father, ready to spring into action if needed, or fade away from sight if not.

As long as she made it back before he did, he'd be none the wiser. Not even Damien knew where she was headed.

She sucked in a sharp pull of sea air. It smelled of salt and promises and magic. Then she whirled her arms overhead and dove into the waiting embrace of the sea below.

The ocean, warmed up under the midday sun, caressed her like a lost lover. Ever greedy, it first tried to suck her down towards the sandy bottom, but Jo had been swimming these waters since she was a babe, and she knew how best to handle it.

The key was to move with it, not through it, something she had been taught by a flock of pacifist mermaids who had taken shelter in the Jolly Roger's shadow during the early days of the Merfolk War.

She'd been captivated not by the iridescent scales of their tails, but by the razor sharp points of their flesh-tearing teeth and the taut muscles of their backs. They were strong and powerful and Jolie had been extraordinarily envious.

For their part, they liked to spend time twisting her dark hair into long braids and entwining it around her brow as a crown. After the war ended and the sea finally faded from blood red back to sapphire blue Jo kept the braids, but simplified it to one that trailed down her back.

She'd told Damien that it kept it out of her face in a fight, but truthfully she also liked the way it made her look. *Like her mother*, her father had once told her, drunk on what would have been their wedding anniversary.

Now, it trailed behind her like a blackened fish as she tore her way away from her ship. She was deep below the surface so that even if someone happened to look her way they wouldn't see her. After four minutes and thirty-six seconds, a number she'd been working on raising every few weeks, her head bobbed above the surface for air.

The crushing feeling of fire against her lungs spurred her on. It was nothing compared to the pain she would feel if she allowed Pan to betray her father.

She reached the shore quickly, ringing out the salt water from her hair and clothes. They would dry easily under the hot noon sun, though the trudge to Hangman's Tree in wet shoes made her grimace.

Get comfortable with being uncomfortable, her father used to say while putting her through drills. Balancing apples on her head. Holding a saber between her teeth while climbing the Jolly Roger's mast. Stealing a coin from his vault in under five minutes. There was no test too strange for the future Captain Hook.

As she stepped off of the sandy beach and into the thick cropping of towering trees, Jolie imagined that this might have been her most challenging test so far. And hopefully one of her last.

Chapter 6

"Fairy tour guides are available in most Neverland ports. Be advised to always keep a sterling coin on your person for payment, lest they extract something more deadly instead."

ADDENDUM: This section has not been updated since the events of the Merfolk War.
- THE MOSTLY ACCURATE TRAVELER'S GUIDE TO THE ANCIENT WORLD OF NEVERLAND

Like any adequate pirate, Jolie knew how to read a map.

But, like any *great* pirate, she also didn't need one. Hook had drilled Neverland's topography into her head since the day she could read the letters on the atlas.

Her home, the Jolly Roger, wouldn't appear on any chart, but those who wanted to find it usually made their way up to Skull Rock in the northeast. One of the vultures there would listen to their message and take it directly to Smee for the low price of a dead rodent or two.

Neverland proper was a mix of dense forest, rocky mountain, beautiful lagoons, and even a settlement or two along the western shores. Hook didn't keep many books in his office, but there was a beaten copy of a traveler's guide that Jo used to devour underneath her covers.

A magical thing, updated sections used to appear overnight in gold ink, and she always loved any page that mentioned the pirates. Much of it harkened back to the before time, when those in Neverland had been able to make their way to any of the other worlds in the sky, and they had played host to a near-constant stream of visitors in return.

But now they were cut-off. Another thing to blame Peter Pan for.

At some point, a few years after the war, the book stopped updating. Jolie had always wondered whether the author, wherever and whomever it might have been, had died. Or perhaps history had just stagnated since then.

Jo mentally traced her footsteps across the map as she wove through the trees. A few reached their branches out towards her but recoiled when she shot them a glare. She was not a tree hugger like those Lost Boys.

She went over her plan again as she walked.

"Hide, observe, be ready for anything."

She kicked a rock off the path.

"Hide, observe, be ready for anything."

If she was lucky, the current would be in her favor on the swim back.

"Hide, observe, be ready for anything."

Jo's eyes lit as she finally spotted the end of the tree line. Just beyond it would be the Hangman's Tree, its thick, leafless branches reaching outwards like claws, its trunk stained dark red. She carefully peered out at the meeting spot.

"Hide, observe, be—"

Her heart flew into her throat and cut off her words.

Jolie ran into the clearing, legs pumping as she shot forwards. Fury and fear were singing a duet in her ears, raucous and cacophonic and *wrong wrong wong*—

She slid to a stop in front of the tree.

No one was there.

But it was impossible. Her father left before her.

Slowly, she spun in a circle, searching for a sign. Nothing, no one. The Hangman's Tree suddenly let out a shuddering groan from behind her, a warning that came too late.

"Two Hooks for the price of one? I am a lucky boy."

Chapter 7

*"This author advises you against ever making a deal
with Peter Pan."*
- THE MOSTLY ACCURATE TRAVELER'S
GUIDE TO THE ANCIENT WORLD OF NEV-
ERLAND

J o didn't spare a moment before unsheathing a dagger from her side and throwing it directly into her enemy's chest. It was dead on target—except for that he teleported away at the last moment, the weapon *thunking* into the tree behind him instead.

He reappeared, frowning at her, and pretended to pat down his chest. "Ouch, you wound me, Jolie. Not even a hug hello for your dear old friend?"

"We're not friends," she growled, stalking up to him.

He was taller than her, though not by much. Instead, it was his aura that made him seem larger than life.

Wickedness and magic combined.

While her father had been waging war against Pan's Lost Boys for nearly a decade, Jolie had never faced her enemy in person before. Though she had been training in swordplay her entire life, her father's legacy was *"too precious to allow onto the battlefield"*—a stipulation Jolie had always unsuccessfully argued against.

She noticed more things about Pan that the portrait in her father's office had gotten wrong.

His nose: slightly crooked and with more freckles than she expected. His hair was wild and curly, the color of dark caramel instead of sand, and his eyes piercing green like an apple. He was boyish, but his fierce grin and sharp gaze spoke the truth: Peter Pan was as old as Neverland itself.

Unlike Hook and his pirates, who aged slowly but surely, Pan was blessed to stay seventeen forever. Blessed, or cursed. There were even rumors that he was immortal, but Jolie always imagined that once she stabbed him he'd bleed just like any other man.

She reached around him and yanked her weapon loose from the tree, immediately aiming a slice for his belly. She growled in frustration when he disappeared again, taking the dagger with him with a cloud of smoke.

"Too cowardly to fight me?"

"There's a thin line between cowardice and strategy," he said, reappearing behind her. He held his arms out and teetered in place as if walking on a tightrope. "One slip in either direction..." He pretended to stumble, but before he could hit the grass he disappeared. There was a rough whisper in the hollow of her ear: "...and you're dead."

This time she reached for her saber, whirling and slicing at his neck. He ducked, and it slid through the air without resistance.

"Violence is hardly the way to a man's heart, darling girl," he tutted.

"Enough of your games," Jolie spat, eyes tracking the forest behind him for any hint of hidden Lost Boys.

Peter Pan's army may have looked like teenagers, stuck in time from his magic, but the fierce barbarians were anything but. They melded so well with the trees that you didn't know when they were on top of you until it was too late. "Where's my father? And the crew he came with?"

"Enough games? Well that sounds boring," he pouted.

"Where. Is. He."

"Gone."

Jo's eyes turned to slits. "What do you mean, gone?"

Pan's eyes flashed a piercing black that almost made Jolie stumble back. His voice was biting, "Do you see him here? No? Because he's gone."

"What about the rest? Smee? The shore party?"

He grinned. "They were boring so I sent them back to the ship."

"Boring?" she seethed. "And what about me? Am I boring you? Are you going to wave your hand and use some dark enchantment to send me to the bottom of the sea?"

He paused, took in a breath and closed his eyes. When they re-opened it was back to mossy green. He hummed in thought. "Jolie Hook...would you like to play a game with me?"

"I said enough–"

"Win my game," he continued, his voice a playful trap, "and I'll tell you where your father is."

Jo considered his words. She knew better than to play anything with Peter Pan. He was a trickster. He was an enemy. He could not be trusted. But...she searched the grass near her feet. There were no blood spots. No broken sword points or wayward feathers from Hook's hat. It was almost as if he really had vanished.

"What are the rules?"

Pan rolled his eyes. "Come now, say yes and I'll tell you."

She gritted her teeth. The bastard was crafty, and he knew he had the upper hand. But Jolie wasn't afraid. He was nothing more than a boy, maybe with a few more bells and whistles, but a boy nonetheless. And Jolie Hook would never be intimidated by him.

"Fine. I agree to your game. You'll tell me where my father is once I win."

"So confident!" he laughed, his tone a chiming of bells in the trees. "I do love that in a competitor." He tapped his finger to his lip and Jo noted stacks of gold and bronze rings. "Now, what shall we play?"

She resisted the urge to snap at him to hurry up. Her father could have been bleeding out somewhere or running from the wylde-beasts she knew roamed the forest. But Pan was the only link she had—and she didn't fancy running into the Neverwoods without a sense of direction to lead her on.

Still, she couldn't stop the look of annoyance from crossing her face when he began to circle her like one of Damien's pet sharks.

"Ah!" he said finally in a sing-song voice. "A game of the senses, I think."

"What do you–"

Her words died as Pan swept out his arms to the side and tilted his head back. His eyes, cast upwards towards the sky, turned black, and a smoky ichor began to pour from his mouth and encircle them both.

Jo tightened her grip on her weapon as she shifted into a fighting stance. She should've known better than to trust Peter Pan to keep his word—the villain was calling on his dark magic to no doubt snuff her out and send her to the watery afterlife.

Let him try, she promised, readying herself. The smoke surrounded her so thoroughly now that she couldn't see the world beyond it anymore. She jabbed out with her sword, but it only slipped through the air.

"Fight like a man!" she hissed, spinning in place. Then the smoke condensed into itself, forming five identical figures around her.

"I am not a man," they all said as one. Each Pan's eyes remained black as they looked at her and tendrils of dark smoke still shifted around their feet.

"I am a Lost Boy," said the one to her left.

"Or am I?" answered the one behind her. Even their voices were identical.

"Which of us is the real Peter Pan?" said the third.

"Which of us is the unaging boy?" called the apparition to her right.

"Choose carefully. I'll give you three questions to ask, but you only get one guess," said the final, the one who stood right in front of her, so close she could almost reach out and tug on one of his wayward curls or flick his slightly pointed ear.

"It's your choice," they all finished in unison.

Chapter 8

Hook had always told her that Peter Pan liked to prey on your fears.

His illusions came from a dark place where nightmares overtook reality, and he was so powerful that even the most judicious of opponents would have trouble breaking through and finding what was real.

Pan underestimated her, then, if he thought that five copies of himself would scare her. No, Jolie Hook loved a challenge, and Peter Pan seemed very willing to give that to her.

"Five Pans," she said, slowly spinning in the circle of illusions. "One is real, the rest are not."

"She's a bright one."

"The daughter of Captain Hook has to be."

"Yo ho ho and all that."

"But is she brighter than us?"

"Oh no, no, no, no."

"Will you just shut up," Jolie huffed, trying to block out the irritating conversation. It was bad enough dealing with one Peter Pan, five might make her finally lose her marbles for good.

The one in front of her raised his eyebrow. "Well, what's it going to be then? Ask your three questions. Make your choice. And," he added, "they have to be yes or no questions. To make it more fun."

Jo pointed her sword at him. "How about I run you all through and see who bleeds. That should end your stupid game."

All five of the Pan's sighed and shook their heads. "That," they said as one, "would be CHEATING!" The final word burst from their mouths in the form of fire, heading straight towards her to incinerate her where she stood.

Jolie held out her arms in a mediocre attempt to shield herself from the burn, but instead of heat all she felt was a cold breath of air caressing her skin. And then a small pinch as the sword in her hand popped out of sight.

She startled, twirling around to see where it had landed. She must have somehow dropped it. "Where–"

The Pan's descended into mad laughter. "Gone for now! Gone to the dark place where all our treasures go. Maybe that's where we put your father, hm? Come now, darling girl. Time is ticking. Make your choice."

"I expect that *back* when this is over, Pan." The boy only smirked, five sets of deliciously red lips pulling together. It could have been a beautiful mouth, if not for the vitriol and villainy Jolie knew was bound to spew out of it. "And you failed to define a time limit when you explained the rules of this game, so I'm going to take however long I please to make my decision."

The Pan to her left opened his mouth to argue but then thought better of it. He gave her a sullen nod instead—clearly he didn't appreciate when she turned his game around on him.

With a few moments to think, Jolie took turns staring at each of the figures. Not a single hair was different between the lot.

All of them had black eyes—though she knew that a brilliant green was hiding underneath—and each wore the green tunic, brown pants, and soft brown slippers customary of the leader of the Lost Boys.

Her eyes turned to slits. "Where's your hat?" Like her father's elegant plumage, Peter always wore a cap as well, though his was decidedly smaller and less lavish. Still, the absence of the accessory made her pause.

They scowled in return. "Bird stole it."

"Really?"

"Yes," said the one behind her. "But that's a silly waste of a question, darling."

Dust, she seethed. He answered where his hat was freely, but only to trick her into using one of her yes/no questions like a fool. Pan was as sharp as a sword and twice as shiny it seemed.

She held up her hands and pointed at the two nearest boys. "Am I pointing at the real Peter Pan?"

"No."

She spun slowly and pointed at the next two. "Am I pointing at the real Peter Pan?"

Again, "No."

She turned to the last one. If none of the other four were Pan then it only left this one. The same copy as the rest, except for the wicked glint in his eye.

"Am I your guess then? Remember you only get one, I'd hate for you to waste it." His voice was a trill, full of barely held back mirth. He was enjoying this game far too much, and Jolie longed for her sword so that she could carve the smile from his face. He kidnapped her father yet he dared to play this game?

Jolie stilled as the cogs in her head turned.

Peter Pan was smart. Smart enough to rule over most of the forested area of Neverland. Smart enough to have the support of his Lost Boys and the last remaining fairy, and smart enough to have never been caught by her father after so many years of fighting.

He was too smart to risk himself like this.

She reached out towards the nearest one and, like a ship through the misty ocean fog, her fingers went right through his chest. "That tickles," he winked.

"You're not really here at all, are you?" she said. "None of these are the real Peter Pan."

The small smirk on Pan's face bloomed into a wide grin as all five shapes converged back into one apparition. "Well played, darling girl. You're right, I'm not here. Did I have you fooled? Oh, please say I did. It would be boring if this game was all for nothing."

"How is it that I was able to feel your breath then, if you aren't really here?"

He winked. "Magic."

"Tell me where my father is." Jolie was tired of talking, tired of the mind games. It was a neat trick, one that none of the pirates even knew about, but it made sense; of course Peter Pan wouldn't have actually come to Hangman's Tree himself. Why would he, when he could stay locked up safe in his castle?

She admitted, though, that he had her fooled for most of it. His magic was truly breathtaking.

His eyes—dark still, and perhaps even stormier than before—bore into hers for a moment too long. It nearly stole the breath from her lungs with its intensity before he finally shrugged. "A deal is a deal. He's in the dungeon of my castle."

This time, the air really did leave her.

The dungeon?

If Pan was telling the truth, which she still wasn't sure he was, then...it would be suicide to try and break her father free. His castle was covered in enough traps and tricks to send even the most dedicated explorer running. Not only that, but he'd have to know that she would be coming. Him and all of his Lost Boys would be on the lookout.

"You lie."

"I am many things, darling girl, but I am not a liar."

"You lied to my father about wanting peace."

"I never said I wanted peace," he admitted, sly grin sliding into place. "I said that Neverland has been at war for too long and I wanted to meet. It was his poor foresight that took those words to mean a truce."

He turned to leave. Jolie's heart clenched, she couldn't let her father end like this.

She couldn't let their legacy be dictated by some forest boy. But with no way to hurt Pan, with no way to follow him or otherwise command that he release Hook she was at an impasse. Her mother's voice rose unbidden in her ears.

You can have anything in life if you're willing to sacrifice everything else for it.

It was something she used to say when Jolie was younger, whenever she felt like she was facing unsurmountable during her father's tests. It was a reminder of everything she fought for, every moment of fleeting pain or brief loneliness. Her goals were worth it all.

"Wait!" she shouted, reaching for his arm and stumbling as she fell through him. She caught herself at the last moment.

He raised an eyebrow. "Yes?"

"What are you doing with him? What do you want from him?"

"Want?" he mused. "Well, nothing really. He's just a grande treasure to have in my vault, don't you think? My sworn enemy at my mercy forever...has a nice ring."

"Forever?"

"Immortality loves company," he shrugged. "Now, this has been fun, but I must go. Ta-ta!" His face began to fade from view as he dissolved his magic. Jolie's fear, the small, icy ball that she kept shoved down into the very darkest pit of herself, clawed its way up her chest.

"I want to make a deal!" she shouted in a strangled yelp.

In a flash, Pan solidified again. Curiously, his eyes were back to green, and they sparkled at her in anticipation. "What kind of deal?"

"I want my father back."

He shook his head, his wayward hair flopping across his forehead. "That's a demand, not a deal."

Jolie glared. "Make me an offer then."

"Oh, you are a treat, aren't you? But are you wise, or foolish?" Pan mused. He leaned in close enough to her face that she could almost see herself reflected in his eyes. It felt strange to be so close to him without being able to stab him—it felt claustrophobic.

Would her father approve of this? Making deals with the enemy?

This whole mess started because he wanted to make a deal with the enemy, she reminded herself. Still, she felt like she was jumping directly into a vortex. "What are your terms?"

He paused, no doubt thinking up the best way to manipulate her into a trap. "Make it to my castle within three days, and I will let your father go."

Jo was taken aback. "That's it?"

His gaze sharpened. "The forest will not be kind to you...and neither will I. It won't be as easy as you seem to think." He paused. "The question is: is your father worth it?"

"He's worth everything," she bit back.

He smiled and leaned in close. "Jolie Hook," he whispered into the hollow of her ear. She shivered at the intimacy; her name spoken like a dangerous secret on his tongue. "Do you agree to my terms?"

Her determination wavered, just for a moment. "And what if I can't do it?"

His gaze sharpened to the point of a sword and Jo felt all at once the slimy, cold sensation of having made a mistake—worse, of having walked willingly into a mistake. "Well then I suppose I get to keep you, too."

Jolie sucked in a sharp breath of momentary fear before remembering herself. She had nothing to be afraid of: Jolie Hook did not fail. "Yes, we have a deal."

Peter Pan smiled, and it was at once soft and sad and happy and intrigued. "My darling girl, I think you might be my new favorite toy."

The world erupted into black smoke around her.

Chapter 9

"Do not venture into the Neverwoods without a guide. Do not venture into the Neverwoods at night. Do not eat or drink anything in the Neverwoods, no matter how much it begs to be tasted."
- THE MOSTLY ACCURATE TRAVELER'S GUIDE TO THE ANCIENT WORLD OF NEVERLAND

J olie hit the forest floor with an uncomfortable "Oof!", throwing her hands out in front to break her fall.

Her fists caught a handful of crunchy brown leaves, which squealed in annoyance until she dropped them and they skittered back up into their tree. Tracking their movements, Jo caught sight of two yellow monkeys lazily picking butter-and-toastflies out of each other's fur.

It smelled of rain and damp dirt, but also of that sweet sugared lemon aroma of magic and possibilities. Jolie knew exactly where that villain Peter Pan had whisked her away to. She was in the Neverwoods. And she was in trouble.

Most people never ventured into the woods that made up a large portion of Neverland's southern shore. Those who did usually came back watching over their shoulder and being spooked by the smallest of noises. It was Peter Pan's territory, and not even her father liked to enter it.

Except it was more a 'who' than an 'it', because the Neverwoods seemed to groan and sigh and move just like a person would.

In fact, Damien had a theory that its borders were constantly moving and shifting, and that some days it was bigger than others. His explanation was that Pan funneled his magic into the dirt, and the trees gobbled it up like roast dinner.

Wrapping her arms around body to stave off a sudden chill, Jolie felt like Damien was right. There was something magical about the woods, and magical things, more often than not, were wielded against her.

"Pan!" she shouted, searching the thick trees and foliage for any sight of the rogue. He had dumped her fairies-knew-where, with only the clothes on her back. No food, no compass, no weapo–

Jo blinked as she spotted her sword twisted deep into the side of a tree. Had Pan given it back to her? She stepped over and noticed that the sword was actually pinning a note:

> *Three days, darling girl.*
> *My castle is somewhere in*
> *the woods, and your fa-*
> *ther is somewhere in my*
> *dungeon. Better hold on*
> *to this sword tight—who*

*knows what kind of night-
mares lurk behind the trees?*

"How generous," she muttered sarcastically, pulling the saber out. Jolie, having polished the weapon for years any time her father allowed it, immediately noticed a slight difference in the metal. She peered closer and scoffed.

Peter Pan had carved a cartoon of his face into her sword, complete with freckles and a smug smile. Though it felt tainted now, Jo decided that it would serve her well: each time she'd look at the sword she'd imagine that one day soon she'd have Pan's real head on it.

For now, she used it to carve a giant X into the wood. X marked her starting spot, should she get turned around.

Truthfully, she had no idea which way to go. She assumed the castle would be in the middle of the woods, but having been so unkindly teleported to her location, she wasn't sure which way was north and which way was south. She could wander for hours and end up back at Hangman's Tree.

She sighed, realizing that she had dug herself into a near inescapable pit.

Her crew didn't know where she was.

She hadn't even told Damien that she was going to follow her father—though he was smart, he'd probably figure it out.

No one was coming to rescue her from her own foolish choice to play this game. She almost wished that the emerald-eyed boy was with her now, if only for someone to yell at.

Jolie scanned the forest. Beyond the monkeys—who now looked at her with faces that she suspected meant they were about to throw clods of dirt her way—she was alone. It was such a drastic departure from her normal life, where the hustle and bustle of the Jolly Roger had her wishing for one moment of peace.

But this was not peace. This was war. And she would bring Peter Pan down.

Yes, Jo decided. *I will free my father. And then I will kill Peter Pan.*

Chapter 10

"Unlike other worlds, Neverland has no formal governing leadership. Every few decades, control of the island shifts between the various factions, though fairies have historically held the tightest grip."
- THE MOSTLY ACCURATE TRAVELER'S GUIDE TO THE ANCIENT WORLD OF NEVERLAND

J olie Hook stayed in her starting position for over half an hour with her head craned directly upwards, watching the sun. It rose in the northwest and set in the southeast, so she stared up until her retinas began to burn, eventually picking out which way the ball of fire was slowly lowering itself to.

She carved again into the tree, an arrow pointing southeast this time, and, with a hand firmly on her sword, began to trek deeper into the Neverwoods.

Pan had given her three days, which meant that his castle was most likely at least four days away. She would have to keep moving as best she could and hope that she wouldn't drop from exhaustion before she got there.

It was almost stiflingly hot. She nearly cursed her pants and long-sleeved tunic, but Jo knew that come the chill of nighttime she would be glad for the extra layers.

"Dear Father," she narrated as she sliced through a particularly thick cropping of branches. "I am on my way to save you after you so diligently *didn't* listen to me when I told you it was a trap. Peter Pan has bested you, and that's not a good look for the Hook family."

She grunted as a stinging fire bee buzzed by her face. "I expect a large reward when I return you to the Jolly Roger. I take coin, jewelry, and the deed to the ship."

Jo wiped the sweat forming at her brow.

Was she losing it? It felt too early in the journey for her marbles to have been so thoroughly smacked about. It didn't help that the forest was a maze of similar looking trees and rocks. So far she hadn't run into any of her marked branches, which at least meant she wasn't accidentally backtracking, but she also hadn't made it to anything she might call a good sign.

No sprinklings of fairy dust, no riddles, no sleeping Lost Boys—though for that last one she was glad.

Her stomach growled as Jo ducked under a low hanging branch. She'd only had a soulfruit tart and a mouthful of bitter blackleaf tea for breakfast and now she was regretting it. She couldn't last three days without food or water, but most of the things in the Neverwoods that looked safe to eat never were.

As if waiting for her to think it into existence, the sound of a bubbling creek nipped at her ears. Jo immediately diverted from her path to follow it, nearly moaning in delight when she stumbled onto the source: a winding, crystalline loop of water flowing through the trees.

She sunk to her knees, itching to dunk her entire sweat-soaked face in and drink her fill, but remembered her survival training.

First: the look.

Her eyes roamed the slowly moving water, searching for any dark shadows or glittering dust that might indicate it had been touched by magic. But there was nothing, it was so clear that she could see straight through it.

Next: the smell.

Jolie drew her nose as close to the edge of the creek as she could and inhaled. It didn't have the tell-tale smell of sugared lemons. It didn't smell like rust or dirt or any other manner of ill intentions.

Finally: the sound.

So often the malicious things in Neverland tried their hardest to convince you otherwise. Poisonous mushrooms would sing soft lullabies, deadly snakes would tell jokes.

This water was temptingly silent, and she took that for a good sign.

Slowly, Jo dipped a single finger in. It was cool to the touch, and soft like goose feathers. She plunged her entire hand and splashed the water up towards her face.

She was attempting her best to scrub away the dirt from her brow when she spotted him sitting across the other side of the water.

"Is it too much to ask for you to leave me alone?" she scowled, aiming a splash of water towards Pan that sailed right through his ethereal form.

He smirked, "Would you ask an audience member to close their eyes during a captivating play? To cover their ears and block out the sound of a tavern singer?"

Jolie pursed her lips. "I hardly think watching me drink water will satisfy your curiosity for entertainment."

His eyes flicked down to the gently rushing stream by her feet then back up to her face. Emerald green jewels roamed across her brow, down her cheeks, passing over lips and chin. "You'd be surprised."

She had been cupping a new handful of water, intent on finally satisfying her thirst, when his words made her pause. "You know something that I don't."

"I know many things that you don't."

"You know something about *the water*," she stressed, trying but mostly failing to keep the annoyance from her voice.

Pan lifted a hand and she watched in awe as he conjured a small ball of shadows, flicking it between his knuckles like a marble. It looked like the blackened eye of a storm, condensed down but just as dangerous.

Jolie shivered. Pan was being cordial to her now, but that could change at any moment. He could decide to renege on their deal and use his dark magic to ensnare her just as he did her father.

Finally, he let the ball dissolve back into nothing. "The first two times you drink, it will not be pleasant, it will not be kind."

Jolie nodded. Of course there would be a challenge, a test. Nothing in the Neverwoods came for free. "And the third?"

Pan shrugged. "No one has yet tried a third time."

"It's your magic that helps these woods grow, are you saying you don't even know what it does to the waters and the trees?" Jo growled, aggravated at his non-answer. When the day came that she could finally acquaint Pan with her sword she wouldn't be surprised if it was riddles that spilled from his veins instead of blood.

"I appreciate how omnipotent you believe I am," he said, winking. "Now I'm curious, will you drink? High risk, but with your rate of dehydration and your journey just beginning..." He tsked and shook his head. "I would get some water fast, if I were you."

She glared, but she knew he was right. How could she save her father if she wasted away from thirst first? She brought the cupped hand to her lips. "Will it kill me?"

"Probably not."

She muttered a curse under her breath and then swallowed the water in one gulp.

For a moment, she wondered whether Pan had made the entire thing up. She felt no different than–

A harsh squeeze against her abdomen was her only warning before she doubled over and emptied the thin contents of her stomach on the forest floor. Bile and blood and a watery black substance poured from her lips, again and again. In an instant, Pan was at her side, a mockery of concern on his face as he pretended to pat her shoulder.

"There, there," he sighed. "I did warn you. Though your determination is quite impressive."

She slapped his hand away—or tried to, seeing as Pan was an apparition and not truly there—and groaned as her stomach twisted again. This time, nothing came up.

Sweat slicked down her back as she painstakingly straightened, moving away from her steaming pile of sick. Her arms shook as she tried to retie her braid out of her face, quickly abandoning the efforts when she couldn't get her fingers to cooperate.

"What foul magic was that?" she mumbled, wiping her mouth. She looked up at Pan from where he stood overtop of her. "Did that entertain you enough, then? Are you satisfied?"

He raised an amused brow. "Maybe you'll feel better if you drink some water."

She threw him a crude gesture but turned back towards the creek anyways. He had said that the first two times wouldn't be kind, but the third might be worth the risk. Could she do another sip? What might it do to her? Cause her skin to peel off? Her bones to twist and break?

Knowing the depths of Pan's vicious magic, she doubted this second sip would be easier to swallow than the first.

"If I die, I'm coming back to haunt you," she sniffed, bringing a fresh handful of water to her mouth. She vaguely noticed his face blanche at her words before he schooled his features back into a look of detached amusement.

Interesting, she thought, before downing the second sip.

This time, the effect was immediate.

It was in the way that the leaves on the trees around her suddenly became swirls of glittering greens and purples, in the sound of children's laughter bubbling up from the creek. Her jaw slackened as all around her she could feel, could almost sink into, the magic of the Neverwoods.

She giggled, and an embarrassed part of herself demanded that she slap her hand over her mouth and pull herself together. But the lull of the water sloshing through her body was louder.

"Wow," she sighed, running a hand across the grass by her feet. "It feels like silk." She wanted to touch something else, see what other things might feel nice. Her legs were no longer shaky as she rose, heading towards the nearest tree. She cried out in amazement when her fingers touched the bark. "The softest cotton." Jo leaned in and smelled the tree. "Smells like lemons."

"You seem to be enjoying yourself."

She turned, shrugging. "Is this what magic feels like all the time?" she asked Pan, suddenly not minding his presence as much. In fact, why had she ever minded it at all? He captivated her; Pan was glowing like a star freshly fallen to the ground. She should wish on him, maybe it would come true.

"What do you feel?" he asked quietly, coming close enough to her that she could count the freckles on his cheeks.

She hummed and closed her eyes. "Like...a warm bath. A soft bed. Like the comfort of home." When she opened her eyes again, Pan was looking at her with such interest it should have made her angry.

But why would anyone ever be angry?

"No," he said, tucking a wayward lock of hair behind her ear. "That is not what magic feels like all the time."

"You smell like lemons," she hummed, leaning into his touch. His fingers lingered by her chin before tilting it up so that she was once again caught in his gaze.

"Your pupils are completely blown out," he said. "I could ask for your darkest secrets right now and you'd probably tell me. I could make you do awful things, whatever I wanted."

"How are you touching me?" she asked. "I thought you weren't real."

She frowned in disappointment when he stepped back, wishing to wrap herself back up in his warmth. His eyes flashed that strange emotion again. She reached out, certain that if she could just grab it that she could figure out what it was.

"Magic," was his only reply.

She grinned. "I like magic."

He shook his head. "No, you don't. It's time to wake up now, darling girl."

Pan disappeared from her sight.

And so did the magic.

Without the light touch of the world around her to hold her up, Jo sank against the tree, fingering her now pounding head. Pinpricks of self-consciousness stabbed into her. Had she just told Pan that he smelled like lemons? That she liked his magic?

"I hate this place," she spat, pulling herself up. Given the choice, she'd take the vomiting over whatever strange trance that had been. Sure, she had felt good, but she also hadn't been in control.

Jolie Hook was *always* in control.

Without hesitation, she moved back to the water and dunked her entire head into the stream. Mouth wide, she drank her fill until she could nearly feel the sloshing in her belly.

She waited one minute, another, then smiled. Nothing happened. No vomiting, no hallucinations.

"If only Pan were here to see this." It felt like a cruel irony that would see her high and giggling over trees but not her conquering his foolish challenge. "At least this journey is looking up."

She turned back into the forest and began her trek once more. After several minutes she took a slight left turn on her path and pulled out her sword to carve a new positioning mark. Her heart stuttered wickedly off beat as she saw that there *already* was a thin arrow in the bark. She had been there before.

"No...no no no!" she screeched, hacking at the tree with her weapon. "Dust take these trees! Dust take that blasted Peter Pan!"

"Peter Pan? Are you looking for Peter?"

Jolie whirled, raising her weapon. She blinked when there was no one behind her.

"You won't find him in that tree, silly," a second voice chided. This one sounded younger than the first, who itself couldn't have been more than a child. A Lost Boy?

"Show yourself!" she barked.

"We're up here."

Jo looked up in confusion. There was nothing to see but a bird.

"Hi!" it said, flapping down and landing on the dirt in front of her. It was about the size of two fists, with blue and white plumage, small yellow feet, and a sharp beak.

Jolie's mouth fell flat. "Go away bird, I don't have time for your songs today." She was usually more than happy to converse with the various winged creatures of the island, who often whispered wonderful gossip in her ears, but now was not the time.

"Aw, she doesn't want to play with us John?"

"I guess not, Michael. Too bad, we could've shown her the way to Peter's castle."

Jolie startled for two reasons. Firstly, The bird was tempting her with directions, and secondly she realized the bird actually had *two heads*. One larger, with two round markings over its eyes like glasses, and one smaller, with yellow feathers by its ears. "Wait!"

"Oh, she does like us!" the face with the almost-glasses chirped.

"You know the way to Pan?" she prompted, crouching down so that they were at eye level.

"Oh yes, couldn't forget it if we tried!" said the smaller head.

"And believe us, we've tried," added the larger.

Jolie paused, studying them. They could have easily been spies, but something about the innocence on the feathery faces made her think otherwise. Could it really be that she had stumbled across a tour guide for the Neverwoods?

"Can you tell me?"

"No–"

"–but we can show you!" The bird squawked and jumped up into the air, flapping its wings and steering off to the left. "We can't take you all the way, but far enough!"

"What do you want in return?" Jo called, rising to her feet and jogging after the quickly departing guide.

"Return?" the smaller one—she recalled that the other called him John—asked. "Oh, nothing."

"Nothing?" Jo asked. "No one does anything for nothing."

"We do."

"Why?"

The bird with the glasses turned to look her in the eye. "You remind us of someone we've forgotten. Maybe if we stay with you long enough, we'll remember."

Chapter 11

"It rains in Neverland for precisely one hour and one minute every day, but your timing may vary."
- THE MOSTLY ACCURATE TRAVELER'S GUIDE TO THE ANCIENT WORLD OF NEVERLAND

"Why do you have two heads?" Jolie asked after an hour of wandering the woods.

The bird—John and Michael—had grown tired of flying and were now perched on her shoulder. Jolie was surprised that she didn't seem to mind. In fact, talking with the two had settled her nerves somewhat. If she was thinking of them then she wasn't thinking about all the nefarious things that hid in the Neverwoods, and she also wasn't thinking about the next time she'd see Pan.

He sent her heart thumping and she refused to admit that it was fear, or curiosity, or something even more sinister.

"Why do you only have one?" Michael asked back.

"Fair play," she snorted.

They were taking turns asking each other questions, the bird assuring her that they were on the right track every few minutes. Night would be falling soon, and she hoped that they could stumble across some sort of shelter before then—otherwise she'd be sleeping in a tree and might wake up with lightbugs nesting in her hair.

John asked his next question: "Why are you looking for Peter?"

Jo's pace faltered slightly but didn't stop. "He stole something from me. I intend to get it back."

There was a gentle nuzzle of feathers against her shoulder. "He stole something from us, too," John admitted quietly. "And it must have been special, for our heart to feel so sad about it."

"You don't remember?"

John shook his head. "I always thought that absence made the heart grow fonder but in our case it's made us quite forgetful."

Her own heart gave a painful squeeze. Was there no one safe from the whims of Peter Pan? He lorded over Neverland like a king, taking whatever he pleased and hunting those around him in the process.

"If I find it, I'll get it back," Jo said. "I promise."

"Just remember to keep away from the water!" John trilled.

"What?"

"I don't know why I said that," the younger half of the bird said. "How strange."

Jolie sighed, kicking a cluster of stones out of their path. "Yes, well Neverland is strange."

A rolling boom of thunder sounded overhead as a gray cloud slid into view, covering the sky in its entirety. "Shoot," she muttered. It was about to rain, and unless they found shelter it would be a miserable 61 minutes ahead of them. "Are there any caves nearby?"

The birds looked at each other, thinking, until Michael's eyes lit up. "Yes! If you run we can make it. This way, hurry!" The bird dove from Jolie's shoulder.

She stumbled over a wayward tree branch but kept pace, dashing under leaves, passing by glowing toadstools with fat purple frogs sitting underneath, brushing by an old abandoned firepit of some sort.

"Up here!" the bird cried with both voices, taking a sharp right turn and disappearing through a wall of vines.

For a moment Jolie's brain screamed at her that the vines were too thick, that she would bounce off of them like a coin or get stuck in them like a fly to sap, but strangely enough it almost felt like they were made out of ribbons as she dashed through.

There was a yawning mouth to a stone cave only a few feet ahead. She dove in just as the first raindrop pinged off of Neverland's forest floor.

Jo breathed a sigh of relief—it was never fun to get caught in the Neverains. It took twice as long to dry off from as regular water and sometimes smelt of unsavory things. Today, though, the rain had the aroma of freshly baked bread and the sound of small diamonds when it hit the ground.

"John? Michael?" she called, turning in place to face the interior of the cave.

Her breath left in a short, panicked burst. Her bird friend was no longer there. Instead, the back of the cave had two wooden doors. Both were pearly white, with knockers the shape of fairies. In the middle of each one read: *Shortcut to the castle.*

Jolie's throat went dry. She glanced back at the mouth to the cave and the icy pit in her stomach grew. The opening to the forest was gone, as if the cave had closed in on itself in the five seconds that she had looked away. She was trapped inside, with only two suspicious ways out.

Chapter 12

"While travel in and out of Neverland is restricted by the use of the Star Portals, it is possible to travel internally via many means: by boat, by animal, by foot, or by magic door."

ADDENDUM: The Star Portals are closed indefinitely.

\- THE MOSTLY ACCURATE TRAVELER'S GUIDE TO THE ANCIENT WORLD OF NEVERLAND

"I should've known better than to trust a talking bird who says it knows Pan!" she seethed, unsheathing her sword.

It seemed impossible that Michael and John wouldn't have led her to these untrustworthy doors on purpose and then disappeared, no doubt flying back to their master.

Never trust the Neverwoods, she thought. Jolie knew better. Her father would've been disappointed by her brash actions. But desperation made a fool of even the mightiest of pirates—his *peace treaty* was proof of that.

"Never again," she promised herself, inching towards the set of doors. "A Hook does not rely on others. A Hook takes matters into their own hands." Her father had said those words often enough to her that she kicked herself for forgetting the advice in the moment it had mattered most.

As she slowly moved forward she caught a sniff of sweet sugared lemons: the smell of magic. Specifically, the smell of Peter Pan's magic.

He was messing with her.

The forest will not be kind to you. And neither will I, he had said. Was this another of his obstacles?

"I am not afraid of you, Pan. I'm sure you're listening."

"More than listening, darling girl."

Jolie shot out with her sword towards the apparition that popped up to her left, but it sailed right through the center of his torso.

She scowled.

He looked the same as when she had seen him at the creek earlier, except the smarmy grin on his face was possibly even bigger now. The same riotous curls, the same light smattering of freckles. His eyes were the normal green, though Jolie noticed a slight black ring around their edges that she wasn't sure was there before.

"Are you planning on following me around like a dog?" she sneered, lowering her sword. It was useless against a ghost anyways.

Peter shrugged. "You're very entertaining, Jolie Hook. Would you begrudge a boy his fun?" He leaned towards her and she got a full face of his smell: lemons, earthy dirt, pine. Somehow, even though he was an apparition, Pan's scent had followed him.

"I'm not an actor in some strange play."

His smile grew. "No, you are a player in some strange game."

"My father's life is not a game," she snapped. "Maybe if you came here yourself I could let you know just how serious this all is for me."

Peter waved her words away. "Everything is a game for me, darling girl."

"And everyone your playthings."

His eyes turned to slits for a moment, then he relaxed again, leaning back against the stony wall of the cave.

He crossed his arms and Jolie was surprised at the pull of the fabric against his biceps, though she quickly shook the thought away. "You impressed me earlier. I've never seen anyone so thickheaded in their determination that they drank three times. You've turned out to be a remarkable plaything. But the beauty about playthings is that they're easily replaceable. For example..." Peter looked towards the two doors, "make the wrong choice here and I might have to find a new toy earlier than I'd hoped."

Jolie swallowed down her ire. She was no one's toy, but she needed Pan to abide by the rules of his idiotic game. She needed to play along until she freed her father, but if he said anything more she might just snap. She turned her attention back to the doors.

"They look the same," she murmured to herself.

The only two things strange about the doors were the words on them and the fairy knockers, which seemed to have been blown from glass.

They were forged in miniature, with dainty wings shown mid-flight. Fairies had two forms, one smaller than a palm, the other nearly indistinguishable from a human. The ability to change between them was one of the reasons the fairy council had ruled over Neverland for so long, and why fairy assassins were some of the most deadly. They could slip through door cracks, wait in tea cups, hide in your bed until you fell asleep; and then they would strike.

The flash of face mottled red, ice blue lips, a trickle of blood down the corner of her nose—

Jolie slammed the thought shut and threw it deep within herself.

"Do they both really go to the castle?" she asked aloud. She hadn't been expecting an answer and nearly jumped when there was a whisper in her ear: "They both go to the castle."

If he was an apparition, then why could she feel the heat of his body against her back? Why did his breath leave a chill down her spine? There was no magical water coursing through her veins this time to blame it on.

She would've elbowed him away had he been real, so instead she just turned her sharp gaze to his. Her heart thumped at their proximity. "I can't concentrate with you this close."

"Which rule says that I can't interfere with your concentration?" he smiled, but moved an inch away nonetheless.

His charm was baffling at times but, Jolie supposed, that was how Pan had gained so many loyal followers for his army. That was why they used to say his name in other worlds with reverence. Peter Pan knew how to play the hero. But Jolie knew the truth. He was nothing more than a villain in her story. A murderer with no remorse.

Something wet splashed against her boot and she jumped back. It was...water?

"Uh oh," he tutted. "Looks like it's raining." He gave her a smug side glance. "Better pick a door fast."

Jolie cursed as the water rapidly began to rise. Clearly some foul magic was at play, causing raindrops to fall from the cavern's ceiling—and fall fast. It didn't smell like bread or twinkle like diamonds anymore either; this was pure salt water. She could smell it in the air, and when she held her hand out and then to her lips she could taste it on her tongue too.

"I'd tell you to walk the plank, Pan, if I didn't think you'd make the sharks sick," Jo said, shivering as the cold water reached her shins.

Quickly, which door would it be?

"Tick, tock!" her enemy sang. She noticed that he had conjured up a small floating stool to perch on as the water kept rising. "Tick, tock, Hook was on the clock! To save her father or let him rot!"

"Shut up and let me think!"

Jolie liked competition and, under normal circumstances, she liked games. But this was a game of chance, not skill, and she *detested* those.

Damien used to beg her to play dice with him, but after constantly losing her best pixie stick candies to the malicious six-sided fiends, she had sworn off games of luck. Jolie Hook was not lucky—she worked hard for what she had, and she reaped the rewards. Unlike Pan, who merely snapped his fingers and had it handed to him.

Two doors. There had to be a clue, something that told her which path to take. Sure, they both led to the castle, but there had to be a trick somewhere. She waded through the water, now up to her hips, and pressed her ear against the first door.

Nothing.

No...wait...

It almost sounded like a drum, or a heartbeat. It thunked steadily against her.

She moved to the next, catching Pan's curious look as she did. The second door, again, made no noise for a moment and then: water. Like the crashing of waves.

"I don't know which one!" she yelled over the rush of the swirling water, which had quickly swelled in size and now reached her neck.

"Sure you do!" he called, appearing right next to her, untouched by the rain and far more relaxed than she felt. "Don't let me down, darling girl—make a choice and entertain me!"

"I am not–" but the rest of her words were caught up in a mouthful of water. The salt hit her teeth and her tongue and threatened to rush down her throat before she clamped her lips shut. Her entire body was below the water now, her hair floating around her head like a macabre near-death halo.

Without another thought she reached for the closest door—was it the drumming one or the waves? She was disoriented now—and yanked it open.

The water rushed out, pulling her body unwillingly along with it, she heard Peter shouting from behind: "Excellent choice! The other would've brought you right to my front door, and where's the fun in that?"

Then she was tumbling from the cave and smashing into a new place.

Chapter 13

"The war between the Merfolk and the Lost Boys was, at the time, one of the bloodiest conflicts in Neverland's history. Causing the death of hundreds of mermaids, sirens, and aquatic warriors, the war also displaced many Merfolk from their homes. Those who could not flee Neverland often found shelter amongst settlements and ships. In the early days of the conflict, the Jolly Roger was notable for having sheltered three dozen siren families after a hostile takeover of their traditional lagoon homeland, a benevolence they later helped repay in kind with blood when the pirates entered the fray themselves."

- THE MOSTLY ACCURATE TRAVELER'S GUIDE TO THE ANCIENT WORLD OF NEVERLAND

J o cried out as her shoulder smashed into something hard and sputtered as a whirlwind of water collapsed onto her from above. She groaned and tilted her head to look around. She had made it through the door...seemingly alone.

Not unscathed though. Jo rolled onto her back and then up to her feet, wincing at the pain in her arm. She moved it a few times—not broken, just bruised. And the rest of her was now wet, again. Right as she thought that, though, a gust of warm breeze blew by and dried her off.

As it passed, she could faintly hear Pan's familiar voice: *Thanks for the entertainment, darling girl.*

"Insufferable, egotistical, annoying..." she muttered. She had failed his game, clearly this was not the castle, but she was alive and that's what mattered. She could still save her father.

Jolie took in her new surroundings, lips parting in surprise.

She knew this place. Her mother had taken her here, once.

Once, back when it was whole and beautiful and unspoiled by villainous hands.

Once, back when she was alive.

The mermaid's lagoon had been the shoreline entrance to a sprawling undersea city. It was rosy pink sand and shining green sea glass around a deep blue hole—swim down far enough and you would reach the city itself. It was giant statues of merfolk, huge stone pillars with seakelp vines, dias' carved with art and maps of worlds beyond their own.

When Jolie had visited, she was surprised by how many creatures had been there. Mermaids brushing each other's colorful locks with carved coral combs as they lay out on rocks half submerged into the water. Schools of fish that danced between tail fins and raced up and down the blue hole at their leisure. Sirens with lutes and lyres that strummed songs—said to be hypnotically enchanting to those not born on Neverland's soil.

It had been an oasis, like a hidden gem, the pearl nestled in the oyster. Jolie remembered crying when her mother finally pulled her away from the blue hole, telling her that they'd return soon and that no, she couldn't ask a siren for her seashell necklace.

The very next day, the Lost Boys had declared war, and Jolie never got to return.

Until now.

There were still remnants of the place she remembered; stone archways had crumbled but the bases, cracked and dirty, still stood. The sand, once rosy, had been long stained dark red with the blood of merfolk and Lost Boy alike.

There were no mermaids, no sirens, and no fish. There was only the blue hole, made as a doorway to the undersea city, now boarded up with miles of stone—a last ditch tactic to prevent Pan's forces from wiping out the sea creatures entirely.

Of course, Jo's father would soon help turn the tide in the Merfolk's favor, but they never came back to unplug the entrance, preferring to keep as far from the Neverwoods as they could.

Jolie scowled at the ruin of what had once been such a beautiful place, one that she always associated with her mother.

Checking to make sure that her sword was still sheathed and hadn't been stolen by Pan, she searched around for anything that might help her resume her journey and, more urgently, could give her shelter from the rapidly approaching dusk. It was never safe to be near the woods at night.

She scowled as she spotted a large sandcastle along the beachline, complete with turrets, a drawbridge, and even a small miniature of

Peter Pan himself. So he hadn't been lying when he'd said both doors would lead her to his castle.

"He hadn't really been telling the truth either," she grumbled, jumping down from the stone dais where she had landed and marching over to it. She assumed that it must bear a striking resemblance to Pan's actual castle and, giving in to her incredible annoyance and frustration that she had been yet again tricked, she knocked the entire structure down with a vicious kick.

She smiled as it collapsed back into a pile of sand, even giving a condescending wave to the Pan miniature, who she could've sworn bore a face of horror before he exploded into dust.

"Ha! Take that–" she started triumphantly, but was cut off by a low rumbling sound that threatened to shake her off her feet.

Jolie spun and immediately found the source: what she had believed to be a giant piece of moss-covered stone. Only, stone didn't look at her with twin yellow slits, or peel back its lips to show rows of wickedly pointed teeth, or amble up onto four legs and stand at least four times her height.

It roared, and a slew of birds bolted out from their homes in nearby trees, leaving Jolie frightfully alone with this new nightmare.

Her mouth turned as dry as the sand where she stood, the back of her neck rendered clammy. It had not been a stone after all. It had been a sleeping crocodile, and it looked ready for dinner.

Chapter 14

Peter couldn't remember the last time he'd had so much fun.

Not only did he finally have Captain Hook in his possession, but his daughter was currently fighting tooth and nail to rescue him—whether through familial duty or some sense of love he didn't much care. All that mattered to him was that a delightful game was afoot, and he was so pleased with its star.

He knew that Jolie Hook would be the cure to his raging ennui when she had successfully discovered the truth to his little apparition trick at the Hangman's Tree. Her eyes, so stormy when turned towards him, sent thrills down his spine.

What new dark magics could he throw at her? What nightmares could he create to elicit those beautiful strong emotions: hate, rage, determination. She was a marvelously violent person. He mused that she could've made a great Lost Boy, had the cards been dealt differently.

As it was, watching her trudge through the Neverwoods was keeping Peter's spirits well high. Whenever he stole away from Tink's incessant strategy talk to peer in on Jolie, he found he couldn't keep from just…looking at her. He wanted to know what made her tick.

When he had first agreed to her desperate bargain, it had been mostly born from a sense of curiosity. How far would she get into the belly of his domain until she failed?

He'd first thought she wouldn't make it an hour—especially when she'd been strung out so amusingly on the magical water—and then thought she wouldn't outlast the rain. But she had surprised him. His curiosity then turned into a stronger emotion, the beginnings of which might have frightened him.

After all, he'd thought he'd grown out of those feelings ever since the incident–

No. He wouldn't think on that.

He'd turn those thoughts into something that better suited his legacy. Possession. *Yes, Jolie Hook was nothing more than a prize to be possessed*, he decided, shoving all other thoughts aside.

He felt almost predisposed with a sense of eagerness to see her succeed in his tasks. And also a sense of competitive spirit to create something new to torment her with. He would find out which illusions would unravel her.

That would scratch the damnable itch under his skin.

The first step was to observe her, and Peter had gladly locked himself away in his room for the better part of the day doing just that. He would never physically follow her, but his apparitions could fly everywhere on the island, and that was even better. Like now. Though his body was sat crossed legged in his bed, his illusion self was hanging from a tree branch, watching an irate pirate kick over a sandcastle.

He stifled a laugh. Her reactions were just so entertaining! Had she thought for a moment that this was the castle she was being led to?

Of course not. She probably assumed that both doors would've led to false castles, though that was wrong.

Peter Pan was a trickster, but he was still a man of his word. Had she chosen the other door she would've ended up right at his doorstep. But he was glad she hadn't—that would have ended the fun too soon.

He also wanted to see her reaction to the lagoon. Hook's allegiance to the Merfolk had been a turning tide during their bloody war. Would she be pleased to see this place? Furious at its crumbling architecture? Saddened at the state of those who tried to go against his Lost Boys?

He didn't have long to reflect on that thought, however, because something soon happened that he hadn't anticipated: one of Neverland's most ancient beasts was awakening.

Peter immediately let go of the tree branch and crouched down low between some foliage.

"Dust," he swore under his breath.

The crocodile was old and powerful, but it had been sleeping for nearly fifty years. The fact that it was now awakening—now when Jolie Hook stood looking like a delectable snack not twenty meters away, was nothing short of bad luck. It opened its jaws and gave a mighty roar.

Peter watched in abject horror as it advanced on the raven-haired pirate.

"What will she do now?" This wasn't one of *his* challenges, but rather one born from Neverland itself. *Intriguing.*

He watched with bated breath as the beast stalked closer and closer to her. Was she not going to move? Turn and run? She hadn't even taken her sword out for fairies sake. At the final moment, when the word "Move!" was on his lips and the croc was only a few feet away, she finally regained her senses and dove to the side, into the shielding arms of a nearby broken archway.

The croc lunged after her, but he was weighed down by his massive body—huge after years of eating any creature who crossed its path, and then hibernating until its next slumber. He was known to wander the island and Peter supposed he must have chosen to rest here because it was quiet and untraveled.

Until now.

He caught a whirl of dark hair as the girl spun towards the beast, though now, blissfully, with her sword drawn high. Peter was both shocked and awed by the look on her face: not a trace of fear.

Her eyes shone brilliantly clear and her mouth was set into a grim line of determination that Peter himself had come to recognize from her father. He searched for a wobble in her sword arm, a tremble in her knees, but found none.

Had Captain Hook truly made such a formidable champion out of his heir?

He watched as she slashed towards the beast and, judging from its roar, she must have hit something. She followed up with a sharp clap of her curled first against its snout. Peter had to reign in a laugh. Had she just punched the croc? He shook his head. Only Jolie Hook, fearless and fatal, would dare to do that.

It only served to enrage the beast, though, because it reared up and swiped at her with its sharp claws. It seemed to happen in near slow motion as Peter watched. Claw met arm, blood met skin, and Jolie Hook's body was lifted off the ground and flung into the closest stone pillar where she crumpled to the ground, unmoving.

She laid prone as the beast advanced, slow but determined in its lumbering gait.

Peter then did something that he didn't quite understand, and that Tink would surely shout at him about later: he teleported his physical body into the lagoon. Standing in front of the knocked-out girl, he blocked the path of the beast.

"That's my pirate," he sneered, raising his hand and pulsing out a wave of magic that knocked the crocodile back.

Angry, it approached again, raising its snout and snapping its jaws. "I said, back off!" he roared, flaring his fingers. This time, the croc exploded into a hundred small purple bubbles, which then floated upwards and disappeared into the wind.

Peter's knees buckled and he caught himself on the stone arch. Strong magic took a lot, and banishing a Neverbeast? That took strong magic. It would be back someday, that he knew, but it bought him time. *Them* time.

He turned to look at the crumpled figure on the sand. Her hair had come loose and was splayed everywhere. Peter resisted the strangest urge to run his fingers through it. Instead, he knelt down over her body.

"You look terrible, darling girl," he sighed. Her arm was gushing bright red, and what breath he could see rising from her chest was shallow.

You should just leave her.

But then the game would be over.

There's plenty more games without needing her.

But there's something about Jolie Hook...

He scooped the prone girl into his arms. It felt odd to feel her against his real skin. He hadn't left his castle or the Lost City in years, but he found that he didn't mind it.

Her head lolled against his chest and he brushed a finger against her cheek with a surprising tenderness. She looked so soft when she was sleeping, he decided. So unlike the fiery girl he knew. Any moment now she might wake up and try to stab him.

Just looking after my toys, he decided. But Peter knew that if he had a heart it might've beat for Jolie Hook at that moment.

Chapter 15

"Legend has it that Neverland was once a part of a bigger, greater world located on a distant star. One day, the people there decided their land was too vast, so they cut it down the middle and tied one half to a dozen massive beasts. The beasts pulled the land across the stars until it finally settled, becoming what we now know as Neverland. What happened to the beasts, none can say—though many believe they still slumber somewhere on Neverland's shores."

\- THE MOSTLY ACCURATE TRAVELER'S GUIDE TO THE ANCIENT WORLD OF NEVERLAND

 t first, all she had was flashes.

A behemoth of a beast with mossy green scales lumbering towards her on knuckles tipped with vicious claws.

Her sword, shaky at first and then unbreakable. She was a Hook and she would not be afraid.

Blood. Darkness.

And then...brown curls. Freckles. A soft look and a charming mouth. Whispers of *"You'll be alright, just hang on, darling girl. I've got you,"* that somehow made her feel safe before she slipped back under the lulling pull of waves.

She woke up again in pain. Her entire arm was on fire, something was burning her skin straight off her bone. Her voice tore against her throat until it was nothing but tatters, even as cool hands pressed damp cloths against her brow.

"It's not working–"

"Keep going," a sharp voice answered. She recognized that voice.

"P-pan?" she croaked. "G-get away-y from me–" But her protestations were drowned with another cry of pain. Her flesh was ripping itself into ribbons, fluttering uselessly to the floor.

"Come on, darling girl. Don't tell me you'll give up this easily?"

She finally managed to peel her eyes open, even as the motion tore a whimper from her mouth. Everything was fuzzy, but she could still make out twin emerald eyes staring at her flashing bright with determination and...fear?

Was he saving her?

Pain like the thunder of wild stallions raced through her, and she fell back beyond the dark.

In her dreams, she was plagued with visions of her father. Not of him trapped in Pan's dirty dungeon, but of him resplendent as the captain of the Jolly Roger. He was strong and he was confident, and she was so proud to be his daughter, to share those qualities.

Except it wasn't a dream at all, but a nightmare.

"You will never live up to my legacy," he sneered. "What have you sacrificed? Nothing. You didn't know pain at all." Her father waved his hook in her face. "You will never be a real Hook."

"I–I–" she stammered, her heart beating wildly.

He reached forward for her left arm. "If you want to captain this ship, sacrifices must be made."

He raised his hooked hand—now not a hook, but a sword—and swung it down across her wrist, and Jolie screamed and–

She woke up with a strangled yell amidst the tangle of soft green sheets stained with sweat. Her mouth was dry and her chest was tight, but she grasped her hands together and was thankful that they were still whole, still attached.

"Just a dream," she tried to calm herself. Her hair was plastered to her brow in thick clumps and her shirt clung to her body in sticky, uncomfortable places. She paused. *This is not my shirt.*

Gone was her maroon tunic and worn-in pants; she now had on the soft green uniform of Peter Pan's Lost Boys. Even his gaudy golden leaf pin at her shoulder. She frowned and immediately ripped that off and tossed it into a shadowy corner.

She took in the room. It was small but comfortable. Not much more than the wooden bed she laid in, a well-made dresser, a pot of unidentifiable flowers, and a small jug with two cups. She realized that her old clothes and her sword were nowhere in sight.

Kidnapped by the enemy then?

Her fingers fluttered gently across the arm where the crocodile had sliced her. The short-sleeved shirt did little to hide the scar running down from shoulder to elbow, but she was surprised at how invisible it seemed. Someone with a deft hand had stitched her up. Or...it was magic.

Jolie shuddered at the thought of magic fingers creeping their way into her skin and veins. Especially if it had been Peter Pan.

"Pan!" she realized with a small start. She had seen him, sometime during her snatches of awareness. Had he saved her from the beast?

She frowned and shook the thought away. No, that would be altogether out-of-character. The man who threw her into danger was unlikely to be the one to save her from it. Jo scowled as she realized that she'd had to have been saved at all.

She scrubbed her hand down her face. She was exhausted. Physically and mentally. She wanted to be back on the Jolly Roger gabbing with Damien and training with her father. She was tired of games, tired of the Neverwoods, and tired of trying to figure out Peter Pan.

"One good deed doesn't redeem him for a lifetime of evil," she reminded herself, throwing off the sheets and swinging her legs onto the floor. As she stood, a rush threatened to send her collapsing back into the bed, but Jo gritted her teeth and forced herself to remain standing.

She was most likely in enemy territory. She would not appear weak.

Jo spent the next few moments ransacking the small space.

There was nothing under the bed except for spiders and dust—the non-fairy kind—and the chest of drawers only had more uniforms like she was wearing, though she did swap her slippers for a pair of black boots. She didn't find any clues to her whereabouts, any intel on her enemy and, more importantly, couldn't locate her sword.

Unarmed and lost, Damien will never believe this.

Seeing no other option but to move forward, Jolie crept towards the unassuming wooden door and pressed her ear against it. Hearing nothing, she slowly twisted the knob—almost surprised when it opened beneath her touch—and peeked out through the crack.

Jolie instantly knew that she was in trouble.

Chapter 16

"Entry into the Lost City is restricted to Lost Boys and prisoners of war. Unauthorized travelers will be taken to Cannibal Cove to await judgment. (This author firmly advises against any attempts to visit.)
- THE MOSTLY ACCURATE TRAVELER'S GUIDE TO THE ANCIENT WORLD OF NEVERLAND

She hadn't just been taken into enemy territory, she had been taken into the very brains of her enemy's territory. If Pan's castle was the heart of his kingdom, then the Lost City was the mind.

From her father's reconnaissance she knew that it was here that his generals converged and talked strategy. How best to overrun a settlement. Where to strike the pirates next. How to get away with murder.

Jolie nearly wanted to retreat back into the room, what small comfort it posed, but forced herself to slip out the door and take the city in; it would come in handy when she reported it back to her crew later.

She was loath to admit it, but the Lost City was breathtaking.

The entirety of it was made up of tree houses, built from neverwood and connected via lengths of rope and plank bridges. Jars of captured star-bugs seemed to almost float in the tree branches, the creature's glowing wings gently fading from white to gold. Curling staircases made of thick interwoven vines could be seen creating pathways further up into the trees as well as down to the ground which, as Jo stole a look, was at least sixty feet below where she stood.

Her gaze tilted upwards, where she could make out the sliver of the moon casting its light between the treetops. She cursed under her breath. While the cover of night would make it easier to sneak out undiscovered, it left her completely exposed to the nightmares that lurked the forest at twilight.

But she would take monsters over Lost Boys any day.

All of the treehouses had fences of wooden beams to prevent you from falling to an unfortunate death, and Jolie crouched low behind one now so that only her eyes and the top of her head were visible. She scanned everything she could see and frowned.

It was nighttime, but there was no one around. Would the Lost Boys not have posted guards? Sentries? The fact that there had been no one waiting outside of her room to throw her back in had itself been a surprise.

She glanced at the nearest vine ladder. She could easily climb down and run for her life, though she might not make it far without her sword.

And will you ever have the chance to snoop around the Lost City again? Imagine what you could learn about the enemy!

"This could be a trap," she muttered, but she knew it didn't matter. A Hook wouldn't run from this chance.

She moved with the fluid grace drilled into her from years of training. Flitting from shadow to shadow, Jolie Hook melded with the trees and the houses. At the bridges, she crouched down as low as her aching knees could afford her, though she had a feeling it was an effort for naught. There was truly no one around but her and the bugs.

At each treehouse, Jolie tried the doors. Unlike her own, these refused to open, and the windows were too small and too high for her to do anything with them.

There has to be something here, she repeated to herself as she ventured further, her hackles rising with every step. The longer she dallied, the more likely it was that she'd be discovered.

At first she attempted to take note of her path, but the city was like a maze with its crisscrossing bridges and dead ends. At more than a few points she had to double-back and ended up in a place she was sure she had been before. Curiously, not once did her arm even twinge of pain, and Jolie again marveled at its healing.

Pan would no doubt regret not leaving her to die.

Suddenly she spotted it out of the corner of her eye: an open door.

Again, her instincts yelled *TRAP* and again Jo stuffed those thoughts down. So what if it was a trap? She could get out of traps with her hands tied. Without a sword. Without allies.

She crept steadily forwards. Upon further inspection, this treehouse seemed larger than the others, and older.

Yes, as she approached she could see that the towering oak must have been centuries old, and centuries strong. The treehouse itself had marks in it, some that must have been from blades, but others that looked almost like drawings. Jo frowned and tried to make one out in the dim light. Four figures holding hands. And...a dog?

"Strange," she muttered. But it wasn't what she was looking for. She needed war plans, maps, anything that could give her crew an edge over the Lost Boys. With a look around to make sure there were no sudden eyes on her, and a listen for any noises coming from the hut, Jolie crept inside.

It was mostly barren, though there was a touch of cozy to it.

The same wooden bed that Jolie had woken up in, but with a clearly hand-woven blue blanket thrown haphazardly over top. A dresser of drawers, but none of them closed because they were so full. Curiously, she peered inside, and nearly laughed when she saw not clothes at all, but piles of junk! Acorn shells, nuts and bolts from a welder, a pile of mismatched socks. On top of the dresser she was disappointed not to find marching orders, but rather a yellowed piece of paper, clearly torn from some book.

She didn't recognize the author, but the page was creased enough that she assumed someone must have read it a hundred times over.

> *And who could play it well*
> *enough*
> *If deaf and dumb and*
> *blind with love?*
> *He that made this knows all*
> *the cost,*
> *For he gave all his heart*
> *and lost.*

And then, scratched at the bottom in faded black ink: Never forget where you hid it, and never give it away again.

Jolie wasn't sure what to make of the cryptic message. It wasn't battle related, of that she was sure, but what did it mean? She slid it closer and traced her fingers over the words, wishing she could glean some secret code from their letters.

As she reread it again, her nose twitched with the smell of sugared lemon and pine.

"You're not where I left you."

Chapter 17

Jolie spun to face Pan, schooling her features into a cool mask. He seemed refreshed. His hair looked freshly washed, his clothes unwrinkled. His eyes were clear green, lighter than she'd ever seen them, and crinkled at the corners as he smiled at her.

"Why am I here?" she asked, taking a step away in tandem as Pan took a step forwards.

A ghost of a frown kissed his lips. "You got a little too friendly with an overgrown pet, that's why." He ruffled his hand through his hair and Jolie's heart gave a pitiful stutter—he looked so innocent when he did that. Like nothing more than a human boy.

"I was fine," she bit back.

"Liar," he teased. "You would have become lunch...and I feel like you're more of a dessert girl, hm?"

"Back off," she snapped as he took another step closer. "You saved my life, maybe, so what? I don't owe you anything."

His brows rose but his amused smile didn't fade. "Owe me?" He laughed. "Not at all, darling girl. I'm just taking good care of my things."

"I'm not your *thing*."

Pan winked, and the urge to punch him intensified. "We'll see about that," he said softly. "I think I've grown quite fond of you, I'd hate to let you go."

She swallowed, her throat feeling as thick as the tension in the air. Had she truly believed that he had healed her from some hidden good nature? Some kindness? No. Peter Pan was doing what Peter Pan did best: stealing things.

"You're unhinged." She darted to the right to try and squeeze around him. The door was nearly in reach when he caught her by the waist, spun her, and pinned her against the wall. His hands were hot and rough against the thin fabric of her clothing.

She refused to cast her gaze down, instead opting to stare at him with all of her fury—she hoped that the heat of it was palpable.

"I think we're all a little unhinged in Neverland," he murmured, tightening his grip for a moment. Whatever emotions he was feeling flitted across his face so fast that Jolie couldn't pick out any of them in particular.

For herself, she made sure that her mask was thick with anger, but underneath she was fighting cracks of confusion and chips of nerves.

"You...you're touching me. You're not an apparition. Why?" She cursed herself for not having found her sword soon enough.

"Why are you in my room?" he countered. Jo was a little surprised, though she tried to hide it. This room was his? The mess and the chaos and the whirlwind of who she had assumed was a young boy?

"You live in your castle," she said, a statement not a question.

"Sometimes," he nodded, his eyes trailing up her face, pausing in certain places: her lips, her cheeks, her eyes. She wondered what he saw there, if he wanted to stuff her into one of his drawers amidst his other collections.

She cleared her throat. "I was in here looking for my sword," she admitted.

He huffed a laugh. "Of course you were. It's off being cleaned."

"Cleaned?"

"It was stained with croc blood," he shrugged. "You can have it back later."

"Why not now? Afraid I'll be able to finally kill you now that you're not some untouchable ghost?"

He leaned in closer and grinned, then tucked a lock of hair behind her ear. Jo startled at the movement; it was far too intimate. Something had changed within Pan since she last saw him, something more raw, honest.

It scared her even more than if he was being malicious.

That she could deal with.

But a coy, tempting Peter Pan? "If you want me to bleed so badly for you," he said, voice rough, "all you have to do is ask."

She batted him away and crossed her arms over her chest, melting back further into the wall.

Again, he smiled. Like everything he did was another of his little games, and he was always excited to see how she'd react.

He can see how well I'll react when I get my weapon back.

As if sensing her thoughts, Pan straightened. "Come on, we'll be late."

"Late? To where?" She spared a small, quick glance at the yellowed paper on the dresser. She had a feeling it was more important than she knew.

"Why, to dinner of course."

Chapter 18

"Neverland has many delicious dishes native to the island. This author recommends the glowfish cakes with a side of soulfruit salsa. Don't forget to wash it down with Captain Hook's favorite spiced rum, as well as some fairy cookies from the gift shop on your way home!"
- THE MOSTLY ACCURATE TRAVELER'S GUIDE TO THE ANCIENT WORLD OF NEVERLAND

In the time that it took Pan to wind Jolie down a sloping ramp, through two empty huts, and across a bridge, she had come up with eight new ways to kill him—none of which seemed a violent enough end fitting for her enemy.

But amidst the swirls of red clouding her vision, tendrils of confusion wormed their way into her thoughts as well.

Jolie had no idea what Pan was doing. He had undoubtedly saved her life, but why?

She wanted to understand him, to unlock the secrets that made him tick.

Better to know your enemy than to not, she told herself, but it was a weak excuse even to her.

Truly, she was far too curious for her own good.

She thought back to the poem she'd found, turning the words over in her mind and wondering what they meant to him. She had a feeling her mother would have enjoyed reading it, she'd always had an affinity for books.

She glanced up at Pan as he pushed aside a curtain of woven daisies and tugged her inside. Would he remember her mother? Or was she just another long line in his tally of casualties?

Was *she*?

Your father's waiting for you. Damien's waiting for you. Your crew's waiting for you, she reminded herself, straightening her spine and turning to face whatever fresh nightmare Pan had cooked up.

Jolie blinked. True to his word he'd taken her to dinner.

To a feast, was more accurate.

Beyond the daisy veil was some sort of outdoor dining space. Surrounded by trees but with the sparkling sky visible overhead, they walked towards the massive rectangular oak table in the center. It had at least space for two dozen people, and enough food piled onto platters for twice that. More glowing bugs in small jars were laid across the wood and hung from curved sticks around the circular space.

"What is this?" she asked.

"This is dinner." He steered her towards one end of the table, where two high backed chairs, not unlike the one in her father's office, were placed side by side. They stood in stark opposition to their plain birch siblings around the table, though Jolie noticed another elegant chair at the other end, one with a small pink bow attached to the back.

"Can't I sit over there?" she grumbled, sliding into her seat beside him. "Away from you?"

"That seat's taken," he replied, waving his hand until magical sparks crackled over his knuckles. At his bidding, a curl of rope appeared and knotted itself over Jo's left hand, binding her to the arm of the chair.

She huffed and rolled her eyes, pulling against the rope uselessly. "Afraid I'm going to attack you?"

"Not me."

"There's no one else here. Probably put off by your foul appearance," she sniffed, trying to tug her elbows as close into herself as she could. She didn't want to risk bumping into Pan in any capacity.

It did seem wasteful though, all the food for just the two of them? She could see grilled meats and steaming roast vegetables, at least six pies of various fruits, and pitchers of liquids in every color of the double rainbow. A variable smorgasbord, though Jolie would trade it all for a single bite of Damien's veggie stew.

Instead of answering her, Pan cupped both hands around his mouth and let out a loud, sharp caw. The wind rustled and for a moment Jolie wasn't sure anything happened, until the rumbling started. Soft at first, just the patter of slippered feet, and then louder and louder until she was sure they were about to be besieged by an army.

"Pan..." she warned, twisting and turning in her seat. If she was about to be attacked she at least wanted to be on her feet, but his warm hand clamped down on her arm.

A yell, nearly a battle cry, sounded and then a stampede of people flocked through the daisy curtain. If not for the rope binding one hand down, and Pan's grip binding her other, she would've grabbed a fork and readied her defenses.

In the blink of an eye, each chair around the table went from empty to full and she was surprised at who she saw. Lost Boys.

Chapter 19

"Those looking to join the ranks of Lost Boys might find themselves disappointed to learn that it is a highly exclusive, by-recruitment-only army. Only Peter Pan can say what qualifications one must possess to join his ranks and, at this time, the elusive boy has declined all interview requests."

- THE MOSTLY ACCURATE TRAVELER'S GUIDE TO THE ANCIENT WORLD OF NEV-ERLAND

"Lost Boys" was partially a misnomer, since quite a few of Pan's army were in fact girls, but Jo knew not to discount them. The Lost Boys had been as much a part of Pan's bloody legacy as the unaging rogue himself. They were vicious, they were unyielding, and most of all, they were loyal.

They were also staring at her.

Unfazed, Jo stared right back.

They were wearing the same uniform as she was; some were dirty and ripped while others seemed freshly washed. It was the same for the Lost Boys themselves: a few looked like they had just come from the mud pits while some sparkled and grinned at her with pearly whites. There were blondes, brunettes, redheads. There were some younger and some older, though none seemed older than Peter Pan himself and she wondered if they aged at all.

Jolie refused to back down from their threatening auras. Even though she felt as though she'd just been flung into the viper's pit, she somehow doubted Pan would let his army do anything permanent to her.

"Who's she?" one of the nearest asked. She had half of her hair shorn close to her skull and a white tattoo of a rose was inked onto the ebony skin of her neck.

"A guest," Peter answered. He seemed to remember at that moment that he was still holding Jolie's hand because he let go, wiping the sweat from his palms onto his trousers as he did so.

"I know 'er." Jo turned to the new voice, grimacing at the boy who immediately reminded her of a pig. Wide, round face. Beady eyes. A snout nose. He was one of the most unkempt of the entire dinner party. "She's one of 'em. A pirate." He sneered the last word like a curse.

"Rather a pirate than a Lost Boy," Jolie snapped back.

"Oh ho! She's got bite!" he chortled, the sound animalistic. "What's the plan Peter? We gonna use her as a...whats-it called? A hostage?"

His words echoed across the open aired space and the entire table began to murmur. Some excited, some nervous, a few confused.

"She's a guest," Pan stressed again, his voice hardened. "And she will be treated as such until the time she leaves."

"Which is when?" Jolie asked.

When his gaze slid to hers she noticed a small smudge of black in his green eyes. "When I say so." He turned back to his crew. "Now eat!"

They had clearly been waiting for his order, because as soon as the words left his mouth all of the Lost Boys began slamming food onto their plates and slopping drink into their cups. A few didn't even bother with utensils, ripping instead into chicken with their teeth and fingers, swiping globs of butter straight from the dish with their thumbs. Food went everywhere, but no one seemed to mind the chaotic mess of a ritual.

She watched in awe as someone crushed nearly an entire baked potato into her mouth at once, chewed twice, and then swallowed with a satisfied grin.

"Hey, *guest*, mind passing the peas?" the ruddy-faced boy asked, gesturing to a wooden bowl filled with green spheres. She rolled her eyes and slid it as far in his direction as she could.

"It's Jo, not *guest*, and I'd mind how much you shove into that gullet, wouldn't want to choke."

He glared as he dove a massive soup spoon into the bowl and then into his mouth. He chewed with his lips wide and his teeth gnashing, spittle and green flecks flying across the table.

"Watch it Conroy," the girl with the tattoo hissed, wiping a pea shell from her shoulder. She glanced at Jo, "Boys, such pigs."

"Guess his parents never taught him any manners," Jolie muttered in return, scratching idly at the table. A silence oozed through the dinner party like a poisonous cloud as two dozen eyes shifted her way. "What?"

Peter ducked his head towards her, murmuring in her ear, "These are Lost Boys, darling girl."

She resisted the urge to turn her head and face him directly, wanting to avoid a set of piercing eyes she knew would ensnare her. Instead she shrugged. "So?"

He chuckled and pulled back to face his crew. "So? Parents?" he shouted.

The crown erupted back at him: "Don't have 'em! Don't need 'em! Don't want 'em!" Jolie jumped at their cheer, at the way they banged their forks and cups against the table as they did so.

No parents? She looked across the table at each of the Lost Boys, people her father had fought against for years. She recognized some faces, and some scars. A particularly nasty cut that ran from nose to shoulder of a boy nearby was her handiwork—a trap she'd set on the beach that the enemy had waltzed right into.

Her father had grounded her for a week for disobeying his orders to stay on the ship but it had been worth it.

"How do you find them all?" she asked Pan, her curiosity getting the better of her. The leader of the crew had a huge smile on his face that made his freckles dance across his nose; he was basking in his army. She wondered if they were his family, like the pirate crew was hers.

"They find me."

She clicked her teeth. "Doubtful."

"It's true," he replied, shrugging. "Ask Azalea." He nodded to the girl next to Jo, the one who had spoken to her twice now.

Azalea. Another name to add to her list of enemies.

She looked only a year or so younger than her, but the mounds of hardened muscle beneath her tunic meant that she'd be a tough foe. She'd be a challenge in a fight, but no more than Pan himself had proven to be.

"Second star to the right and straight on until morning," the girl said back, nodding to Pan and putting down her forkful of potato.

"It's second star to the *left*," Jo corrected.

"Not when you come from off world. *To the right*, that's the calling. Something in here," she pointed to her chest, "was screaming at me to follow that call. I ended up in the woods, and Peter found me the next morning."

Jo squinted at her. "A calling? What spell did Pan use to lure you all? Or is it more apt to call it a curse?"

Azalea laughed. "Is it a curse to work for the pirate tyrant Hook? I'm sure to you it is a privilege—what does he and that daughter of his pay you? Gold? Jewels?" She peered at Jo, "Immortal life?"

Pan's hand was at her thigh then, a firm, warm touch. A blush rose to her cheeks as she tried to pry him off but he just gripped tighter. She flicked her eyes to his, surprised to see that they were already on her, a warning in their gaze.

A warning that said not to start this fight. Not to expose herself as Hook's daughter. Was he protecting her? Or merely protecting himself from his crew's reproach?

"Why do you call him a tyrant?" she asked back, squeezing his fingers in recognition of the demand. He loosened his grip somewhat, but his hand stayed on her leg—from the spark that lanced between her skin and his touch, it was almost as if there were no fabric between them at all.

"Look at what he's done," Azalea scoffed, spearing a slice of red juiced meat on her fork and stabbing it in Jo's direction. "Pillaging? Looting sacred treasures? Murder?"

Jo ignored the last charge. War was hardly murder, soldiers in the Merfolk war knew what they had been signing up for. Both sides had lost countless; Mer, pirate, and Lost Boy. The other charges irked her though.

"Pillaging? Hardly," she scoffed. "Claiming treasure chests from the watery depths isn't looting, it's bringing things that were once lost back to the surface. Without pirates, they'd be sunk forever. At least we polish them up."

Azalea's gaze turned icy. "It's not yours to take."

"No one else is taking it, why not us?"

"Classic pirate attitude," she snapped. "Why can't you just–"

"Ladies!" Pan interjected, his fingers a ghostly trail along Jo's thigh. She repressed a shiver. She should shove him off, yell at him—but in front of this easily rioted crowd? She'd need to plan her actions carefully. "Why don't we calm down and remember that we're at the dinner table. Leave it for the battleground, yes?"

Azalea said nothing, pursing her lips.

"Officer Azalea." His tone was commanding, strong. It sent chills down her spine.

"Yes, Peter," she answered after a long, rebellious pause. "I'm sure this one's...not like the other pirate girls, hm?" She tilted her head at Jo, a hunter stalking her prey. Jolie raised her nose slightly and angled her gaze down its bridge. She wouldn't be intimidated by some second-rate fighter.

"Give me my sword and I'm sure you'll find I'm exactly like other pirate girls," she replied, reaching for a goblet of water and taking a thin sip.

Pan barked a laugh, his hand finally leaving her skin and reaching to tug on the ends of her hair instead. "What did I say? She's got spunk." When he looked at her it was with humor and joy. "My darling girl."

"Don't call me that," she hissed, elbowing him in the side and trying to scoot her chair. He smiled but let her move away and, for a moment, finally far enough away from his scent and his heat that she could breathe, Jolie could almost imagine she was back on the Jolly Roger with her own crew. Eating, laughing, living.

"Do you do this every night?" she asked, taking in the swirling din of conversation. Sadly, nothing was useful. There was no talk of strategy or battle, just the weather, what people did that day, who was dating who...

"They do," he answered, filling a cup with something that smelled like wine and nudging it towards her. She ignored it, not wanting to dull her senses. He shrugged and took the goblet himself.

"You don't eat with your crew?"

Pan said nothing, but placed a heap of meat pie on a plate along with a spoonful of a thick red sauce.

"Oh, I get it," she realized, her anger from the entire situation beginning to leak through to all parts of her. "Hard to eat when you're an apparition, is that it? This must be a real treat for them, seeing their leader in all of his red-blooded glory. And here I was thinking you were agoraphobic or something."

"Your mouth would be better suited for eating," he sighed, sliding the plate of food in front of her, along with a spoon. Jolie noticed there were no knives in reach.

"My mouth would be better suited cursing you," she said, but couldn't deny the empty expanse of her stomach. It had been a full day since she'd eaten–

"Wait, how long was I unconscious for?" she realized with a start, trying to mentally roll back her internal clock. She'd only been on her journey for one day when the croc had attacked.

"A full day."

"What?!" she cried. "A whole day? But that means I only have..."

Pan nodded. "One day left to reach your father. Like I said, you'll want to eat up."

Without another word Jo dove into her meal. Her appetite took hold of her like a wild, vicious thing as she shoveled the entire pie into her mouth and then reached for a steaming platter of fried clams.

She had to admit that it was all delicious. The perfect amount of spice and cooked to perfection. It was possibly the best food she'd had in months, and she was glad. She needed the energy, she would have to spend the entire day running if she hoped to find her father before midnight the next day.

Her hand stilled, a morsel of clam poised a few millimeters from her lips. *Her father.* What was he eating for dinner? Anything? Nothing? Dust and rat carcasses? Rain water?

How could she even be there, enjoying Peter Pan's tainted food while her father was locked up in his dungeon?

"Problem, darling girl?"

She dropped the clam as if it had scalded her. Her free hand clenched at her stomach, almost expecting the food she ate to come spewing out in a fiery torrent of shame. Like it or not, she was having dinner with the enemy.

A slim finger went under her chin and tilted her head up. Angry tears welled in her eyes but she furiously blinked them back, trying to rip her face away but finding Pan's grip too tight.

"I want to leave," she hissed. "I want to leave this city, I want to leave this farce of a dinner. I want to find my father."

He scowled. "Your father? You go out into the Neverwoods at night and you'll die. In fact, you've proven yourself quite capable at being able to nearly die during the day time too. So no, you'll stay right here where I can keep an eye on you."

"We had a deal—"

He let her face go and waved off her words. "You'll have plenty of daylight tomorrow to continue your journey."

"I don't believe you. I want to leave."

"Tough," he snapped, nostrils flaring. "What? Not used to getting everything handed to you on a golden platter? Boo hoo, the daughter of the fearsome Captain Hook has to beg and work hard for once!"

The dining table stilled as the Lost Boys caught on to his words. Hushed murmurs erupted until finally Azalea stood, unsheathing her sword and pointing it straight at Jolie. Her secret was out.

"She's the daughter of Captain Hook? Not just some pirate?"

"Put the sword down, Azalea," Pan said tiredly.

"If what you say is tru–"

"PUT the sword DOWN!" he roared, smashing his fist on the table. The warrior girl slowly holstered her weapon but did not sit.

"Is there a reason why she is having dinner with us, instead of being locked away in the dungeon?"

"Yes."

Azalea narrowed her eyes. "A good reason?"

"Yes," he snapped.

Silence as she looked first at her captain, then at Jo, then at the rest of the Lost Boys. The silence was wide and stifling.

Finally, she returned to her seat, but with a pointed look that Jo interpreted as "this better not end in a disaster."

And it might. But only if Jolie wasn't quick enough.

As Pan stared down the rest of his crew, Jolie, having been working on twisting her arm free from the magic ropes for the better part of the standoff, finally tugged herself loose.

Before anyone could notice, she uncovered the fork that she'd stashed under her shirt and jammed it into Pan's ribs, briefly smiling at his groan of pain.

And then she made a mad dash out the daisy curtain.

Chapter 20

"There is a handy topographical map at the end of this guide to help orient you. Be warned that maps often lie, however, and will lead those who aren't careful astray. One recent traveler even walked clear off the world itself."

\- THE MOSTLY ACCURATE TRAVELER'S GUIDE TO THE ANCIENT WORLD OF NEVERLAND

Jolie didn't know where she was going but she knew that she was dead if she stopped running.

From the shouts and crashes that ensued following her escape, there was probably an army of angry Lost Boys storming after her. Not to mention the angry magical villain now dripping blood in the dining room of the Lost City.

She smirked, ducking through a bramble of branches. She knew a fork wouldn't kill Peter Pan, but it sure had felt good to finally see him bleed. After years of war, where she and her crew had unknowingly been fighting nothing more than an illusion, she could finally say she bested Pan. At his own dinner table, no less.

Her feet felt like they were spurred on by the wind itself as she flew down a set of twisted stairs made up of old wooden planks. Her lungs ached for air but she refused to slow down and give in.

The food in her stomach was stuck in her like bricks. But Jo didn't stop— not until the path turned into a dead end before her and she was forced to skid to a halt, lest she smack her face into the tall fence that penned her in.

"Dust!" she swore. The fence was too high to jump, too thick to knock over, too smooth to climb up. Her head swizzled as she looked for an escape. Behind her, the tell-tale flickering of torchlight was coming around the bend. She was dead.

As she dropped her stance and readied for a fight she saw it, barely visible in the darkened forest: a trap door. She flung herself to the ground and stretched her fingers across the wood planked floor until she found the handle, so well hidden it had looked to her like nothing more than a leaf.

The interior was a terrifying black hole with a scraggly ladder but she could hear the chanting of angry Lost Boys getting nearer, so Jo didn't think twice about squeezing herself in.

She dropped the trapdoor and, not wanting to risk her enemies hearing the pounding of her heart or smelling the lick of sweat at her brow, she began to descend further. She couldn't be sure if she was above ground or below ground; with the way Pan had laid out his tree houses and bridges she had lost sight of her cardinal directions and sense of place. It felt like a cave though.

Slick moisture clung to the ladder and more than once her feet slipped out beneath her before she reached the bottom. When she finally did, she felt around for the walls: mossy patched stone.

What was this place? A secret way out in the event of war? An unused cellar? It was hard to tell in the pitch dark. She could very well be walking into an oubliette: a place they threw prisoners to forget about. Jo slowed her steps and made sure to feel ahead for anything designed to kill her—but all she felt were cobwebs.

Slowly, she shuffled further. The ladder had let out into a hallway of sorts, but as she followed it she felt no branching pathways left or right; she could only move forwards.

Her breath came out in short huffs. It was hot. The walls nearly felt like they were trying to suffocate her; at times they pressed in so tightly she wasn't sure she would be able to wriggle free at all. Another one of Pan's magical traps?

Suddenly, the hand she had been using to feel ahead crashed into something hard. She pulled back with a hiss of pain, massaging her bruised fingertips. Gently, she reached out again. It was just a wall.

Jo frowned. Another dead end?

She used both hands to feel around. By all accounts it felt exactly like a stone wall of any other cave. She should just turn around and head back the way she came, hope that the Lost Boys had given up their search. But beyond the stone, beyond the slick walls and the mildew smell...she could sense something.

Father used to say that there was star-stuff in her veins, and every so often Jolie believed him. In moments like this, when something hummed out to her, and her body sang back. Potent, powerful, promising...yes there was still a secret to be found in this cave.

She closed her eyes—for what good it did since the entire way had been too dark to see anything—and trailed just the tips of her fingers across the barrier. There was no knob, no handle, not even cracks of where a door would be. But somehow she knew that there was something worth seeing just beyond this rock.

"Open," she whispered. After a moment, "Please."

There was little fanfare. In one moment there was a rock wall, and in the next her fingers were clutching only at air. She gasped and her eyes flew open before she immediately shut them again.

It was bright.

She peeled one eye back, then another. Her mouth fell open as she walked through the open doorway and into what she could only describe as a portal to another world.

A world that was a massive, yawning cavern with a ceiling so high she couldn't see the top.

Everything was illuminated with the light from stars—they looked like stars, anyways—that hung overhead. The floor was grassy, brilliant greens and emeralds, with pushing daisies and marigolds spread around. There was a stream too, with no indication of where it started nor where it ended. It was so clear that it wasn't even blue, instead she could see right to the bottom, where rows of rainbow rocks shone up at her.

There were two trees, giant maples that almost leaned on each other, and a single, lone, blue couch. The cushions were dented inwards and the back had small body shapes pressed into them. Someone had clearly used this place, and used it frequently.

There was a dust to the air, though. A feeling that she had stumbled not into a sanctuary, but into a museum. She was almost loath to touch anything, because somehow this entire palace felt sacred, and she felt like an intruder. But above all, it felt impossible. She whispered the world aloud to herself as she ran her hands along the grass and dipped her fingers into the water. It felt real.

A soft rustling of feet behind her and the smell of sugared lemons. She turned towards Pan. "What is this place?"

She spotted the tear in his shirt from where she had stabbed him, and there were even a few stains from the blood, but it seemed as though he had healed the wound. He looked angry, but it was a cold anger. An icy anger. Somehow that was scarier than a fiery rage.

"This place is a dream or a nightmare, take your pick," he answered.

"Doesn't seem like a nightmare to me."

His eyes were black when he looked at her. "It's about to."

He clenched one of his fists, brought it up high, and slammed it through the air. Magic crackled along his palms and Jo smelled burnt sugar as the world around her changed.

Chapter 21

"Don't be fooled by illegitimate merchants peddling their junk along the settlements. If they offer you a course to teach yourself magic: run. Magic is neither bought nor learned. It is a living, breathing thing, and it itself chooses who to be bound to."
- THE MOSTLY ACCURATE TRAVELER'S GUIDE TO THE ANCIENT WORLD OF NEVERLAND

Jolie was tired of Peter Pan binding her to chairs. She clenched her jaw and yanked against the ropes until they started to rub her wrists raw.

"You won't get out of it this time," Pan said from his place standing behind her. "I made them stronger, just for you."

She shivered. She didn't like that she couldn't see him. An invisible enemy was the most dangerous kind.

"Where are we?" she asked, covering up her discomfort. His magic had whisked her into some strange land of illusion. Gone were the trees and the stream and the stars. Now it was as if she was suspended in pure nothingness. Not darkness just...nothingness. No horizon. No floor. No one around but herself and Peter Pan.

He set his hand lightly on her shoulder. "You tell me, this is your nightmare after all."

"Being trapped with you is enough of a nightmare, thanks, I'm ready to wake up," she sniffed, turning her head as far as she could to catch a glimpse of him. She had begun to notice just how startling his features were. Every inch could have been painted by the brushstrokes of a master.

"We're just getting started, darling girl."

He waved his hand and the entire world shifted, like the rotating stage of a play. The white blank canvas became a much more familiar scene: her own bedroom.

Jo's breath caught. Like a vision pulled from her memories, she watched as her mother tucked a much younger version of herself into bed.

"Now Jo, remember what we said about monsters, hm?" cooed the young woman with the raven hair. She had delicate, beautiful features, but a sharp smile and a curved tongue she often used to cut her enemies down to size. Her hands worked to tuck the thick quilt around the shoulders of her daughter—a veritable miniature of herself.

"Monsters are real," the small girl answered back.

"And why is that a good thing?"

"Because it means we can kill them."

The woman pressed a kiss to her brow. "Exactly, my sweet. Now count your stars and drift off to sleep, and I will be here when you wake up."

But Jolie, the 17-year old Jolie magically bound to a chair, forced to watch her own nightmare, knew that was a lie. Her mother wouldn't see another morning.

"This is cruel," she whispered. "Even for you."

There was no reply except for a fractional tightening of his hand on her shoulder.

In real life, Jo's memories would fade to black here as the drag of sleep pulled her under, but in this illusion something more terrible happened—as her mother exited the room, turning down the hall of the Jolly Roger and slipping into her own, they followed. Like floating spectators in a horrific game, Jolie and Pan watched as Penelope Hook made her way towards her own death.

The bedroom was empty when she entered, though something soon caught her mother's attention. A bouquet of white roses, and a slim card.

Jo closed her eyes, but it was useless, she knew what came next. Her mother would read the card: *'Forever yours'*. She would smile in that way that used to light up the entire ship. Then she would pick up the flowers, and she would breathe their scent deep into her lungs.

And then she would die.

While Jolie could close her eyes and pretend she was anywhere else, she had no one to block her ears. They could hear her mother's tinkling laugh at the card, they could hear the fierce inhale, and then they could hear sounds of choking, or dying.

"Watch," Pan breathed in her ear. "Or you'll miss it."

Jo opened her eyes, but everything was warped and watery. Still, she could clearly make out her mother's shape as she dropped to the ground, the bouquet of flowers still clutched in her hand.

"Mom!" she cried out, even knowing that it was all fake, that her mother had been dead for a decade. She felt like that little girl again, the one who would wake up in the morning reaching for a pair of warm arms that would never hug her again. Who would soon watch the entire ship run itself aground in a tizzy, who would creep into her parent's room to find not soothing, waiting arms, but a face mottled red, ice blue lips, a trickle of blood down the corner of her nose.

She would wear a wrinkled black dress and watch as they lowered her casket back into the sea, and she would cry and her father would tell her that Hooks didn't cry—even though that was a lie. She had seen him wipe away furious tears the night before.

"You've had your fun," she hissed through the tears. "Let me go!" Jo yanked on her bindings, but they tightened more in response.

He laughed, cold and cruel. "Scream all you want, Jolie Hook. No one in the Lost City cares for the scream of another poor lost girl."

"We had a deal–!" She struggled again. Fear, that sickly evil being, was making its way into her heart.

"I know what deal we made, Hook, and if you want to back out do so now. Otherwise sit still and watch, and remember that you brought this upon yourself."

Somehow, even though she couldn't see him standing behind her like a shadow, she knew that his eyes were molten black pits. Whether from his magic or from his malice she wasn't sure, but this was not the same boy who had saved her from the crocodile.

Part of her whispered that maybe she shouldn't have attacked him, shouldn't have ran. Would she be eating dessert with the Lost Boys if she had listened?

No, she shook the thought from her head. *He always had this cruelty inside of him, my meddling or no. He was just hiding it before, using his charm to lull my defenses. And it worked.*

Suddenly, the scene in front of her changed to something she couldn't place. It was her father, bloodied and chest heaving. At his side, his sword dripped...not red, but silver.

Fairy blood.

All around him were dying bodies—fairy bodies. Broken, iridescent wings ripped off in chunks. Delicately tattooed skin scratched and torn. Eyes glazed.

Jolie wanted to throw up.

Death didn't frighten her. She was no stranger to it. But this was not death. This was something far more sinister.

Her father turned, and Jolie gasped at the look on his face. Blank rage. If she walked up to him at that moment, she didn't think he would be able to tell friend from foe. He bent over slightly, peering down at one fairy woman who still breathed, shallow and pained. Her honeyed skin was flush with death's sticky fingers.

"P-please," she whispered.

Hook looked to his sword—one that had never left his side in all Jolie's years—then back to the woman, half his size and dwarfed in his darkness.

So slowly it was torturous, Jolie watched as her father slid his weapon across the fairy's throat. There was a dreadful gurgle, and then nothing.

Hook sneered. "That was for my wife."

The scene went dark and Pan spun Jo's chair so that she faced him.

"I don't understand," she admitted. "What was that? A nightmare?"

He gave her a contemplative look. "You call me cruel, and maybe you're right. But don't forget the cruelty that runs through your veins as well, darling girl. I am not the only villain in this story."

"I don't–"

"Haven't you ever wondered," he interrupted, "where all the fairies in Neverland went after the Merfolk war?"

Her blood froze. She had always assumed that they had fled, seeking better worlds. And once the gateway to the stars had closed...well they'd just never found their way back.

"You're accusing my father of killing them all," she said in a low, foreign voice. The words felt wrong coming from her lips. A traitorous accusation to levy against her own father. Hook was strong, and he was a fighter, but he wouldn't massacre an entire race.

"Smart girl. You saw it for yourself," Pan nodded. "That was no illusion. In the dead of night, Captain Hook stalked to the Fairy Village, and slaughtered each...and every...one." His eyes were blazing with such conviction that she found it hard to immediately discredit his words. Still, she tried.

"You lie."

"I am many things, Jolie, but I am not a liar."

"Then tell the whole truth!" She shot back. "If he did do such horrible things, then it's only because it was to avenge my mother. She was murdered, and I know it was your hand that penned those orders!"

He closed his eyes and breathed for a moment. "Are you certain about that?"

"Y-yes," she stuttered. She straightened her back as far as the chair would allow and put more force behind her words: "Yes. You're the monster who ordered your assassin to murder my mother." She glared. "And what a stupid move that was for you. The pirates joined forces with the Merfolk and we pushed you back to the Neverwoods. You lost the war the moment you poisoned her in her own home. As far as I'm concerned, you killed those fairies, not me!"

"You?" he mused, leaning forward to toy with the tips of her hair. "Who said anything about you? Aren't we talking about daddy dearest?" His eyes were leveled with hers now, his face mere millimeters away. If she leaned forwards at all, their lips would meet. "Afraid of who you're destined to be, hm? Afraid that the legacy of Neverland's villains is painted in the same blood that runs through your veins? All of this happened before, and it will all happen again, only with new players. Death begets death, after all."

Jolie saw red, reared back, and smashed her forehead into Pan's face. He grunted as his head snapped back and his nose, crushed under the blow, spewed maroon. He laughed once, low and rough, and pulled his lips into a smile, rubbing his fingers through his own blood.

"Just shut up about my family!" she shouted, rocking the chair side to side. "*You* are the one who launched that war! *You* are the reason my mother is dead, and my father is dying in your dungeon! *You are cruel and cold and dark and twisted*, Pan, not me!"

"There is a monster prowling in your veins, Jolie Hook," he murmured, cupping her chin in his bloody hand. She tried to jerk away but he pulled her even closer. "I'd love to see it break free. Such havoc it would cause. Such beautiful chaos."

"You're the monster," she spat.

He dropped her chin. "Another game then!"

"No! Dust your games, and dust you!" she seethed, baring her teeth.

"Your game," he continued, bracing himself against the arms of her chair and lording over her like an unwanted shadow, "is easy. Tell me who killed your mother."

"You did."

"Wrong!" he sang.

"Then the answer is your beloved Tinkerbell, but the order came from you."

"Wrong again," he tutted. "Better luck next time, darling girl."

With a mighty shove he threw the chair, and her still attached, backwards. Jolie tried to brace herself as best she could, but she still cried out when she smashed against the ground.

She blinked and the world above her, though upside down and pierced by the glare of a morning sun, was instantly recognizable.

She had been transported back to the Neverwoods.

Chapter 22

"No one has ever successfully cataloged the full range of animal species in Neverland—new ones seemingly crop up overnight based on the illogical, but creative, wishes of any number of imaginative children. See, Chapter 19: The Lion-Headed Snake, for an example of strange animal combinations that have been known to occur."
\- THE MOSTLY ACCURATE TRAVELER'S GUIDE TO THE ANCIENT WORLD OF NEVERLAND

Everything ached, but her heart most of all.

Pan had not only forced her to relive the night that had been plaguing her nightmares for ten years, but then had dropped another crushing blow onto her already bruised self.

Her father, a true murderer?

During the war she knew he had killed, or had ordered to *be* killed, many enemies. But that was different from murdering a bunch of innocent people, a bunch of innocent fairies. He should have just stormed Pan's castle and demanded that Tink pay for her crimes. Better yet, that Peter Pan himself pay.

Peter Pan who now denied taking any part in her mother's death.

"How can I believe that?" she sighed. "He would say anything just to get inside of my head."

And he had succeeded. She didn't know what to trust or who to believe. All she had was herself at that moment, and herself was very much lost.

She had 'lost' Pan's last game, and he had apparently dumped her into the middle of the woods in punishment. Still without her sword, and now without any sense of direction beyond her instincts, Jolie wandered through the trees and over fallen logs.

The magic of the woods—the ever-changing flowers, the colorful hybrid animals—that had seemed so intriguing to her before now held no interest. She just wanted to go home and never speak of magic again.

But first she had to find her father. Murderer or no, she needed to get him out of Pan's clutches. And then…and then she would ask him the truth.

"Dust!" she swore, slamming her fist into the side of a tree. A flying squirrel chittered irritably at her and chucked the casing of an acorn at her head.

"Sorry," Jo muttered, smoothing down the skin of her now red-dened knuckles.

"Don't worry, squirrels never hold grudges."

Jolie turned and eyed the voice—it was that dust-forsaken bird again. Pan's two headed pet, Michael and John, who had led her straight into the trapped cave.

She huffed and tried to ignore them. If Pan wanted to use this animal to spy on her then so be it, but she didn't have to entertain its presence.

"Where's she going John?"

"Well, probably off to the castle, right Michael? But she's going the wrong way."

"Do you think she knows that?"

"Probably not."

"Should we tell her?"

"Maybe she'd rather take the scenic route–"

Jo interrupted them. "Would you both quiet down? I don't fancy having another giant beast attack me because you dodo birds couldn't keep your traps shut."

"Dodo birds!" the head called Michael cried, flapping the shared wings and settling onto Jo's shoulder. She resisted the urge to brush him back off. "That's not accurate."

"And it's not nice," pouted John, as much as a bird could pout at least.

"You know what isn't nice?" she hissed. "Telling me you'll help me find shelter and then leading me to a trap."

"What?" they replied as one.

"That cave! Pan was waiting there, and then he nearly drowned me, and then he teleported me to a freaking croc–!"

"The cave? Oh, the cave!" Michael nodded. "Yes, we went to the cave, but you never arrived! We assumed you got lost."

"And then we searched for you ever since! And now we've found you, and can take you to the castle—oh but you're still heading the wrong way. Isn't she, Michael?"

"Yes, John, she is."

Jo's steps slowed and her eyes flicked over to the bird. It could be lying, but what use would it have to lie?

"Truly? You aren't spies working for Peter Pan?"

Her only reply was a trill and bell noise she likened to the bird equivalent of a laugh. Jo soon found herself chuckling along, and then doubled over in a full belly laugh. It wasn't until a few tears slipped from her cheeks onto her booted feet—she had to be rid of Pan's idiotic uniform soon!—that she spoke again.

"I think I am lost," she sniffed, wiping the tear tracks away. "I refuse to be scared by Peter Pan or his tricks but..." She looked up at the bird nuzzling her neck. "I need help. Will you help me?"

"Of course we will!" John cried, lifting up into the air.

"Follow us and we'll be there in no time!" Michael sang. "Just watch out for the stink sap along the way. Peter likes to use it to trap intruders."

"And watch out for poisonous flowers."

"And talking lion-headed snakes. They'll try to steal your tongue."

Jo sighed. "Anything else?"

"Yes," John finished. "What goes in usually doesn't come out of that castle. So be as quiet as the dead, because if Peter finds you then you might wish you were dead."

Jo grimaced. She still had no sword, no weapon beyond a large, pointed rock she had stuffed into her pocket, and knew she wouldn't be able to beat Pan in a straight up fight. His magic was too powerful for that.

But sneaking around and hitting him unawares? That she might be able to do.

"Let's go."

Chapter 23

"Don't forget to stop by the gift shop at the end of your journey, located between Star Portals 12 and 13, for all your Neverland souvenirs! Postcards of Skull Rock, imitation Merfolk scale, even a miniature of Peter Pan's castle (note: Pan merchandise is not officially endorsed and is an artistic depiction, not reflective of the actual castle itself)!"

ADDENDUM: This section has not been updated since the events of the Merfolk War.

- THE MOSTLY ACCURATE TRAVELER'S GUIDE TO THE ANCIENT WORLD OF NEVERLAND

J olie wasn't sure what she had been expecting of Pan's castle.

Few had ever seen it beyond his Lost Boys, and any time they were captured and questioned about its whereabouts they'd disappeared into a golden plume of fairy dust. Jo had always figured it was a kill-switch failsafe for Pan to keep his secrets, but after having seen how he interacted with them at dinner she wasn't so sure. He seemed to like them too much to kill them like that.

He was a liar and a villain, but at least he seemed loyal to his own people.

John and Michael had made quick work of leading her to the castle, a place she knew she would never have found on her own, even if she'd had weeks to wander the woods instead of days.

It had been past rows of trees clustered so thickly together you couldn't see through them, beyond a gathering of rocks that only parted when they'd asked politely, and through the mouth of a waterfall which poured over their heads but never got them wet.

And then the castle popped into view, like a cloud finally moving away and letting the sun's rays shine through. It was old; weathered gray stones stacked high on top of each other, covered in places by twisty vines and wicked looking thorned flowers. There was stained glass along the facade, a tower with a parapet in the back corner, and a wide, dark moat that separated it from the forest.

Two stone gargoyles watched from atop the high walls.

"If they see you, they'll report back to Peter," John whispered.

"How do I get past them?" Jo asked, eyeing the guardians.

They had wings tucked behind their backs and small horns protruding from bold brows. She shivered as their heads swiveled past the trio's hiding spot in the trees, almost expecting the watchers to light up red and screech their arrival. But they didn't seem to notice them yet.

"There's another way, a secret way," Michael said. He lifted his wing and gestured towards the moat. "They can't see you under the water. There's a door down there. It's spelled shut though."

"You have to solve its riddle, and it'll open," John added. "If we were a two-headed fish we could do it, but I don't think we know how to swim. Do we Michael?"

"No, John."

"It's up to you, Jolie. That's your way into Peter's castle, if you think you can do it."

Jo hardened her nerves.

The moat was big, bigger than it needed to be, and dark. The water must have been magic, because Jo had never seen the ocean look back at her with such malice. But she had been raised on the waves, had been swimming since before she was walking. Her mother's blood was sea water salty, and it ran through her veins. Thicker than anything else, even what might be the blood of villains. Her father's blood.

You can have anything in life if you're willing to sacrifice everything else for it.

"I can do it," she confirmed. She gently took the bird off her shoulder and placed it on the ground. "What will you two do?"

The heads looked at each other, shrugged. "We'll be here, there, everywhere."

"Not going home?" she asked.

"If we had a home we've forgotten it," Michael said, voice thick. "So if you find it inside there, let us know, will you?"

"And that other thing we forget, too," John piped up. "I can't remember, but it seems important."

"Okay," she nodded. "I promise. And I promise that if you ever need help, fly to the Jolly Roger and come find me." She pet both heads fondly—it was strange, how close she had become to a magically spelled set of birds, but Jolie was glad for their acquaintance, and not just because they had known the way to the castle.

She imagined that if she'd ever had siblings, they might act like Michael and John.

"We promise!" they echoed back.

Jo nodded and turned to the moat. It was a good fifteen second sprint from their hiding place to the water, and she'd need to stay out of the gargoyles' sight. They were scanning back and forth along the terrain, slow enough that she could track their movements. All she'd have to do was time it right...

Now!

Her heart leapt into her throat as she dashed out. She pumped her arms in tandem with her legs and all she could hear was the roaring of blood in her ears as she ran.

The water was so close, but from the corner of her eye the gargoyles began turning back in her direction.

Move! That was Damien's voice in her head, and she wanted to cry for missing her friend. His demanding tone worked, and she flew the final few feet before launching off the moat's edge and tumbling into the water.

It slapped her like a firm hand as she went in head first. She tumbled down and quickly lost her bearings. It was so dark that she couldn't pinpoint which way was up; her eyes might as well have been closed. Jo flailed in the nothingness for a moment, before forcing herself to remember everything her mother had taught her.

Swimming was about moving *with* the water, not against it. Slowly, she commanded her muscles to relax and open up her senses. She could feel it then, a gentle caress and the water, not truly stagnant like a moat should be, curving around her body. Where was it going?

Jo's hands turned to points as she carved through it, moving forward only by instinct. She realized then that Pan could have put together any manner of traps in there with her, but it was too late to turn back. All she could do was move forward.

The water urged her to dive down further and she acquiesced, stopping only when the tips of her fingers bumped into something.

Suddenly, bright golden light lit up the space around her. Her eyes narrowed at the glare, then widened. She had found the secret door. Looped cursive letters illuminated in magical light worked their way around a circular barred entry. Only none of the letters formed words at all, it was pure gibberish. Jo frowned, was this the riddle?

She gave the door a push but it was stuck. She'd have to puzzle her way out, and fast, before the tightness in her lungs became unbearable.

She peered at the letters:

Lal hte rlowd si dema fo iftha nda usttr adn yfiar sudt

It made absolutely no sense to her. Which meant it probably made perfect sense to Peter Pan.

She racked her brain for any hint. What would Pan have done?

For some reason, her instincts honed in on the letters *yfiar*. There weren't many words with y's in them, and even less that might be notable to the rogue.

It had to be an anagram for *fairy*.

Jo reached out to the word and was only marginally surprised when her hunch was right: the letters were moveable. She shifted them into the right spot and smiled in triumph—but her work wasn't done, and the presence of the water against her chest was starting to hurt. She had maybe only another minute before she'd have to go up for air, and at that point she'd most likely be caught by the guardians.

This was realistically her only chance to get in unseen.

Her fingers started sliding the other letters around, trying to make sense from nonsense. Slowly at first, and then in rapid succession she created word after word.

Jo kept sliding the letters until *All the world is made of faith and trust and fairy dust* was written along the outer edge. Internally, she cheered at her own cunning. Externally, she waited for a sign. *Any* sign that she had done something right.

But nothing was happening. The door didn't glow or open or move in any way. It was like she wasn't even there.

A hot, rough feeling was bubbling up in her lungs; like a cough that needed to get out. She was going to drown if the dust-forsaken thing didn't open. With a growl and a curse to Pan and his ludicrous castle, Jo slapped one hand at the door.

All at once and all of the sudden, the porthole disappeared, and a fierce tug of pressure at her navel was sucking her through the opening and into Pan's castle where the moat let out into a darkened waterfall of nothingness.

She stifled her scream as her body was flung through the air, tumbling head over foot down down down—

She finally stopped. She opened her eyes—not having realized that she had ever closed them—and parted her mouth in surprise.

There was no waterfall, no vastness of air and riddles. There was only damp, stone walls and the moss that slowly slithered across it, leaving green slime in its wake. Floating yellow orbs cast some light across the room—which was more like an antechamber. There was a suspicious brown wooden table with straps in the room's center, but besides that she saw only doors. Thick, wooden beamed doors with metal locks and steel bars over tiny window slots.

She had made it to Peter Pan's dungeon.

Chapter 24

*"There are many species of plant flora native to Never-
land, though it is hard to catalog them all. Most have
legs, and aren't afraid to use them to move across the
island whenever the whim arises."*
- THE MOSTLY ACCURATE TRAVELER'S
GUIDE TO THE ANCIENT WORLD OF NEV-
ERLAND

The instinct to shout for her father was strong, but Jolie knew better than to assume it was safe to announce her presence. Pan could have traps, trolls, or tricks—in fact she was counting on it. She had made her way through the Neverwoods, escaped the Lost City and the Lost Boys, outsmarted Pan at every turn—and now she had made it into his very castle. It would be one of the crowning achievements of her lifetime.

I am not the only villain in this story.

She shook the phantom words from her head. No matter if what Pan had shown her was true or not he would still be her enemy until the day he died. She had missed her chance in the Lost City, but she wouldn't let it slip by her again. As soon as she had the opportunity, she was taking it.

Her borrowed boots were thick and sopping as she slunk towards one of the walls, careful not to disturb any of the creeping moss or sleeping mice.

Jo stilled as a scratching noise, like the movement of clawed feet, sounded from a darkened corner opposite her. She drew back tighter into the wall, hoping that the shadows might conceal her from whatever nightmare Pan had concocted to guard his treasure. She didn't have her sword, but she did have her fists, and she curled them tight, waiting on the balls of her feet to spring into action the moment her enemy did.

Another scratch. Her heart pounded in her chest. She would not be afraid. She did not come this far to succumb to that wretched emotion.

A black snout was the first thing she saw, entering by the glowing light of the dungeon. Then padded feet, bigger than her hands. A shaggy gray furred body. Yellow eyes on a wide face—staring right at her.

A dread wolf.

Her knees shook for a moment before she locked them together.

Pan had a dread wolf?

Of course he did.

The beasts were vicious and violent. They did not injure or maim, they merely killed, and their saliva was said to be a poisonous toxin that rendered you completely immobile while they attacked.

She had to give it to Pan: this was an impressive entry in his bag of tricks.

She didn't dare move until it did, while it tilted its head back and forth, listening for something.

The beast took a step forward, sniffed, and turned towards her.

Dust! It must hunt by scent too. She pressed further into the shadows.

It growled, a thick drip of drool edging towards the cement floor. One paw shifted forward as the wolf's shoulders drew together, readying for an attack. An attack Jo wasn't sure she'd survive.

Then: a scuffle from somewhere overhead, the banging of a door. "Nana!" Jo's breath caught. That was Pan's voice.

The wolf's ears perked at his voice, and he called out again "Nana, where are you girl!"

Had Pan truly named his beast Nana?

She would have laughed at his cheek had she not been inches away from probable death.

It growled in her general direction once more, then a sharp whistle sounded and the wolf—Nana—turned tail and bounded away, back into the darkness and up the stairs.

Jo's legs nearly crumbled beneath her. She shot out a hand to steady herself, grounding her thoughts against the rough wall. That had been too close. And now that she knew Pan was nearby, she needed to move quicker. Shoving off the last vestiges of fear, Jo ran towards the first door, peered through the bars.

There was nothing inside. No one.

On to the next and the next she went, around the room like a clock hand. "Father?" she dared to whisper.

"Jolie?"

Her heart leapt at the familiar voice returning her call. She raced towards the next door. "Father!" She couldn't stop the cry fleeing her lips at the sight of the once great Captain Hook. He was sitting at the end of the cramped stone cell, reclining on the dirty wall. He looked awful.

Pan had left him in his pirate's clothes, but they were stained with blood, torn at the shoulders, and caked with dirt. His shoes were gone, as was his hat, and she stifled a gasp when she saw that his hook had been removed too; all that remained of that hand was the stump.

But it was his face that got her, that brought fierce twin streams of hot angry tears to her face. He was gaunt, with pale, sunken caverns for cheeks and blue ocean smudges under his eyes. His lips were so fiercely chapped they looked like paper, his hair so mottled with muck and gore that he was barely visible under its wiry chaos. He did not look like her father; he looked like a prisoner.

"Jolie," he croaked, reaching for her with his good hand. "You came."

"Of course I came," she half-laughed, half-sobbed. "I need to get you out of here, how does this door open–" As if responding to her words, the door swung inwards. She stepped towards her father, kneeling down next to him and pressing her hands into his cheeks.

"What has he done to you?" she cried. "It's okay, I'll get you home. You're safe now."

Hook's head threatened to slump forward but Jo caught it. His lips parted, but it took him a moment to draw enough breath to speak. "Trap..."

"I knew that meeting was a trap!" she said. "I'll save my I told you so's when we're back home, okay? Come on." She tried to reach under his arms to haul him up, but he was as limp and heavy as a sack of grain. Heavy, and yet her fingers could easily tell that he was malnourished.

Three days with no food, probably no water save what he could suck free from the stones.

Every single moment in the past few days where Pan had shown her kindness washed out of her mind with the growing tide of her anger, until there was nothing left but the vicious undertow of her hatred.

She hated him.

"Father, come on–" she groaned, unable to lift him up further than a few inches. "I can't drag you home like this–"

"Looks like Nana was right, we do have a new house guest."

Jo let go of her father and whirled. Pan gave her a look of amusement, his eyes a darkened green, though not the nightmare black from their last liaison. At his side, the dreadwolf nuzzled into his leg. He looked Jolie up and down, taking in her drenched outfit. "Most people usually knock on the front door, though."

Chapter 25

"In case you didn't heed my advice before: this author advises you against ever making a deal with Peter Pan."
- THE MOSTLY ACCURATE TRAVELER'S GUIDE TO THE ANCIENT WORLD OF NEVERLAND

"I suppose congratulations are in order," Pan said lightly, stepping into the cell.

Between his tall frame and that of his deadly pet, the way out was sufficiently blocked. "I don't know how you made it into the castle..." he eyed her dripping clothes and narrowed his eyes, "but I guess that shows how you should never underestimate the powerful Hook family." The last words were said with an acidic splash that told Jo he still wasn't over the whole stabbing incident.

Which was fine by her. She would never be over his tricks and schemes. There had been moments in the Lost City when she had almost forgotten that Pan was her enemy—when he had just seemed like some charming boy who'd invited her out to supper.

And then he had pulled the nightmare over her eyes in the cave.

And the depth of his mistreatment of her father had become clear.

"Remember this feeling, Pan," she snapped. "This is the feeling of you losing at your own game. I won your challenges, I've beaten your traps. Let us go."

Pan gave a dramatic sigh but waved his hand towards her father. "I am a rogue of my word. Your father can go. For what it's worth, he'll recover in a few days. Right as rain. Swift as starlight. I'll even give him his hook back."

"Am I meant to thank you for that?"

He rolled his eyes and snapped his fingers. Bright golden sparks shot from his palm and in the next instance her father disappeared from the cell.

Jo's mouth fell open and she whirled on Pan. She grabbed him by the front of his green shirt, noticing how the dark color matched his eyes; not quite black, not yet. "Where is he?!"

He only smiled in return, so Jolie cocked back a fist and aimed for his nose; Pan caught it in midair and used it to pull her flush against his own body. Her neck craned upwards to meet his eyes, her weight resting along his torso.

She growled and made to kick at him instead, but with a snap of his free hand she found that her legs wouldn't—couldn't—move.

"What is this?" she panted, trying furiously to yank her feet free. A vicious flush was working its way up her neck; part anger, part something else. "Where is my father?"

Pan lowered her fist but didn't let go. He held onto her upper arms, rendering her effectively immobilized. How had he caught her so unaware, so fast?

"You forget that this is my home," he murmured, trailing his fingers down her arm. She ignored the electric trail of lightning and shivers that sprung up—the feeling was strange, but not unpleasant. "This is where my power comes from. I'd advise you not to test me within these walls."

His words relit the kindling in her belly. She shrugged off his wandering fingers and made to claw at his face, but he merely stepped out of her reach.

"Fight me!" she said. "Enough with your games!"

"Fight you?" he asked, cocking his head. "That doesn't sound nearly as fun as you claim to make it."

"Then let me go."

"I would talk with you first," he replied, leaning against the cell wall.

Nana, the dreadwolf, had yet to move from her spot guarding the door, but with a look and a whistle from Pan she bounded off somewhere, leaving the two of them alone in the darkness.

"Tell me where my father is or I won't say a thing more."

"He's back on the Jolly Roger, drinking a buttered rum and, I expect, readying his plans to attack me back. He'll need a few days to recover though, if he hopes to join in on the fun."

"You teleported him back? Just like that?"

"Just like that."

Jo chewed it over. She supposed it was...nice...of him to teleport her father home and not make him walk the whole way. She didn't know if she'd have been able to drag him back through the woods unscathed.

"Will you talk with me now? Drop the scorned pirate princess act?"

She scowled. "It's not an act. I really just hate you."

He hummed, flicking some dirt from his pants. "Why?"

"Why do I hate you?"

He nodded.

"You want me to list the reasons?"

"I'm all ears."

She blew out a huff and started ticking off her fingers. "You're my father's enemy, therefore you're my enemy. You send raids out to our ships without a care. You started an ill-conceived war on the Merfolk that the crew got sucked into. You kidnapped my father and made me play your twisted game to get him back. You murdered my–"

"Alright, I get it," he interrupted, raising his hands in surrender, a cheeky smile playing on his lips. "But besides all that..."

"Besides all of that, I just hate looking at you," she barked. It was mostly a lie, Pan was actually half decent to look at.

More than half decent, if she was truly honest with herself.

Between his curls and his freckles, his playful smile and his lithe fingers, Peter Pan made some distant, cold and echoing hollow in her heartbeat. A purely physical reaction born from knowing no men her age except for Damien, she was certain.

"You wound me, Jolie," he mourned theatrically, holding his hand over his heart. "Is there truly nothing redeeming about me at all?"

"Why do you even care?" she parroted back, her feet starting to fall asleep from their magic hold. "We'll always be enemies. It's easier if we just imagine each other as horned monsters with no hearts."

In a flash, Pan peeled himself from the wall and set himself inches before Jo. He leaned in close, their breaths intermingling, his eyes so wide and clear green she could nearly count the swirls of jade. "Tell me, then, how do you expect to kill an enemy with no heart?"

Her chest stuttered in reply. She somehow felt even more immobile under the weight of his gaze. Not a single muscle wanted to listen to her commands to push him back or slap the dark look from his face. His eyes roamed hers searching for answers.

No matter how hard she tried, how many strategies she wrote or plans she made, she could never figure out Peter Pan. His actions made him a villain, time and time again, and yet his words seem to yearn for something else. Approval? Love?

He raised his hand as if to touch her, and Jo withheld the urge to flinch. She wouldn't shy away from him, now or ever. He dropped his fingers before they reached her though, his mouth falling into a flat line. "Why don't we play another game?"

"No."

"You haven't even heard the rules yet."

"I don't care. Unbind me and let me walk free of here."

He gave her a sorrowful look and stepped away, his hands clasped behind his back. "She seems to be working under false assumptions, Tink. Wouldn't you agree?"

Jo's jaw clenched as Pan's second in command materialized behind him, stepping out of the shadows and into the light of the cell. How long had she been standing there?

"It's not her fault, all pirates have fish for brains," the fairy snorted. Jolie glared.

Tinkerbell was almost as infamous in Neverland as Peter Pan.

She was short, at least a few inches shorter than Jo, and curved in places Jolie was abysmally straight. Her blonde, nearly white, hair was worn in a tangled mess of braids and waves.

Colorful tattoos stood in stark contrast to her pale skin; a dragon that writhed down her arm, imbued with magic to appear like it was really breathing fire; a cluster of berries painted her elbow; a branch with flowering white petals across her chest.

She wore a pair of tight black pants and a matching tank top with twin slits out the back for her wings. Red and nearly see through, they were folded in close to her shoulders, but Jo knew they were powerful enough to knock her off her feet if the fairy wanted. At her side were two wickedly sharp knives with darkened steel blades.

Pan's lieutenant hardly ever graced the front lines of any fight. The assassin preferred to sneak through the shadows, to use poison and traps. One such poison was the one that killed her mother. She was a monster with loyalty only to her unaging master.

She was the last remaining fairy on Neverland soil. The image of her father slaughtering the entire fairy clan raced through her mind before she could shut it out.

Stop falling for his treacherous lies, she admonished herself. What he showed you isn't real. Your father would never stoop so low. The fairies fled before the portals closed. That's what happened.

"She doesn't look so scary," Tink said, crossing her arms as she took stock of Jolie just like Jo did of her.

"Unbind me and give me my sword and I'm sure you'll change your tune."

Tink laughed. "I'm sure you would. Sadly, I think Peter fed your sword to the croc, and my schedule of charity fights against poor pirate princesses is fully booked up this month."

"Now, now Tink, she's a guest not a prisoner of war."

"Really?" Jo laughed, trying and failing to kick up her feet. "Feels like I'm trapped to me."

Pan rolled his eyes but snapped his fingers and Jo immediately fell to the floor as her knees buckled. "Bit of warning next time would be nice," she muttered, pulling herself to her feet. "Thanks for whatever strange interrogation this has been, I'm leaving now." She made to push past Pan but he caught her arm in place instead. "Get off of me."

"But you haven't heard the rules of the new game yet."

"I don't think she cares, Peter," Tink pointed out, pulling out one of her knives and balancing its point on her finger.

"Your sadistic friend is right," Jo agreed. "I don't care."

"Too bad," he snapped, tightening his grip for a moment as his eyes flashed dark and then settled into green again as he relaxed. "Would you like to play a game?" he said as he crushed her fingers tighter to his chest.

Jo pulled her hand away and put a step between them. "No, no more games. I know you, I know there's some trap here and I won't play into it. I'm going home."

"Don't you see, pirate girl," Tink drawled. "There's no *going home* for you. You're afraid of a trap but haven't realized you've been standing in one all along."

"What are you talking about? We had a deal–"

"*Make it to my castle within three days, and I will let your father go,*" Pan said, mimicking his words from the Hangman's tree. "And I did, your father is a free man." His face shuttered close, and when he next opened his eyes they were two pools of ink. "I never said anything about letting *you* go."

"You..." Jolie breathed, realizing the depths of her mistakes. It had been fatal error to cut a deal with Peter Pan, she should have known better.

You were never the winner when the odds weren't fair.

A scream bubbled up in her throat and she launched herself at the magical boy, hands grabbing around his throat and knocking him to the ground. She squeezed her fingers over his airway, knowing that it would amount to nothing in the end but still gaining pleasure from it. "I'll kill you!" she growled.

"You'll have all the time in the world to try," he whispered out, closing his hands over her. "That's the game. There's only one way to kill me, and I'll give you one free chance. Choose right and I'm dead, and the magic binding you here will break. Choose wrong...you're mine forever."

She hated him, his whispered words of honey and of vinegar, his two faces and how fast they shifted between each other. She hated her father for starting this mess, and she hated the Merfolk for not throwing Pan out of their world when they'd had the chance.

Jolie Hook was rage and fire and madness swirling together as one, she was going to kill–

Stars blossomed before her as Tink slammed the hilt of her knife into the side of her head. She grunted and toppled forwards onto Pan, who caught her gently in his grip. He hugged her to him with one hand, the other smoothing down her hair.

"It's okay, Jolie. It's all just a game."

Chapter 26

"Do you think you're making a mistake?"

"Am I?"

"I think history is repeating itself."

"It's nothing like that."

"No? Beautiful girl living in your castle? Only this time it's against her will—can't imagine how this will end."

"Even if it is like last time, so what? I won't make the same mistake twice."

"Don't tell me you love her."

"Don't be ridiculous."

"Infatuation then."

"She's a prize, nothing more. The only thing more valuable than her father is her."

"Don't insult me by lying, we've been through too much for that. This is just like before, only this time you're twisted inside. You think that if you trap her here she'll forgive you for years of being her ene-my–?"

"I know."

"She's not her, you know. Gaining Jolie Hook's forgiveness won't absolve you of your guilt."

"I know."

"One of you is going to end up dead at the end of all of this. This game? Why bother."

"Because it's no fun if there isn't a bit of danger involved."

"I don't think this is fun for you. I think this is what happens when you've worn a mask for so long it becomes fused to your face."

"...."

"You know I can't let her actually kill you."

"I'm hoping she won't want to. Maybe she'll come to realize that we're all villains in this story, one way or the other."

"That's a lot of pressure on a hope."

"Maybe. Maybe that's all we have left now."

Chapter 27

"If you ever find yourself in an inescapable situation, make sure that you try and plead your case to the stars. They have been known to show benevolence every once in a while."

- THE MOSTLY ACCURATE TRAVELER'S GUIDE TO THE ANCIENT WORLD OF NEVERLAND

When she woke hours later, Jolie expected to be chained to a slab of stone, perhaps with a rack of torture devices for company.

She expected Tinkerbell to be crushing up black death daisies to put in her tea and for Pan to be teaching his dreadwolf on how to chase her down should she try to escape.

She didn't expect to wake up in a guest room with silky green sheets, thick beige curtains, and handcrafted furniture. She winced and gently touched the bump on her head as she sat up in an extremely comfortable four poster bed—comfier than she had ever been in.

Apparently, Pan had seen fit to gild her cage but not to heal her with magic.

That was fine. The pain would be a reminder of who he was: her enemy.

She pushed back the covers and stilled. Just like last time, she woke up in new clothing. That in itself didn't bother her—magic seemed more likely than Pan, or even Tink, undressing her—but it was the clothing themselves that had her ears turning red.

It was a dress.

Pale blue and with billowing bell sleeves, it had a wide leather belt that cinched at her waist while the rest of the fabric fell to just above her knees. Below that, someone had laced up a pair of beautiful black boots, though she frowned at the impractical two-inch heel jutting out from the ends.

To anyone on the outside looking in she appeared like a guest, a friend of Pan's that had been given new clothes and the nicest room after a long journey.

But Jolie Hook was not a guest, she was a prisoner.

She cursed and threw the blankets off, swinging her legs to the side and testing her legs on the new shoes. Surprisingly, they seemed comfortable. So did the dress, though Jo knew the skirt would be a hindrance in a fight.

A fight she was itching to get started. If she believed what Pan had said about only one way to kill him, though, it would have to be a fight of the wits. She would only get one chance to try, so she'd have to make very certain she knew his weakness before she did.

She calmed her shaky hands as she gripped one of the bed columns. If she couldn't figure it out she'd be his prisoner forever. Of course, she would fight it, she would rebel, but magic had ways of crushing even the most determined of spirits.

Magic had a way of ruining *everything*.

"A Hook is not afraid," she whispered, latching on to the words like a lifeline in the storming seas. So what if Peter Pan had the upper hand? A game like this could easily topple in her favor at any moment, she just had to find a bit of leverage.

She'd have to be careful and play her cards close to her chest. If there was anything she should have learned by now it was that Pan did not play fair. She went over the rules of the game in her mind:

1. There is only one way to kill Peter Pan.

2. If she finds that way, she can kill him.

3. She'd only get one shot. If she guessed wrong he'd never let her go.

There was nothing in the rules stopping Pan from interfering or trying any way possible to guard his secret weakness from her. She had a hunch he wouldn't actually put her in physical harm though—otherwise why go through all the effort to trap her here?

Just another prize for his collection. In the corner of the room, a fireplace roared. She grabbed the iron poker next to it, gripping it like a sword—a makeshift weapon, but better than nothing in this castle of horrors.

She walked up to the door and paused, reaching for the brass knob—what if it was locked? But it popped open at her touch, not a single creak to be heard as it swung outwards.

Instead of the dark corridors of the dungeon, her room emptied into a warm hallway. A length of forest green and gold carpet ran along underfoot and glass sconces lit the walls with yellow light. With a closer look and she noticed there was no flame. More magic.

Seeing no guards nearby, she swiftly stepped out of her room and clicked the door shut behind her.

Was she truly free to explore the castle as she wished?

Not waiting for anyone to tell her otherwise, Jo made quick work of investigating the other doors along the hallway.

All were guestrooms; beautifully decorated just like hers but with thick blankets of dust resting across the furniture and a stale quality to the air that told her the windows had not been opened in a long time.

Still, she riffled through them as she went, but the only thing of note was a pair of circular glasses in one's nightstand.

She picked them up, careful of their thin wire frames, noticing a spider crack on one of the lenses. Pan didn't wear glasses and neither did Tinkerbell. She wondered which unlucky person had taken residence in this room and what had happened to them.

A curiously cold breeze from nowhere stole past her shoulders and she shivered, putting the glasses back and sliding the drawer shut, the room suddenly feeling dark and pressing—altogether wrong. She slipped back out and closed the door.

The end of the hallway was a left turn that opened up into what must have been the main atrium of the building. A massive, triple wide set of stairs made of polished mahogany and decked out with another lavish rug cascaded downwards into an open space, across from which were the grande front doors. They were probably locked, and she could probably pick them, but Jolie knew three things.

She was no coward.

She couldn't give up the chance to kill Pan.

And his magic would drag her back to the castle if she broke the deal anyways. She ignored the doors. Overhead, a glittering glass chandelier was lit up with hundreds of candles—undoubtedly spelled to never drip wax or burn out.

She realized that if the guest rooms were on this second floor, Pan's room might be too—and that was her biggest guess as to where she would find his weakness. He was the type to keep it where he could best keep an eye on it.

She frowned. She had been assuming it was an it, but maybe it wasn't. It was just as likely to be a dagger as it was to be a magical beast, she supposed. Or maybe it was something curiouser altogether.

Jo descended the stairs and continued across the landing where she spotted another door. There was a golden plaque at eye level that read: *Library.*

She smiled, partially surprised that Pan would even have a library. Still, it could prove useful to rifle through whatever tomes he deemed keepsake worthy. She pushed open the door and gaped at the sight that welcomed her.

Pan not only had a library, he had a pristine, awe inspiring, museum of a library.

Each wall wasn't a wall at all, but a towering bookshelf. They stretched so far overhead that Jolie noticed a handful of wheeled ladders you'd need to use to reach the top. Book spines of all shapes and sizes were housed neatly in place, not a single one askew.

There was a sunken seating area in the middle of the room with piles of jewel-toned pillows and blankets, and even a tea tray that still bore crumbs of cookies and dregs of green tea.

She moved reverently through the room, trailing just the tips of her fingers along shelves and glass cabinets, past a globe of a world she didn't recognize and an entire floating display with vials of strangely glowing liquids.

Along the far wall, a window stretched across between two full shelves, the top of which was made of stained rose and orange glass that turned the flooring into a sunset. Looking out, she was delighted at the view: a glittering vastness of ocean that reminded her so much of home she had to clap her hand to her mouth to keep herself from crying out.

She had never been away from home. Ever. And now she was on...day three? Day four? She couldn't even remember.

Was her father okay? Had he recovered? Did he miss her?

She thought of Damien, and Smee, and the cook and the deckhands and of all the people that she had left behind on the Jolly Roger and might never see again. Not for as long as the beast had his claws in her.

She wiped a hot tear from her cheek and turned away from the ocean view. Tucking the fire poker under her arm, Jolie reached for the nearest book on the shelf.

The Myths and Stories of Midgard

She frowned at the cover. She had no idea what Midgard was. A place? A person? She turned to the first page and blinked. Though the cover had been easy enough to read, the inside was...gibberish. Or foreign. She traced her eyes over the dried ink words and phrases, trying to unlock their meaning.

"What do you think you're doing?"

Chapter 28

"The literacy rate in Neverland is 77.9%."
- THE MOSTLY ACCURATE TRAVELER'S
GUIDE TO THE ANCIENT WORLD OF NEV-
ERLAND

The muscle in Jolie's jaw twitched as she set the book back down on the shelf.

"I was looking around. Aren't I a guest?" she said, eyeing the fairy as she uncurled her wings and floated to stand right in front of her, the pet dreadwolf padding along behind.

Tinkerbell gave her a flat look. "With a fireplace poker?"

"I'm trapped in a house with my mortal enemy, an assassin, and…" she looked down at the wolf, "that thing. Forgive me if a poker gives me a sense of sanity amongst the madness."

"Okay one," Tink snorted, cocking her hip, "I'm retired. And two: her name is Nana." She punctuated her words with a pat to the top of Nana's head. "She won't hurt you as long as Peter says you're safe here."

"And I'm just meant to believe the honeyed words of Peter Pan?"

"Yes."

Jo frowned, though her grip did loosen somewhat on the makeshift weapon. "The dog's not going to try and kill me?"

Tinkerbell sighed, refolding her wings back against her. "Nana, go show our guest some hospitality."

Before Jo could react, the dreadwolf bounded over, knocking hard against her knees and slobbering wet animal kisses over her hands. Each time she tried to push away, Nana came back even more determined, until Jolie was laughing along with the excited yips and barks.

"Alright! Nana. Nice to meet you." She set the fire poker down. "This space is beautiful," she admitted. "I wasn't expecting such finery from..."

"From a villain?" Tink supplied, draping herself languidly onto a pile of cushions in the sunken area. "Let me guess, your father says that we live in a gruesome cave eating bugs and grubs, and we only ever come up to shed blood and feast on human flesh?"

"You did kidnap and starve him in a dungeon for three days," Jo shot back. "Clearly there's some truth to his stories."

Tink shrugged, the dragon on her arm moving up and down her skin as she did. "That's the thing about stories, they change every time they're told."

"Is that why you have so many books?" she said, crouching down to get a better look at the rows on the bottom shelf. Cookbooks, history books, even some romance novels—none with so much as a single speck of dust. "Once a story is written down there's no changing that."

There was a silence punctuated only by Nana's pants and the chime of a faraway clock. Then: "I doubt you'll find Peter's weakness in here."

She half turned to the fairy lazing on the cushions. "Doubt? So you're not sure?"

"I don't know his weakness, if that's what you're getting it."

"Then there's no use to torturing you for information except for fun?" Jo smirked. In a flash, Tink crossed the room and whirled her into the nearest shelf, pinning her with an iron beam of an arm around her shoulders.

"I'd like to see you try, pirate scum," she hissed. "I'm being cordial to you because Peter asked me to, but don't think for one second I haven't forgotten who you are. The daughter of the tyrannical Captain Hook—the man responsible for the murder of my people."

Jo's vision flashed red. "Don't talk about my father, especially not with a mouthful of *lies*."

"Lies?" she laughed, dropping her arm "It's not a lie to say that your father broke into the fairy enclave. It's not a lie to say that he murdered them all—without even giving them a chance to defend themselves. It's not a lie to say that they begged for their lives!"

Jo shot off the shelf and tumbled in Tinkerbell, the duo slamming backwards over a side table and into the pile of pillows.

She vaguely heard Nana's bark and then the clipping of nails as the wolf sped along the hardwood and out the library door.

"Shut up!" Jolie screeched. Tink girl was smaller in height but bigger in stature than her—and decades, *centuries* her elder. The fairy squirmed and bucked her off. Jo reached for her hair in return and tugged, the white blonde locks fisted in her hand as she sent the assassin's head crashing into the floor.

Tink reached up and clawed at Jo's face, missing her cheek but glancing across her ear and drawing blood. Jo's heartbeat thundered as she ignored the pain, flipping the girl over and straddling across her chest with her full weight.

"Don't talk about my father when you're a murderer too! You went after someone who wasn't even involved, you—you poisoned her and she wasn't even a fighter! She wasn't even involved!" Tears clouded her vision as she reared back and landed a punch to Tinkerbell's cheek.

"What in dust's name are you talking about," she seethed, legs flailing under Jo as she tried to scrabble for leverage. Finding none, she reared her head back and smashed her forehead into the pirate's nose.

There was a loud crunch as it folded under the attack, and Jo fell backwards off of her foe, clutching a hand to the waterfall of blood dripping from her face.

"You murdered my mother to hurt my father," she hissed. "So if my father needed revenge then–then–"

"I didn't touch your mother, you daft naive princess," she hissed, both of them rising to their feet. "And neither did any of the other fairies."

Tinkerbell straightened, her wings flaring in anger behind her, eyes shooting deadly sparks. "I've killed 633 people and creatures in my life. I remember every single one. I feel guilty for more than half, but that's what war does to you—and Neverland runs bloody with it. I know all of their names and all of their lives. Your mother is not one of those 633."

"Stop lying!" Jo yelled. From the corner of her eye she noticed her discarded fire poker at the exact same time Tink did. They both lunged, Jo sliding on a duo of pillows before launching through the air–

"Enough!"

She slammed into a dark force field mere inches away from the weapon, Tink hitting the same on her side, as Peter Pan stormed into the fray. Nana yipped at his heels. He looked furious.

His gaze went to Tinkerbell first. His second in command was heaving like a beast and had a blooming black eye but seemed relatively unharmed. Pan offered her a hand up but she slapped it away, standing on her own account.

"Keep her away from me," she hissed, giving Jo one final glare and storming from the room, pulling Nana along behind her with a mutter of "traitorous guard dog".

Pan sighed and ran a hand through his curly locks, seeming both so much older and so much younger than usual. His steps were light as he came to stand in front of Jo's prone form. "Will you let me heal your nose?"

She could only blink at him as her emotions drained out the bottoms of her feet. Anger, betrayal, sadness.

"I don't know why I'm here," she said quietly as Pan crouched down to her level. "Or what plans you have for me. But if I could ever ask you for anything I'm asking you for it now. Tell me the truth. Did my father kill those fairies?"

Pan's face blanched but he nodded.

"Did you or your army kill my mother?"

This time he shook his head no, and it was enough to dislodge the bubbling sob that had been brewing deep in Jolie Hook's chest for days. She felt pain, most of all. Pain from the shattering glass that had been her world.

Her entire life she had believed Peter Pan to be her mother's murderer—whether it was by Tinkerbell's hand hadn't mattered, he was her leader. Her father's crew—her crew—had been warring with him for a decade. A war born on the idea that he had taken away their most precious thing.

Peter Pan had been her villain her entire life. Her father had been her hero. Why were the lines so blurred now?

"Why?" she sobbed, her tears mingling with her bloody nose as her thoughts raced. "Why would someone do that to her? She was my mom and—and–" Her breath caught and she couldn't form any more words. Her hand went to her chest. It felt like her heart had been ripped out.

"Jolie—Jo—you need to let me heal you. Hey–" He caught her hand in his. "Deep breaths. You'll be okay, I promise."

"N-no," she stuttered out, chest heaving. She took her hand back and gripped the skirts of her dress. "I c-can't–"

He made to put his hand on her arm and she jerked. "Don't touch me! Don't touch me, don't–"

"Okay! Okay," he placated, raising his hands in surrender. "I won't touch you. But you need to calm down. Jo, I need you to breathe."

Her skin was hot and her fingers were shaking. How much more of her life had been a lie? Why had no one told her any of this?

Peter tried to tell you, a quiet voice in her mind whispered. *He tried to help you.*

"He tried to kill me first," she whispered back, both hands gripping her head. She felt like she was going crazy, and Pan must have felt it too because he waved his hand and suddenly they weren't in the library anymore.

They were outside, in what must have been his back garden, under the shade of a giant willow tree. Yellow buttercups and purple tulips lined her view.

"Look, we're outside, okay? Wide open sky. Breath in the air, fresh air. Come on, in…" he soothed.

Jolie found herself complying, too tired to fight against the lull of his voice any longer. She sucked in a shaky, uneven breath.

"And out," he said. She let it loose. They repeated the motion until her limbs stopped shaking and her heart no longer felt like a cannon.

She looked up at Pan through thick lashes. Though he wasn't touching her, like she'd asked, he was close enough that she could still feel the energy between them.

In a moment of pure exhaustion, she rested her head on his shoulder. Her tears were drying up, but she knew she must look like a mess with a scratched ear, a bloody nose, and a bird's nest of hair.

Pan cleared his throat. "Are you...are you alright now?" He sounded nervous. Like he was afraid if he made a wrong move she'd close in on herself again, tear away from him like prey from predator.

The ridiculousness of the situation was not lost on Jo. A week ago being this close to him would have been a nightmare. Now, she drew some strange comfort from having him near, but she needed to remember her place. Prisoner, not guest. It was just so hard when he smelled of the forest and lemons, when he was warmth to her aching chill.

"I don't understand," she said, finally finding the strength to lift her head from his shoulder. "Someone killed my mother. If not you then..."

His gaze was soft. "I've done a lot of bad things in my life, Jolie, but killing your mother was not one of them. I'm sorry for your pain."

She turned away, distracting herself with the feel of the soft grass under her palm. The garden was beautiful—someone clearly took the care to prune the weeds and clip the hedges. She smiled, imagining Pan in gardening clothes, wrestling with a tree root.

"What happened to *your* parents?" she asked, suddenly curious. Peter Pan had always simply *existed* to her, but he must have been born like anyone else.

His answer was rough and slow, like drawing blood from a scab. "I never had any."

"Oh." She scratched at her arm awkwardly. The four words were heavy with history, with a story that she didn't feel comfortable trying to untangle yet. "I'm sorry."

"Don't be," he shrugged. "I'm better off alone anyways."

"Doesn't really seem like you're alone," she pointed out. "You have Tinkerbell, Nana, the Lost Boys."

"And now you."

She shot him a look. "Your kidnapped guest hardly counts. I'm only here for as long as I need to be."

"As long as it takes for you to find a way to kill me."

She swallowed, giving him an indecipherable look. "Exactly."

Chapter 29

"Watch your clocks closely, they have been known to lie."
- THE MOSTLY ACCURATE TRAVELER'S
GUIDE TO THE ANCIENT WORLD OF NEV-
ERLAND

She allowed Pan to heal her nose and clear her ruined dress before he left her to her own devices, citing a need to check up on the creatures in the Neverwoods.

Alone with her thoughts, Jo wandered through the gardens. Everything was so well maintained, including a small stone wishing well, a wooden footbridge over a bubbling stream, and rows upon rows of vibrant flowers. It was also quiet; only the faint rush of the ocean in the distance and a few birds interrupted her thinking.

And she had a lot to think about.

Her heart was a tangled mess of brambles. Of thorns that she had grown herself, of a disarming smile that had started to worm its way into her hidden places. She didn't know truth from lies, history from stories, and she didn't know why she wasn't clawing at Peter Pan's eyes every chance she had.

Something in her, some preconceived idea of herself and the world around her, had started changing ever since she stepped foot off the Jolly Roger. Some things were crumbling, some growing, but nothing was any clearer than fog on the horizon.

She wished she could talk it over with Damien.

"Dear Damien, I'm sure you're rightly angry that I came all this way to save my father and ended up a prisoner in his stead. Well, I never pretended to be lucky. Anyways, it turns out that all my years of pent up anger against Peter Pan for murdering mother might have been misconstrued. Oh, also father single handedly was involved in wiping the fairies out of Neverland. Ta for now!"

She kicked at a rock and watched it skitter towards a cluster of small black flowers and paused. Could Pan's weakness be poison?

It seemed unlikely given who his second in command was, but Jolie still stepped over to the plants. There was a small wood sign that read "Chrysanthemum", and upon closer inspection they weren't black at all, but a deep, mournful purple. Below the name something else was written, though Jo had to squint to read it properly.

For Wendy.

She frowned. Who was Wendy?

She tucked the question into her back pocket as she made the rounds of the garden and examined the rest of the flowers. None of the others had dedications on them and, more disappointing, none were of the poisonous variety. Tinkerbell would have to be able to source botanical poisons in her line of work, though Jo remembered dismally that the fairy had mentioned she had "retired".

A rumble of thunder overheard stirred her from her thoughts.

"Dust," she swore, picking up the edges of her skirts and dashing towards the nearest door back into the castle. She threw it open just in time for the day's rain to hit the ground: today it was in many boulder sized clumps of murky water that smashed into the grass without mercy.

Jolie still wasn't convinced that Pan's weakness wasn't hiding in the garden but she also wasn't keen on getting soaked to her skin. You could never trust Neverland's rain to be safe. Once she'd had to spend a whole day pressing ice chips to Damien's skin after the rain had turned acidic on his exposed arms.

The warmth of the castle was a pair of inviting arms as Jo closed the door shut behind her with a quiet snap. She had entered into some kind of vestibule, an in-between space where she might have shed her raincoat if she'd had one.

The small square room held nothing more than a spindly bench and an oval mirror within which she caught her expression.

She was surprised at the blank look in her eyes, the flatness of her mouth. Jo made quick work of herself: eyebrows tilted up, mouth snagged somewhere between a smirk and a grin, nose upturned. No longer blank, but determined.

Then she frowned. Pan was much taller than her, and yet the mirror was hung nearly perfectly in line with her face. Why?

"Must be Tinkerbell," she murmured, the excuse flimsy but enough to settle her mind for the moment as she crossed the vestibule and pushed open the interior door.

What was on the other side of it sent her mind back into its spiral.

It was a room filled with nothing more than dozens and dozens of clocks. The warm lighting of the magical sconces lit up every detail on their rich wooden bodies, their delicate faces in marble and gold and scintillating, shifting colors. Her steps made no noise as she moved between them—or maybe they did but she just couldn't hear it over the sound of the ticking.

It was a marvel that there were maybe sixty, seventy clocks in this room—a room she couldn't see the edges of so maybe there were even more—and they all ticked together. Like a heartbeat.

Tick.

She trailed her finger along the smooth edge of a particularly large clock. There were mice and butterflies carved into the wood and shining glitter painted across the glass that encased the swinging pendulum. 2:11pm.

Tick.

A small, palm sized watch face laid on a simple pedestal. The hands not hands at all, but a wolf chasing a hare around. Or was it the hare chasing the wolf? She picked it up. 2:12pm.

Tick.

She paused at another clock. Something about it...

"What secrets do you hide?" Jo whispered. "Has Peter hidden his weakness here?" The clock was mostly black, sinewy lines of thick, carved ivory stone. Veins of gold licked through, racing up towards the face, which was the most delicately blown rose glass, the hands so thin she was surprised they managed to move at all.

Only they weren't moving, were they? This clock had stopped.

She inched closer, her heart thumping widely in the cavern of her chest.

She shouldn't be here.

Around her, the ticking hit its crescendo, but Jo found she was unable to move. The light around her flickered and vanished, so too had the warmth of the room vanished. A chill made its way up her ankles, her thighs, her belly, and wrapped around her mind.

Fear. Where had it come from? It had come on so fast, so suddenly, that Jolie hadn't had time to shove it into her lock box, to send it careening down to the bottom of the ocean like she usually would.

As she stared into the clock face—uncomfortably unwilling to turn away—the glass of the face fogged up, like it would if someone breathed on it. But Jolie herself wasn't close enough to have done that.

Then, slowly, an unseen invisible finger traced words into the fog.

You have all the time in the world when you're dead.

The invisible force wiped the words clean and, behind it, the hands of the clock started to spin wildly, around and around and around–

Something in her snapped and she finally stumbled back from the clock.

Her chest heaved as if she had just ran around the island itself. Jolie took a shuddering, steadying breath as the adrenaline surged like ice water through her veins. With a slowness that showed her frayed nerves, she dragged her eyes back up to the clock and choked on her breath.

The clock was gone.

In her hands, the small watch still ticked. She looked down.

No longer were the wolf and the hare chasing each other in perpetuity. Now, they both lay bloodied and broken at the ends of the clock hands, being dragged around the face as she watched the time tick over.

5:12pm.

Chapter 30

"Please see the back of this guide for a full recipe list of all meals mentioned, and don't forget that if you don't have free-range and organic ingredients at your disposal, merchant bought is fine."
- THE MOSTLY ACCURATE TRAVELER'S GUIDE TO THE ANCIENT WORLD OF NEV-ERLAND

S he was stumbling through the halls trying to orient herself and account for lost time when the phantom bell rang, followed by Pan's disembodied voice: "Jolie Hook, your dinner is served."

She blinked as a brass compass materialized in her palm, surprisingly light for its seemingly well fabricated metal exterior. Instead of the cardinal directions, though, the red arrow was pointing towards a word: "Dinner".

Her first instinct, despite the foggy delirium that still clung to her senses, was to scoff and toss the compass into the wall. She was not some sheep to lead around by her collar.

But then her stomach groaned and reminded her of how empty it sat, and Jolie rolled her eyes.

"Fine," she huffed.

Though she distrusted that the compass was actually leading her in the right direction—or at least it was doing so in the most roundabout way possible—she did eventually reach her destination.

A set of double doors was thrown open to reveal a dining room of massive proportions.

It was as big as where the Lost Boys ate their meals except that the forest flooring was swapped for a plush carpet, the living oak table changed into a fine maple, and the canopy of trees gone. In its place, Jo noticed as she craned her neck upwards, was a fresco, painted in golds and emeralds, azure blues and slate grays.

She spotted Pan first, an artist's rendition of him smiling, surrounded by a half dozen people in soldier's uniform. She recognized trees that only grew in the Neverwoods, fish that only swam in certain spots of the dead sea. She saw Tinkerbell's face amongst a crowd of two dozen fairies.

It was beautiful, but clearly decaying. Chips of paint had flaked off, revealing holes where eyes should have been, cracks where armor should have protected. Even Pan, the clear subject of the art as he stood proud of regaled in the dead center, was missing part of his chest.

If he had been standing in front of her, she could have shoved her fist right through the hole–

"Do you like it?"

She had turned and punched out with her hand before her mind could make sense of the words, nor who spoke them. Inches from connecting with his body, Pan grabbed her wrist.

She gasped, the fresh smell of sugared lemons tickling her nose.

She couldn't help but notice that he was freshly showered. His curls still wet, his skin soft and without a trace of dirt. His outfit, too, seemed like the kind of thing one would wear in the comfort of their own home, which, she mused, he was.

The fabric of his tunic was soft under her palm as her free hand found his shoulder to steady herself.

"We have to stop meeting like this, deal?" he smirked.

"I know better than to make deals with you," Jo scowled, tugging her hand free. "You're a trap wrapped in fine ribbons."

His smile sunk even deeper. "You think I'm fine?"

Twin dots of red flamed across her cheeks. "I think you flatter yourself."

"I consider personal flattery a form of self-care, darling girl."

Jo rolled her eyes and stepped away from him, unclenching her heart as she did. "This is a delusional conversation."

He snorted, pulling out the closest chair and dropping down into it. "The conversations on the Jolly Roger must be dreadfully dull then."

Her chest tightened at the mention of her home. How was everyone getting on without her? Were they remembering to twist the steering wheel back into place after every rain? Were the seagulls getting fed their meals? Had they finally discovered who had been leaving pots of chili in the men's room?

Or was life going on exactly as normal, her presence nothing more than a wisp of memory?

She grew hot at the cavalier way that Pan dropped her ship's name, and she opened her mouth to say so when he raised his hand.

"Would you like an argument now," he interrupted, "or would you like to have your dinner first?"

At the end of his sentence, a wild wind whipped through the room, ruffling the ends of Jolie's hair and sending her hands deep into her skirts to prevent them from blowing up around her. She cursed as she smoothed them back down, and when she finally regained her bearings her mouth dropped.

Magic had caught her off guard, yet again.

Where once had stood a grande but barren slab of wood was now an overflowing cornucopia of a dining table. Roasted birds and glazed boar. Steaming mounds of rainbow potatoes and mashed turnips. A half dozen types of bread and a full dozen types of butter. Three carafe of brightly colored juices, and a bigger one of what looked like cider.

It was like the dinner in the Lost City, but perhaps even more tantalizing because this time she didn't have to worry about being attacked during dessert.

Her eyes trailed down to the silver plate and crystal goblet placed at the seat nearest her, clearly waiting for her to start ladening it with goodies.

"Hope you don't mind eating with just a spoon tonight," Pan said, nudging a chair out towards her with his foot. "I vividly recall your affinity for silverware shaped weaponry."

She plopped down into the offered chair. "I'm not going to stab you with a fork."

"Not this time."

"You're immortal anyways. Unless you're telling me that your one weakness is cutlery?" She raised an eyebrow.

"It still stung," he replied, winking before turning to the feast. "Eat before it gets cold."

She was too hungry to deny him, and she loaded her plate up with abandon. Vegetables on top of carbs on top of protein. A giant serving of a dark, salty sauce covered her plate like the thick fog after a storm.

She tucked into the spiced corn stuffing first, barely having time to chew before washing it down with the sweetness of the cider. Pan quickly refilled her goblet as she drank.

Once the gnawing feeling of catastrophic starvation mellowed out, Jolie took a breath and slowed down.

She might not be ready to stab Pan tonight, but she would have to vomit on his shoes if she didn't pace herself. "Tell me, Pan, since we're being so cordial. Why are you the way you are? A tornado wrapped in chaos? Darkness bathed in tricks and riddles?"

He shrugged, sipping his drink. "Because life would be so boring otherwise. Don't tell me you don't love a good riddle."

"A captain has no time for such foolery." Jo busied herself trying to slice off a hunk of boar with the edge of her spoon, ignoring the blooming sly grin that twisted across her companion's lips.

"Lies don't suit you, darling girl." He snapped his finger and her meat fell into perfectly sliced pieces. "Come now, one riddle and I promise to give you your fork back next meal." He held his palm to his heart. "Lost Boy's honor."

She considered it for the briefest of moments before scowling and shoving a piece of meat into her mouth. She held back the moan of delight at the pops of caramelized sauce and bright citrus notes—she could easily eat magical food for the rest of her life. "Your honor means nothing to me."

"Why do you do that?"

"Do what?"

"Not allow yourself to have fun. It's there, a flicker in your face and then...poof."

"Because we're enemies," she snapped. "I'm here against my will."

"Not really. You're here because you want to kill me. Otherwise you'd have tried to escape by now."

"Maybe I'm just waiting for the right moment."

She held his gaze, steady and unyielding. It was both hot and heavy, like the weight of the sun was pressing out against his eyes and boring into hers.

There was so much history behind them, and she was suddenly reminded that Pan had spent his life stuck as a boy. How long had he been unable to grow, unable to change?

It made a part of her sad for him.

"What's the riddle?" she finally said, caving under the pressure from his emerald eyes.

"It's one I've been saving just for you," he said, leaning back in his seat. "*I am a drum. I am a star. I am a flame. I am not a drum. I am not a star. I am not a flame. What am I?*"

Jo blinked. A drum, a star, a flame? She was baffled. What was at once all of those things and then none of them? She could almost feel the wheels in her mind turning and then snag, twisting on a stop block.

"I..." A drum, a star, a flame.

Pan leaned forward on his elbows, watching her curiously. Was this some kind of test? And if so, did she even want to pass it?

Of course you do, her inner voice snapped. *A Hook does not lose, especially not to the likes of Peter Pan. Think Jolie!*

Her fists clenched into the fabric of her skirts. "It's nothing," she said at last. "That's your answer. Nothing is a drum. Nothing is a star. Nothing is a flame."

For a second his eyes crinkled into what Jo thought might become a smile, an admittance of defeat, but then his face morphed into that sallow, sinking expression she was all too familiar with: disappointment. "Oh darling girl, I thought you more clever than that."

Her nostrils flared. "You wouldn't know the first thing about me or being clever. Without your magic you'd be nothing more than a boy traipsing about in britches too big for him," she answered, hot ire quickly splashing from her tongue.

His eyes darkened, his fingers splaying out on the table. "Don't mistake my kindness for foolishness, Jolie. I could strip you of these pleasantries and confine you to the dungeons."

She leveled him with an indecipherable look. "Maybe. But you won't."

He stood at her words, coming to stand directly between her legs in front of her, his hands braced on the arms of the chair, his face hovering over hers. A hot flush raced down her spine as his scent filled her nose.

"And why," he whispered, voice husky, "pray tell won't I?"

She swallowed, refusing to back down, inching her own face closer to his so that there was nearly no space between them at all. "Because this is all a game to you. It would spoil your own fun to send me away."

There was a silent space after her words when all he did was look at her with clouded, blank eyes. What was he looking *for*? What did he see behind her masked expression?

Finally, his lips turned upwards into a dark smirk and he straightened. "You're right. It's all a game. This means nothing." He looked down his nose at her, his eyes a dark miasma. "You mean nothing, beyond what entertainment you can provide before your use expires. Don't forget your place in all of this, darling girl. You belong to me."

Chapter 31

"Before visiting other worlds, please make sure you read the Traveler's Guide for each, otherwise you may commit a scandalous faux pas on foreign shores."
- THE MOSTLY ACCURATE TRAVELER'S GUIDE TO THE ANCIENT WORLD OF NEVERLAND

Jolie was sure that she was dreaming—but something felt off.

The curling edges of the dreamscape felt foreign to her. The gray smoke on the ground, hiding her feet, was cold and unyielding. And the scene before her....an oddity.

She was not in Neverland.

She was in some sort of claustrophobic space between large stone walls, an alley? She reached out to trail a finger along it, crinkling her nose as she pulled back. It was wet, like it had just stopped raining.

She craned her head upwards and let out a sigh of slight relief. The sky, at least, was familiar, each star twinkling down on her with a friendly face.

She frowned. The north star was in the wrong place. Instead of being the second star to the left, it was opposite.

"The second star to the right...?" she murmured. Where had she heard that before?

Her feet dragged her towards the thin mouth of the alley, curious as to where her sleeping mind had taken her. It was nowhere she had ever been. Her father had never taken her through any of the star portals before they'd closed up, but she imagined at least one of them might have dumped her somewhere like this.

Cautious eyes peered out of the sequestered alley onto a large, cobbled street. There were no people, but plenty of buildings.

So many buildings.

They were all made of thick stone, with beautiful wooden doors and shimmering glass windows covered up on the inside by curtains pulled closed. They almost looked like miniature castles, so far were they from the wooden single roomed homes she'd seen in some of the Neverland villages.

In front of each house was a towering metal tree from which hung a lamp—though as she peered upwards she couldn't quite make out how you'd light an oil lamp hung so high.

There were rows of primly kept flowers lining some of the buildings, a few hedges along the sides, but none of the towering treetops she was used to. And everything felt still. There was no buzz of magic, no flitting of creature's wings, no siren song. It was still and silent and strange.

And then a figure emerged from somewhere down the lane, coming out like a ship into port. Jo shrunk further into the shadows of the alley.

Who was she? For it was most definitely a she. Shrouded in a billowing black dress and wearing a veil of lace across her face, the woman—or girl?—hurried on clicking heels down the cobblestones. Her gait was assured, but the constant turn of her head betrayed her: she was anxious.

As she passed by, her eyes flicking to Jo's spot but passing straight through, the pirate's mouth fell open. The woman was carrying something. Someone.

Wrapped in a thick wool blanket, she could only see the very tip of a nose and a smattering of freckles, but it was clearly a babe. Jolie's stomach sunk low into her feet. Someone hurrying off with a newborn babe at this hour of twilight could not indicate anything good.

Jolie watched as the woman—no, clearly a young girl, now that she had a good look, maybe a year younger than herself—stopped abruptly in front of a building that seemed more worn down, more exhausted than the rest. The stairs were chipping away, the door seemed to hang low on its hinges, and even the sign was in desperate need of repainting.

The London City Orphanage.

The puzzle clicked into place. This girl was leaving her baby.

But why was Jolie dreaming of this? Who was this woman? This babe?

She inched out from her hiding spot, her curiosity emboldening her. She watched as the woman hesitated, shifting nervously on the heels of her shoes. Then, with a kiss to the brow and whispered words that Jo did not catch, the woman cradled the bundle to her heart.

Jolie could almost hear their heartbeats as one. For three blissful seconds it was not a goodbye, it was just a mother loving her newborn.

But then she was resting him on the steps, her finger pushing in on a button that elicited a shrill *briiiiing* noise, and she was fading back into the fog.

Jo's eyes tried to track her as she went but were quickly snagged by something else.

There was someone else in this dream, watching now as a woman with a cross necklace opened the door and scooped the child up.

Jo recognized the curly hair, the slight hunch of his shoulders.

"Pan?" she called into the night. There was no indication that he'd heard her, no tilt of the mouth or cocking of the ear. Just two sad, forest green eyes watching as the orphanage door closed.

A wild wind picked up, shaking Jo around the shoulders as she clung to herself. "Pan!" she yelled again, eyes squinting against the torrent of air.

The scene around her disappeared. Suddenly, she was watching a young boy, not more than three, kneeling before a book, muttering repeated words after the woman with the cross. Her ruler came down across his back—hard—when he stumbled.

It changed.

He was older now, seven maybe, watching out the window as a couple left the building with a small child in tow, their hands intertwined. His face was sadness, desperation, darkness.

The scenes shifted faster, like she was caught in a whirlwind of thoughts and emotions and memories with nothing to anchor her.

The boy getting kicked by four others, ones he thought were his friends.

Desperate teardrops raced down cheeks as he tugged on a woman's skirts, begging her to adopt him.

A shuttered face as he helped yet another bunkmate pack their things.

The woman with the cross rubbing a salve across a purpled eye, *tsking* at a rib that cracked and would never again heal right.

Jolie watched the boy grow up and older, grow sadder and sadder as the years crushed into him everything he had always thought but never wanted to believe as true: *He was not loved. He was not wanted. He did not belong.*

Jo finally found her breath as a final scene slid into place—he was older now and she recognized him. But his eyes were dull, dark, not the captivating charming eyes of the Peter Pan she knew. He was sitting beneath a tree, a small pack next to him.

Jolie fundamentally knew that it contained nothing more than a single change of clothes, a toothbrush, and an apple. He had been kicked out of the orphanage—17 was the time to start growing up, they had said.

He sat there with nothing but his shadow for company, plucking blades from the grass below him.

"I wish to go away," he said, head knocking against the bark of the tree, "to someplace where I never have to grow up."

And from his side his shadow's teeth split into a wickedly curved smile as it replied back: "I know just the place. It will cost you though."

She was hurled out of the dream; the boy, the city, and the shadow all falling away. She tried to cling to what she saw, to make sense of it all, but it ran like water through her fingers. Why was she shown this?

She blinked, coming back into reality, her body feeling heavier, her mind full, her throat parched. She was...*where was she?*

A small room with a mahogany desk, a worn bookshelf, a toy chest stuffed into the corner.

In fact, the whole room seemed just that: stuffed.

Rolled up papers along the desk and poking out of opened drawers. Four rugs, vibrant, gold threaded things, stacked at odds with each other underfoot. A full sized mirror with a crack in the corner and clothing thrown over top, various shades of green and brown making up a makeshift curtain. Candles chugged out smoke on most surfaces, and she wondered how it was they didn't burn everything down. There were paintings on the walls of ships, of stars, of gardens and—

A shifting and a thin, pained moan dragged her attention to the corner of the room. There was a single bed, with a brown comforter thrown off onto the floor and silk sheets wrapped around muscled legs. Her gaze drifted up and she blushed.

Pan was bare chested and sweaty. His hands, such strong looking hands, were twisted into the sheets, straining against something unknown.

She moved closer. His face was screwed tight, his brow slick, his eyes flicking feverishly behind closed lids. He was having a nightmare.

She moved even closer, an unknown force calling out to her as she sat next to him on the bed. Even in sleep, he was handsome. She brushed a damp tendril of curly hair from his brow, frowning at the heat that was coming off of his skin.

Was his sleep always so fitful? So…horrible?

He groaned again, a pained, frightful sound. "W-wen…"

Her hand went to his face again, this time resting lightly on his cheek. A small part of her clung to the feeling of his warmth when he turned his unconsciously into her touch.

"Pan," she whispered, leaning her face closer. "Pan, you're dreaming, you need to wake up. Pan—"

A strangled yell was all the warning she got before his eyes shot open, midnight black and blown wide. Rage. Unchecked anger. Fear.

He launched forwards. Jo was taken off guard as her body slammed backwards into the bed, air crushing out of her lungs.

He hovered over her, eyes wild, his knees trapping her legs underneath him, one hand by her head like a cage, the other fiercely grasping along the column of her throat.

Chapter 32

"Neverland's only national holiday, Opposite Day, usually occurs during the hottest day of the summer month. Don't be alarmed if you suddenly find yourself speaking backwards or loving a food you might have once hated."

\- THE MOSTLY ACCURATE TRAVELER'S GUIDE TO THE ANCIENT WORLD OF NEVERLAND

"P-pan–" she tried to cough out, but the rough hand on her throat only tightened.

Her hips bucked up against him. He was strong, so much stronger than her.

Tears sprang to her eyes but her hands couldn't wipe them away, too busy trying to pry his arm off of her.

Her wild, frightened gaze caught his. Unfocused, dark, still lost in a nightmare.

"Peter please!" she strained out, a last helpless plea as dark spots forced their way into her vision. She did not want to die like this. On her back. Captured. Alone. This was not an honorable death, this was not a pirate's death.

Suddenly, and all at once, the grip of her throat released.

Jo immediately turned her head to the side, her legs still straddled and trapped, coughing and sputtering as air came back to her. Her chest heaved as she dragged it down, wheezing coughs the only sound until–

"Are you okay? Dust, what happened. I don't...can you breathe? Can you talk?"

She turned her head back to look at her attacker. His eyes, back to green, back to focused, staring at her, pleading with her to answer him. To tell him she was okay.

Was she okay?

She couldn't quite steady her breathing, nor her heart, which railed violently against her chest.

Then he was grabbing her around her shoulders and pulling her up.

She tensed at first, nearly expecting another onslaught, but he fit her so perfectly against his chest that for a moment she wondered if he had cast some spell.

He was sweaty and clammy but, then again, so was she. He was strong where she was soft, holding her up where she wanted to slip over and fall away. He tucked her head to his chest and cradled the back of it, smoothing his hand across her hair.

"I'm sorry, I'm sorry, I didn't mean to," he chanted in a hush, over and over. Jolie's hands finally started working again and she reached up, putting them against his chest, laying them flat on his heart. Was it exploding as hers was?

"I'm okay," she muttered, voice hoarse, so unknown to her that it might have belonged to someone else. She cleared her throat and tried again. "I'm okay."

Peter only repeated his words, stuck on them like a skipping record. Jolie tilted her head up, pulling back slightly so that she could see into his eyes. Green eyes.

"I'm okay," she whispered.

He stopped his muttering. His eyes tracked over the lines of her face, the red spots on her cheeks, the rosebud mouth, the wide eyes. "You're okay?"

She nodded. "I'm okay."

A sigh, soft and full of relief. His eyes slotted shut and she caught the brief flash of peace flit across his face.

When he opened them again, he seemed to realize their compromising position. He wore only thin linen pants, and her day dress—which she must have fallen asleep in—was riding high up on her thighs.

Their faces were close, their breaths intertwined. The revelation was clear in his eyes as he dropped his hold on her and shot off the bed, leaving Jo in such a state of disarray that her mind spun. Hours ago they had been frothing at the mouth to cut each other down, and she'd been more sure than ever that he deserved a sword to the gut.

But now all she felt was a desperate coldness, a twitch in her fingers that wanted so badly to reach back for him and his warmth.

Pull yourself together, Hook, her father's voice rang in her ears.

He's hurt. Take care of him, that's what you do, Jo, countered Damien's.

The king of the Lost Boys hardly needed a pirate girl to take care of him. But as he walked over to a side table she noted the thin shaking in his legs, the hunch of his shoulders.

He picked up a beautiful ochre tea pot. With a wave of his hand two matching cups appeared. She could hear the fine porcelain knocking against the saucer as he lifted it.

"Are *you* okay?" she finally asked, throwing her legs over the side of the bed—his bed —and smoothing her skirts back down. At this point in her life she felt fairly familiar with the many emotions of Peter Pan. Usually he was cocky, relaxed, charming with a deadly point. She had seen him angry—molten hot rage. She had seen him confused and shocked and happy.

She had never seen him afraid. Until now.

Was it the nightmares that had this lasting effect? Or was it that with a single twitch of his hand he could have killed her?

Some deep, sacred part of her hoped it was the latter, but she refused to entertain the *why*.

"Am I...me?" His laugh was hollow. He turned, passing her a teacup. She noticed that he sat himself down in the chair furthest away from the bed, as if not trusting himself to be close to her. "I nearly kill you and you're asking me if I'm okay?" He downed his tea in one gulp. "You never cease to amaze me, Jolie."

Jo clicked her tongue, setting the tea aside untouched. "Sorry for being concerned."

"How did you even get in here? This room is locked."

She thought on that and shrugged. "I must have sleep walked...I guess." She tapped her chin thoughtfully. "One minute I was in bed and the next I–" she cut herself off. Should she admit that she had, by all her best guesses, been intruding on his dreams? His nightmares?

A picture of that little boy sprung into her mind. Had that child had any idea where his life would end up? "I wound up here," she finished lamely.

She felt almost embarrassed to have intruded on such personal thoughts. To know such intimate details of a childhood so poor, so alone. A sense of pity stirred in her belly, but more so was a near reverence at the fact that he had survived all of that and been made stronger for it. Peter Pan was impressive. No wonder he commanded an army.

He gave her a look that said he knew there was more to the story, though truthfully she didn't have much more to give. If his door was locked like he said then she wasn't sure how she got in, nor how her sleeping feet knew to take her there in the first place.

"Do you have nightmares often?"

There was a moment where they both understood that their relationship stood on a precipice. Peter could ignore her, tell her to leave, kick her out and solidify that they were nothing more than enemies in a long, tiring fight.

Or he could tear down the shield of gamemaster that he had so carefully built up over the years and freefall off the edge—to what end, neither of them knew.

"Sometimes. When I have a lot on my mind," he said finally, voice raw and honest. Jo nodded in understanding.

"I get them too."

One eyebrow rose at her confession.

She didn't know why, but she desperately wanted to share something with him. Something real, something tangible between them to prove...to prove what?

That he wasn't the monster? That *she* wasn't?

"Usually about my mother," she continued, fiddling idly with the hem of her dress. "That I could have saved her. That I was the one who killed her. Sometimes..." she trailed off, breathing out from her nose to resist falling back into the dark spaces. "Sometimes I have nightmares about my father."

Peter's attention was wholly on her, spurring her on. "What about him?"

"That I *am* him," she admitted slowly. "That one day I wake up with a hook for a hand and a feathered hat on my head...only everyone sees right through it. They know I don't measure up to his legacy. They tear off my hook and throw me to the sea, and I sink into the graveyard of the water and their memories of me fade away."

Her hands itched for something to do beyond picking threads out of her clothing so she reached for the tea and took a sip. It tasted like mint.

She set the cup back down on the end table and turned in surprise as the bed sunk next to her. Peter took her hand lightly, dragging the pad of his thumb across her knuckles.

"You will never be your father," he said. Jo's nostrils flared. She tried to pull her hand away, wanting to smack the words out of his mouth. "You will never be your father," he said again, grip holding fast, "because you are better than Captain Hook can even imagine himself to be. You are a fighter and a warrior, yes..." he looked into her owl eyes, "but what I have seen of you...have come to know of you..." he sighed, dropping her hand. "You will be the finest captain that the Jolly Roger has ever seen."

The blush was spread so far past her cheeks now that she felt it licking along her neck and down her spine. A brutal heat that she did not want to give a name to. She wanted to believe he was lying, wanted to hold on to the thread that he was manipulative, he played games but, sitting there in the early morning hours together, Jolie knew that they had both been stripped to their barest honesty.

"Even if that makes me your enemy forever?"

"I have never imagined myself as your enemy, Jolie Hook."

There was a breath of silence while Jo took in his words. Dangerous, world-view changing words.

"Then why the fighting? Why the false peace treaty?"

"Peace has always been an option. It's just taken me a while to see that it's worth the chance to take it," he admitted, eyes hot against her.

"Peter I–"

"I have nightmares about a lot of things," he interrupted, abruptly changing the subject. He wet his lips and ran a hand through his dampened curls. "But mostly about a girl."

"A girl?" she echoed, spinning around on the bed so that she could fold her legs against herself and lean on the headboard. Peter did the same on the footboard.

"She is—was–" he corrected himself, "the kindest person I knew. Kinder than I deserved."

A girl. Her brain snagged on the word was. "What happened to her?"

She saw the words stuck in his throat as he worked up the courage to say them, saw the way his mouth opened fractionally then closed. Saw the terror flash across his eyes before settling into guilt.

"I killed her."

Chapter 33

"The traditional Neverland funeral rites include the burning of sacred pine and the drinking of elderflower syrup by all who knew the deceased."
- THE MOSTLY ACCURATE TRAVELER'S GUIDE TO THE ANCIENT WORLD OF NEVERLAND

Jo was dizzy.

Her body was dizzy with exhaustion.

After she had left Peter's room she hadn't been able to sleep, her own bed turning into a fitful pile of abandoned blankets.

Her mind was dizzy.

With what Peter had said: *I killed her.* He shut off after that, refusing to say more and gently ushering her out of his room, asking her to get some rest now that dawn was on the horizon. She was dizzy with the fact that she had dream-walked *with* him and sleep-walked *to* him.

But, most of all, her heart was dizzy.

It was being pulled in two.

Duty to her legacy that she would find a way to end the life of her enemy. Duty to her father, and to her crew for all the strife Peter had caused.

But another, rapidly growing part of her had grown soft and pliable. Had grown warm, comforted around him. There was a tepid kinship between them, a realization, startling to Jolie, that she had spent her life hating someone that might not have deserved to be hated. There was goodness, hidden beneath a cracking exterior, and she so desperately wanted to pull it out, to let it shine.

She had seen his monstrous side, but then again he had seen hers. He had seen her vicious appetite for success, her cunning, her win at any costs mentality.

I have never imagined myself as your enemy, Jolie.

When she woke up hours later, finally having succumbed to sleep, it was to ribbons of morning sunlight streaming into the room and a curious note on her side table.

Jolie stretched, enjoying the pleasant pops as her joints shifted back into place. She reached for the folded slip of parchment and flicked it open.

Breakfast is served.

There was a large clock—she shuddered as she remembered that room with the tick tick ticking—in the corner that read 8:55am. Jo cursed and shot out of bed. She had slept in so late, usually she'd be rising with the dawn.

Her legs tangled in the sheets and blankets as she hopped towards an armoire and ripped out an outfit at random. She had fallen asleep in the bell sleeved dress from the day before, and even she had standards when it came to laundry.

As her nimble fingers worked to do up the length of buttons that trailed down the front of the knee length peasant style dress, she frowned. Why did she care if she was late to breakfast with Peter? For it was undoubtedly Peter who had sent the note. And their last meal had been...uncomfortable, at best.

I need to know him better if I'm to find his weakness, she thought to herself, finishing with the dress and sliding on her slippers. *And since when did you call him Peter?*

Her nose twitched at a faint smell of crispy bacon as she retraced her steps back to the dining room. Except Peter—*Pan dust it!*—wasn't in. No, indeed her nose and, now, the sound of music, called her to a quieter, calmer portion of the grande estate.

The door to the sun room was open and waiting for her. Inside was a quaint, cozy space with a bay window, a set of plush green armchairs, and a coffee table absolutely laden with delights. Jo's eyes sparkled as she took in the steaming pot of coffee, the cherry danishes, the soulfruit scones. There was the bacon that called her there, but also sliced ham, seabeast sausage, and a meat-alternative fritter she knew had been popular with fairies.

There was enough to feed an army, and yet when she finally looked away from the spread, she found it was only her and Peter there.

"Hello," he smiled, lopsided and carefree.

"This is quite a spread," Jolie said, settling herself down into the empty armchair. It sunk under her weight, the cushions clearly well used and loved.

"You don't like it?"

Jo's eyebrow rose. "You did this for me?"

A faint red hue brushed across Peter's cheeks before he attempted to disguise it by pouring her a cup of coffee. "It's an…apology meal. For last night, and dinner before. I know I'm the bad guy in your story but I promise I'm not all doom and gloom."

"Just kidnapping and mayhem," she replied, but her voice was laced with a surprising lightness.

"Sometimes vandalism." He passed her the coffee.

"Vandalism?" she snorted, waving away his offering of sugar lumps and taking a spoonful of thick cream to stir in instead. Denying herself these pleasures wasn't going to help her find Peter's weakness or break the curse keeping her tied to the castle, so she may as well enjoy it.

"You might want to check out the underside of your ship one day," he smiled slyly. "As long as you won't be too offended by some drawings."

Her mouth fell open. "Peter Pan, are you telling me you carved some crude picture *into my ship*?" Her voice rose to a trill.

Not only was it rude, it meant he had been close enough to the ship to mark it and no one had spotted him. No one had stopped him.

And even more strange, he hadn't done anything worse than…vandalism.

Attempting to ignore yet another inconvenient truth about Peter Pan, she snagged a danish, ripping off the corner and popping it onto her tongue. A sound completely unbecoming of herself erupted from her mouth and she swallowed her embarrassment behind another bite. "This is really good," she offered with a mumble. "Did you make it?"

Peter laughed. "One of the castle's many enchantments. If Tink or I had to cook for ourselves we'd be eating burnt toast and tepid water all day long."

Tinkerbell. By all accounts Peter's closest confidante, and his longest ally. Could she be his weakness? It could be a coup—if Tink was the key to Peter's demise then she'd be able to get rid of them both at the same time.

"You seem close. How did you two meet?" she asked, grabbing a fork and loading her plate with food to hide the weight behind her words. Peter nudged a bowl of sugared lemon wedges closer and for a moment she didn't think he'd answer. Did he suspect why she was asking?

"It's a long story," he finally said.

Jo looked up at him from beneath her lashes.

Did he seem different? Lighter? Or was that just her own coloring of him? His eyes, at least, were such a pale green they almost seemed clear. It felt strange to be sitting down for breakfast with him, after everything they had been through. So many fights, Lost Boys vs Pirates, she could count them all through the scars on her body.

Even though her father forbade her from being on the front lines, she'd still always found a way.

But he had no scars. He had never truly left his safe spaces for open battle and, on top of that, he was probably immortal. What, then, was he afraid of? Capture? Torture? That seemed far more his MO than hers or her father's.

"I'm stuck here with you, you might as well keep me entertained." She blew across her coffee and took a sip, settling further into the cushions.

"Well, first she was hired to kill me, and then she saved my life."

Jo almost spat the drink back out. "She what?"

Peter snickered, and it made the dimples in his cheeks pop in such a way that it roused the sleeping butterfly in Jolie's stomach. "It wasn't long after I first came to Neverland. Apparently I insulted someone badly enough that they hired her services to end mine. I convinced her to join up with me and then we tracked down her employer together and sent him off the edge of the world."

"Harsh," she snorted. "But clearly you have strong magic. What fear did you have of her?"

"Oh, no fear. But I'd rather someone like that on my side of things, wouldn't you? Plus, I didn't tell her I couldn't die until years later." He bit into a steaming golden apple fritter. "She was so angry her hair turned bright red for a week! Tink doesn't take kindly to liars."

"She doesn't seem to take kindly to most things."

Peter sighed, running his always moving hands through his hair and ruffling the ends. "If you just got to know her–"

"I'm not planning on being here long enough to get to know her. I'm not here for friendship," she interrupted, putting down her plate and cup.

He held a hand to his heart in mock defense. "Ouch, darling girl. You wound me. Here I am, with an offering to appease you, a bed to warm you, a castle to entertain you, and you think we're not friends?"

"I'm here against my will," she snapped, though there wasn't as much fire in her voice as she'd like.

Jolie could feel her mood running hot and cold with Peter, but she couldn't stop herself. She'd been sworn to hate him for over a decade, and that hatred ran deep. Even if she believed what he said—that he had nothing to do with her mother's death—he had still fought against her father at every breath. Kidnapped him under the guise of a peace treaty, and made Jolie suffer through his tedious games.

And yet she could feel her sealed heart opening up to his, bit by bit. Two kids of Neverland who were, above all else, lonely. She sighed and grabbed a muffin. "But I will agree that these pastries are phenomenal."

Peter's grin was star bright as he watched her eat—such a mundane task—that Jo couldn't help but twitch her own lips in return.

And it was at that moment that Jolie Hook knew she was in trouble.

Chapter 34

"For the good of the natural wildlife, please do not leave this book unattended. The ink-mice will grow too attached to eating its pages and forget how to hunt and forage themselves."
- THE MOSTLY ACCURATE TRAVELER'S GUIDE TO THE ANCIENT WORLD OF NEVERLAND

"I don't know who he thinks he is," Jolie grumbled.

She had left breakfast full, content, and confused. Confused at her own thoughts and actions, which spiraled into disappointment—in herself and her inability to treat Peter as she knew she should have been. She should not be smiling with someone she was trying to kill for dust's sake. What kind of self-sabotage was that?

Her disappointment had eventually transformed into something she was more comfortable with: simmering, tightly coiled rage. She decided it was all Peter Pan's fault.

"Why is he trying to blur these lines between enemy and...and whatever he thinks we are. He's the one who treats me like a prisoner at dinner and a guest at breakfast! He's the one who is burrowing into my brain like a grubworm! Dust it all these books are useless!"

She tossed the book she had been reading into a fast growing stack. Desperately trying to forget how much she'd enjoyed their meal, Jo had launched herself back into research mode.

So far she had turned up nothing except for an impressive amount of papercuts from flipping through parchment.

She sighed and scanned across another library shelf. There had to be something in the room that could help. What good was having all these books if there was nothing of use to be found in them?

Outside the massive window, the sun was reaching its midday peak. Breakfast was nothing more than a wisp of a rumor in her stomach after a few hours in the library, and while her knees ached from squatting down at the lower shelves Jolie knew couldn't stop until she found something.

She had the incredible feeling that she was running out of time.

Which was a silly thought. Peter had never given her a limit for the game, she could take her time and still make progress.

But every day here makes you wonder if you could really do it, in the end. Can you really kill Peter Pan? Do you even want to?

"Shut up," she hissed at her treacherous brain. She groaned, rubbing her hand across her tired eyes. "And now I'm talking to myself. This place is getting to me." She wondered what her father might say to her at that moment.

Something about not disappointing the Hook name.

Then she wondered what her mother might have said.

She closed her eyes and pictured her mother's face, as it once was. Beautiful, happy, glowing. In love. In love with her father, the ship, the sea, and with Jo.

"She'd tell me to have a cup of tea and use my best asset: my mind," Jolie decided.

There were a thousand places in the castle she might glean a clue to Peter's weakness from, and a thousand more she'd probably not even discovered yet. Sure, she had the time to unravel them all, but maybe she could work smarter, not harder.

Yes, a cup of tea might help settle her mind. Or whisky, barring that.

When she exited the library Jo thought she knew where she was going—Peter had mentioned the kitchen being on the first floor near the gardens—but soon enough the hallways coalesced together into a terrible and unending maze once again.

Jolie had little else to guide her but intuition, which immediately led her into a broom closet. Swearing as she pushed a bucket out of the way and shut the door again, Jo sighed.

Peter had made this place a mess of hallways and doors on purpose, and she had to admit it was a smart defensive tactic. You couldn't kill your enemy in their home if you couldn't find your way to them in the first place.

She could have sworn that even the paintings moved and changed shapes, so that she was never sure which ones she had already passed.

Maybe this is where she would die, withered away to nothing, set to roam the halls forever as a vengeful ghost. She smiled at that, imagining all the chaos she'd wreck on Peter's life as a ghost, when the faint sound of a woman humming reached her ears.

She cocked her head towards the sound. It didn't sound like Tinkerbell, whose voice was scratchy and rough from years of smoking pixie cigars. This was light. Young.

Jolie followed it as best she could until she came to a swinging door. She leaned her ear close. It was definitely a girl humming, and she could hear the sound of the oven door opening, could smell ripe huckleberry and pie dough.

She thought Peter had said that it was magic that cooked all the food—had she misheard?

Somewhere overhead, thunder crashed onto the castle and Jo jumped, heart beating with shock. It was time for the daily rain then, and it sounded like a doozy. Steadying herself, she pushed her way into what turned out to finally be the kitchen.

There was indeed a steaming huckleberry pie on the table in the center of the room that immediately made Jo's mouth salivate. She paused, noticing the dreadwolf Nana lounging out across a brightly colored woven mat, her snout lifted up towards the wafting smell of the pie.

"Are you really not going to attack me just because Peter says so?" she asked, feeling foolish for talking to a dog that wouldn't—couldn't—talk back. Nana rose up on four giant paws and with a massive stretch and a shake of the slumber out of her mind she ambled over to Jo.

They each stared at the other—Jo with her brown eyes, Nana with clear blue.

The wolf made the first move, nuzzling the top of her head into Jolie's thigh, then finding the back of her hand, and finally accepting Jo's palm when she gently reached out to scratch behind her ears.

A floppy pink tongue lolled out of her mouth as pants of endearment and contentment burst from the wolf's mouth.

Jo laughed. "A domesticated dreadwolf. Not the strangest thing I've seen in Neverland, but you're up there." Nana followed along like a happy shadow as Jo moved closer to the island in the room's center. She eyed the pie. The crisp edges, the golden brown crust, the hint of dark purple that peaked out from decorative designs in the dough. It was all enough to send her entire mouth spinning in longing.

"Now, I'm sure you didn't make this, did you Nana?" she asked, tapping her finger to her lips. She noticed another door at the opposite end of the room. "It would be rude to eat this without asking first, too bad the cook isn't around."

At her words, Nana barked, a deep, thunderous thing that sounded even louder than the Neverains outside, and shot off towards the back of the room. Jo startled, gripping at the island to keep from being knocked over.

Nana barked again, jerking her head as if to say "come!" and pushed open the door with her snout, disappearing into a darkened hallway.

"Hey!" she cried, legs pumping after the animal. Where in dust's name was she going? And so fast? A happy bark—echoing, like it came from far away—answered and she raced onwards. She passed by no doors, no windows, not even any forks or splits in the hall.

Nothing except for the gentle downwards slope that told her they were, somehow, heading underground. Peter's castle amazed her.

Something pricked in the back of her mind as her steps slowed, spotting just the tip of the wolf's tail turn a corner off to her right. It was a chill, a shiver, the icy feeling that she was heading somewhere she didn't belong. It sent goosebumps down her spine.

When she looked behind her, the cavernous maw of the pitch black hall—had the lamps blown out when she ran past?—looked too nightmarish to venture back into. No, she'd keep going until she found the dust-forsaken wolf, and then they'd get out of the belly of this beast.

"Nana?" she called out, listening for the returning bark. But there was nothing. No, wait...Jolie cocked her ear and listened. It sounded like...yes, singing.

The same singing she had heard earlier. Had Nana, that daft dread-wolf, brought her to the cook so that she could ask about the pie? It seemed far too unlikely, and yet Peter's companions all seemed to dabble in the unlikely.

Jo sighed, the prickling feeling subsiding, her shoulders relaxing. She hadn't even realized until that moment how tense she'd been, running headfirst into this mystery. "Hello?" she called out, rounding another corner. "Sorry for the bother, I don't mean to intrude–"

She stopped short. The hallway had ended, abruptly and without warning, and without so much as a door, window, or sign to show for it.

But then where did Nana go? And the singing?

Jo glanced behind her. Just like before, it seemed as though all the lamps lining the walls had gone out as she went by, leaving her with just the one lonely candle hanging where the hallway ended.

Her slippers made no noise as she shuffled them along the floor, fingers trailing against the walls, looking for...a secret passage? A hidden door? She wouldn't put it past this place.

"Hello?" she called again, listening intently for a reply.

"Are you here to play with me?"

Jolie whirled at the voice in her ear. She stared into the dark, but no one was there.

"No one has played with me in so long, I've almost forgotten how fun it can be."

Jo turned again, facing the blank nothingness of the hallway. "Where are you?" she asked cautiously.

"Oh, here and there. I've tried to leave but I always end up back at this castle. It's been lonely."

It sounded like a girl. Someone the same age as Jolie maybe, though her voice was lighter, and bore a hint of an accent Jo couldn't place.

Her fingers itched for the sword that had never been returned to her. "Are you going to fight me?"

"Oh no," the disembodied voice laughed, the tinkling of bells. "That wouldn't be very nice. I just want to play a game with you."

Jo's eyes narrowed. "You sound like Peter Pan, saying things like that."

The hallway warmed, like an angry breath had been blown across her body. "We used to play. And now he won't come to see me anymore."

Jo clicked her tongue, thinking. This turn of events was strange to say the least. "Are you a ghost?"

"I'm not sure."

"How are you not sure?"

"How are you so sure that you're alive, right now? The only reason you think you are is because of your mind, because of your senses. Who's to say you're not actually dead, and just going through the motions?"

Jolie rolled her eyes. "I think I'd know if I were dead. Trust me, I've been around death enough to tell the difference."

A figure materialized in front of her. It was the shape of a young woman, her hair pinned back in curls, her long dress trailing to the floor with sleeves to match. She had wide eyes, a small mouth, and twin dimples nestled into youthful cheeks. But nothing mattered more than the fact that from head to toe she was made of–

"Water?" Jo said, conflicted between taking a step back and peering forward. She wondered what would happen if she reached out and put her hand through the figure. Would her fingers come back wet? Was this girl solid, liquid, some kind of half form?

"I don't really look like a ghost, do I?" came the reply from the watery face with the liquid mouth. She lifted a hand, the light from the lamps shimmering through it almost like she was born from the dead sea itself. "But then again, I don't look like you either. One of us must be wrong."

Jo resisted the urge to reply that it was definitely the girl. If she was a ghost—watery form or not—she might be dangerous, and Jolie had been in too many dangerous situations as of late.

"I'm looking for a dreadwolf," she said instead. "Have you seen her?"

"You mean Nana!" the ghost exclaimed, clapping her hands together excitedly. Twin drops of water flew from her fingers as they touched. "She's such a good girl. The only one who still comes to see me—not even my own brothers visit anymore, isn't that rude?"

"Quite rude," Jo nodded. "Well listen, if you could just point me in the direction of Nana we'll be on our way."

The girl's shoulders sank a fraction. "You're not staying? No, that's alright. Oh but–" she looked around, as if about to tell a secret. "Nana's in my room, so you'll have to come down and get her. And while you're there, we can play a game!"

"No, I really–"

"Yes! It will be fun!" the girl insisted, coming close and scooping up Jolie's hands in hers. Jo shivered at the cool touch of water against her fingers. "And if you win, I'll tell you a secret."

Jo rolled the thought around in her mind. "A secret? About what?"

She giggled. "Whatever secret you want!"

"And if I ask about Peter Pan…?"

"Oh! I know everything there is to know about Peter." She tapped on her blue nose conspiratorially, "Even the things he doesn't want me to know."

What were the chances that a domesticated dreadwolf had led her to a water-logged ghost trapped in the castle who might know Peter Pan's only weakness?

Better than the chances of her discovering how to kill him on her own.

And just because she discovered his weakness didn't mean she had to use it. Right?

"Alright," she agreed. "One game."

"Wonderful! This will be so much fun!"

"One game," she repeated. "I don't have all day."

"You have all the time in the world when you're dead," the ghost laughed, before spinning in place and popping out of existence.

Jolie only had a moment to be surprised before the floor opened out from underneath her and she went tumbling into nothingness, her scream trailing like a sail behind her.

Chapter 35

She came to an unglamorous halt in a tangle of limbs, bouncing on top of a mound of fluffy pillows.

"A little warning next time," she grumbled, swiping her hair from her face.

"Oops," came the responding giggle. The girl seemed far too bubbly for someone who was most probably dead, and most certainly trapped in Peter Pan's castle for the rest of time.

Jo glanced around her landing space. She hadn't been sure what exactly to expect. A graveyard? A coffin?

Certainly not a bedroom that looked exactly like Jolie's guest room, only with all the trappings of personalization. A baby blue woven blanket folded neatly at the foot of the bed. A cluster of art supplies on a desk nearby, twin paintbrushes resting in a jar of murky green water. A closet brimming with clothes—though most seemed hideously out of date and, Jo wrinkled her nose, smelled of mothballs even at a distance. There were no windows and no doors in the room.

There was a tea set, though, prepped and placed on a squat table in front of her. There was also Nana, the daft oaf who led her there, lounging on a small couch getting her head scratched by the ghost. Nana gave a small yip of recognition before setting her thick head on her paws and drooping both eyes closed. Clearly *she* felt at ease.

"Do you like it?" the girl asked, leaning over and pouring steaming tea from a pink and gold pot and into two beautifully delicate porcelain cups. "The set was a gift from a friend I once had. A princess." She passed a teacup to Jo, who sniffed at the liquid. Peppermint, and something sweet. Honey?

"She used to tell me that you could get to know anyone over a good cup of tea."

"Used to?"

The girl shrugged. "One day Neverland swallowed her entire village. Gobbled it up whole. Peter said they'd been whisked away to another world, maybe a better world. But I don't know if I believe that."

Jo blew on her tea and took a sip, eyebrows raising at the burst of flavor across her tongue. It was strong but delicious. She took another mouthful. "I'm sorry to hear that," she said finally, setting down the now empty cup.

"Another?"

Jo nodded.

"Will you tell me how you know Peter?"

"Is that the secret question you want answered if you win?"

"No."

"Then I probably won't tell you." The girl smiled. "Keeps things interesting."

"What about your name then?"

"My name?" The girl paused. She lifted her own cup to her blue mouth. Jo was surprised she was able to drink given her...condition. "Would you believe that I had almost forgotten my name! It's been so long since I've used it." She giggled, though it nearly sounded forced. "You can call me Wendy. *Wendy Moira Angela Darling.*"

"Wendy," Jo repeated, the name tingling something in the back of her mind that she couldn't put a finger on. "You can call me Jo."

"Oh, I know your name. I've been watching you since you arrived! Not much else to do, and this is the most excitement the castle's had in ages."

"Watching me? How?"

Wendy shrugged. "I'm invisible to anyone who doesn't care to see me."

Jo hummed on that. It was true that she had wanted to see who Nana was leading her to, though...

"Did you make that pie? In the kitchen?"

Wendy clapped her hands with joy. "Oh I knew you'd put that together! I did! Well, it's not a real pie, is it? It's just an illusion. If you had tried to eat it...poof! It would have been gone."

"Can you do a lot of those? Illusions?"

Wendy nodded. "Only little things. Pies, shoes, even mar-bles—though I tend to forget where I put those."

This ghost—Wendy—was proving to be quite interesting. Jolie desperately wanted to open her up like a book and read through what made her tick. If Jo died in Peter's castle, would she become like her? A specter, bound to the walls and cursed to never leave them? The tricks seemed fun, but she imagined it would get boring.

She wondered what Peter would have to say about this.

"And was that you with the clock yesterday?" she realized. "You wrote on it."

Wendy smiled. "Just a bit of fun. Were you scared? Oh please tell me you were! But never mind that, let's play our game now, okay?" She was nearly vibrating with excitement as she set the tea pot off to the side and made an open space on the table between them. She pulled a deck of cards out from underneath her couch cushion and placed it facedown in the middle.

They were quite a bit larger than the cards her crew played poker with, and seemed quite a bit thicker too. On the back of the deck was a beautiful picture of the night's sky. Jo immediately recognized the second star to the left, drawn a bit larger than the rest. Neverland's sky.

"How do we play?" she asked, watching as Wendy shuffled the deck and dealt out four cards each, face down. Jo itched to pick them up and see if the front was as lovely as the back, but she wanted to hear the rules first. Wendy seemed like a friendly enough being, but Jo still knew better than to trust playing games with those who were acquainted with Peter Pan—she needed to know what she was getting into.

"You've already started playing, actually," she replied, nodding towards Jolie's teacup. "Just a dash of honeypuff flower, enough to open up your mind and connect it to the cards you see. Otherwise it's not as fun."

Jo's jaw dropped. "You did what–?"

"Oh hush, it was tasty wasn't it? And it won't have any lasting effects once you leave here. It'll be our little secret."

Jo bit down on her tongue. *Dust forsaken ghost*. What else was she planning to slip her? She needed to pay more attention from then on. Magic, which Wendy was certainly made of the utmost kind, always had a way of distracting her from the task at hand.

"Fine," she gritted out, though she diligently moved the teacup to the opposite edge of the table. "What next?"

"Next we really get into it," she answered. "You can pick up your cards now, but don't tell me what you have or you'll ruin it."

Jo slid her four cards into her hands. She was right to have assumed that, just like the back, the front of the cards were equally as magnificent. They looked hand painted by a master in perfect brushstrokes and vibrant colors. She looked down at each.

The Tower. A giant marble column that stretched upwards into the sky from a grassy plain. On the top was a single window beneath a dome roof.

The Poisoner's Hand. A pale hand gripping a glass vial of something black and thick. Jolie's throat went dry as she resolutely shuffled that one to the bottom of her deck.

The Broken Mirror. A beautiful mirror encased in a golden frame, completely smashed in the center.

The Heart. Bloody and beating.

"The game lasts four turns, okay?" Wendy said, interrupting Jo's thoughts. "Each turn we put down a card and whichever card is stronger wins. Whoever loses will have to learn a truth about themselves that relates to the card—that's what the tea is for, to make sure you're open and honest. We play until someone loses all of their cards. If that's me then I'll answer one question for you. If that's you then I get the same. Sounds good?"

The rules seemed simple enough to Jolie, though she wasn't sure what kind of question Wendy would ask of her—she didn't think she had anything to say that might interest a ghost. "How will I know which card is stronger?"

"You'll see," she smiled. "Now, play your first card!"

Wendy wasted no time in sliding her own choice facedown, towards the center of the table. Jo sighed and looked over her hand again. She was at a distinct disadvantage having no idea what might be a strong card. She slid out *The Tower*—at the very least the marble column seemed fairly impenetrable—and placed it face down opposite Wendy's card.

"Now we flip them over?"

Wendy snorted, and even that was delicate. "No silly, how dull." She reached out a hand, her pointer finger outstretched so that it was only inches away from Jolie's forehead.

Jo resisted the urge to jerk back, refusing to be afraid of some girl, ghost or no. "What are you–?"

"Now we fall," she whispered, tapping her digit onto her face. Jo felt her eyes roll back and her lids close, felt her lips part in shock, felt her mind break loose from the tether of reality as she was shot into a dream. She was no longer a girl, she was pure undiluted energy.

When the world finally settled, Jo knew that wherever she was…wasn't real. She had left her body in Wendy's room while her soul wandered elsewhere. It felt strangely freeing. Like a lifetime's worth of weight had finally been cut loose.

"Oh wow!" Wendy breathed once Jo finally opened her eyes. "You look like a star!"

She looked down. Her material body was gone. Like how Wendy was made of water, shaped and formed into the body of a girl, Jolie was made of twilight and stardust. Swirling vortexes of purples and white where her feet used to be. Dots of stars along her legs. A blanket of spilled moons and asteroids circling her stomach. She was the universe itself and wondered where Neverland was amidst the endless planets rotating around her.

Jo held her hand in front of her face and twisted it about, trying to find her flesh behind the magic.

There is star stuff in your veins, her father used to tell her.

Her father. Had he recovered from Peter's onslaught yet? Did he miss her?

Jolie shut those thoughts behind a steel door. She'd hear all about it from him when she returned home. She instead looked around the strange space where Wendy had brought her. It was a green field, though the grass was nearly the color of cut emerald in its shine, with a richly azure sky above. It was empty, save for the lone marble building ahead of them. The name *"The Tower"* was hovering above the roof in curling gold writing. The card Jo had played had manifested before them.

"What kind of game is this," she murmured, steadying herself for what was to come. She glanced at Wendy, who was by her side and positively jumping with anticipatory glee.

"This is the best kind of game," she answered. "Watch! Now we get to see whose card is stronger."

Her lips twisted in confusion. Jolie looked from the girl to the tower, waiting for something. Anything.

After a moment, the world around her obliged. With a great rumble the ground before them split in two, a massive crack in the grass that spread out lightning fast and with as many forks and paths. She stumbled back, her body nearly weightless, as she braced for whatever was about to be set upon them.

"This is my favorite part," Wendy whispered, clutching at Jo's arm. "Don't close your eyes, you'll miss it!"

Still, Jo tried to jerk herself away from the watery girl, but there was a surprising strength to her wet grip. "Let me go!"

"Don't be a spoil sport," she snapped back. "You agreed to play, it's too late to back out."

Jolie's response was drowned out by a massive roar as something launched itself out of the crevice, a larger than life mass of green scales and sharp claws, and beady eyes and–

"The croc," Jo breathed.

Her body flinched, remembering the last time she had come face to face with the Neverbeast. It hadn't ended well for her, and somehow she didn't think Peter would come to her rescue this time. Her vision narrowed as dark spots of fear threatened to cloud her gaze. She locked eyes with the croc as it turned its massive head their way. Above its brows, hovering in the air, were the words: *"The Beast"*.

I am not afraid of you, she thought, though her heart was beating too fast and her breaths were coming too shallow. *I am not afraid of you.*

Her body wasn't even corporeal. She was starstuff. It couldn't hurt her, it couldn't–

"Now fight!" Wendy yelled, hands cupped around her mouth, voice louder than a firing canon.

At her words, the croc turned towards the tower, pressed back against its haunches, and launched itself at the marble. It hit, and a thin spider crack bore up at the impact. It growled, repositioned, and threw its entire weight at the tower again. This time, the marble shifted and began to crumble. It raised one clawed arm and swiped—beast against stone—and with a groan of defeat, the column fell into a heap of broken marble and dust.

The croc had emerged victorious.

Wendy looked at her with a smile and touched her finger to Jo's forehead. In the space of a blink, they were both in the bedroom again. It was a dizzying change of scenery that had Jo fighting against vertigo until she was sure that her soul was completely back in her body.

"I win that round," Wendy hummed, pulling her croc card back into her hand. Jolie noticed that the Tower card had been ripped into pieces, which Wendy swept off the table with a flutter. "Time to hear your truth."

Chapter 36

"This author reminds you that dark magic is not some-thing to be played with unless your will and next of kin rituals are fully in place."
- THE MOSTLY ACCURATE TRAVELER'S GUIDE TO THE ANCIENT WORLD OF NEV-ERLAND

Jolie was thoroughly unimpressed by Wendy's game.

"You have an unfair advantage," she snapped. "You know these cards, you know which ones will win."

The ghost plucked a new card from her hand and slid it across the table. "Not really. The cards fight for themselves. Sometimes a card will be strong and prevail over everything. Other times a card is tired. You really can't predict them."

"So it's basically all luck?"

"Aren't most things in life just luck?"

"If that's the case I think I've been decidedly unlucky as of late," she huffed.

"Really?" Wendy asked. "Seems to me like you've had a better time than most."

"Do tell."

She shrugged a slim shoulder. "It's not my turn to tell a truth. You lost the round, it's up to you."

Jo blew out a breath. "What kind of truth?"

Wendy gestured to the pile of ripped up paper that was once *The Tower*. "That card represents protection." She leaned forwards. "I want to know your truth. Who would you die to protect?"

Jolie wanted to think about it. To mull over the question from various angles—who was close enough to her? Who would need her strength, her resilience, to protect them? But something—that blasted tea—pulled the words from deep within her before she got the chance.

"Damien. My father. My crew."

Wendy smiled. "That's a long list. They must mean a lot to you."

"They're my family," Jo answered, her tongue her own once again. "I'd have nothing if I didn't have them."

"That must be nice. I think I had that once but–" the ghost cut herself off with a flinch. "Just because you die for someone you love doesn't make it any less painful."

Jolie swallowed, trying to will away the thick tension that had descended over them. She was infinitely curious about Wendy but she wouldn't pry out painful memories.

She turned back to her cards. *The Poisoner's Hand. The Shattered Mirror. The Heart.* She tried to imagine any of them beating a card like *The Beast*. But if it really was all luck, then did it matter?

She made her choice and put it on the table.

"Do you have to touch my forehead every time?" she asked with a quirk of her lips.

It was hard to tell beneath the constantly moving waves cresting along her body, but Jo was pretty sure that Wendy rolled her eyes. In the next instance, Jolie was out of her body once more, wearing her star skin like a fur coat.

This time they weren't in a field, they were in someone's study. Warm candlelight cast a glow on the thick wooden beams overhead, dragging a golden shine across bookshelves and furniture. There was a desk hugging the far wall and, sitting at it but facing away, was a man.

He seemed unremarkable from behind. Short brown hair. A blue sailor's outfit. He was hunched over a piece of parchment, scribbling away with a quill.

Above his head: *"The Swordsman"*.

That must have been Wendy's card.

Her gaze slid to the ghost. Again, she looked giddy, though she raised a single finger to her mouth to indicate to Jolie to keep silent.

Jo had no problem acquiescing. It felt like all her breath had been stolen anyways. Or maybe it was that in this strange magical realm she didn't even need to breathe at all.

On the opposite side of the room, a door was pushed open with no sound. Nothing to denote any change at all except for a slight chill in the air as a figure shrouded in black robes walked in. Feet bare and hood up, they seemed female, but moved with such otherworldly grace that it was hard to tell.

In her hand, a vial with a glowing liquid.

"The Poisoner's Hand."

The Poisoner crept closer to the Swordsman, who didn't seem to be aware of anything beyond the scritch of his quill. He had no idea that his death was approaching on silent, secretive feet.

When she was directly behind him, she held the vial—now un-corked—above his head. If she tipped it, it would splash on his shoulders.

Yes, yes, come on, Jolie silently urged, watching her card with the taste of success on her tongue.

Slowly, the Poisoner moved the vial and Jo watched a beaded drop race towards the edge of the glass.

There was a crash as the Swordsman leapt to his feet and whirled. He threw his chair back, unsheathed his sword and–

Jolie cried out as he sliced right through the Poisoner's hand, which fell to the floor, shriveled and gray. The apparition screamed, high and sharp, and then disappeared—all that was left was a puddle of black fabric and her mummified fingers.

Jo's shocked eyes turned to the Swordsman. He re-sheathed his weapon, brushed the dirt from his trousers, and righted his chair, before settling back down and picking up his quill.

"Another for me!" Wendy trilled.

Jolie gritted her teeth.

"Are you okay? You seem stressed."

"This game is idiotic," she muttered back. "*This game is idiotic*," she repeated when Wendy was silent. "How am I meant to win something that has absolutely no strategy? No logic? My fate is just left up to the cards."

"So you don't like being out of control."

"I don't appreciate not being able to fight for it," Jo snapped. "I've trained all my life to win, leaving it up to luck is degrading."

When Wendy smiled her dimples were small whirlpools in her cheeks. "You're a very interesting girl, Jolie, I'm glad to have met you."

Jo blinked at the sudden turn. "Oh erm—thanks," she said, fumbling for the proper words to say when a ghost complimented you.

She had to remember that Wendy had been dead and alone for dust knew how long. By her own account her only real companionship for the last little while had been Nana. She deserved Jo's compassion, as much as she could muster, at the very least.

She gently coaxed her frustration back into its locked chest and sighed. "I lost again, what truth do I need to give now?"

Wendy looked at the shriveled hand on the ground by their feet. "*The Poisoner's Hand* represents a lot of things. Death. Decay. Secrets. It also represents revenge." She tapped her fingers to her chin. "Tell me your truth Jolie: what vengeful thoughts lie in your soul?"

There was a hot, fuzzy feeling in the center of Jolie's chest and for a moment she thought she might be dying. Why else would her heart suddenly feel like the sun itself?

But then the heat moved, and soon it poured out of her body altogether in the form of a single palm-sized ball of light. She stared, both captivated and confused, as it moved to the center of the room. It began shifting and twisting, turning into one shape, then many shapes, before settling into a familiar boyish figure.

Hands in his pockets, he had a carefree stance and a mop of disheveled hair. Jolie knew who it was, or rather who it was meant to be. Because instead of the handsome face Jolie was expecting, his features were smoothed over. A blank canvas.

"Oh, it's Peter?" Wendy asked, leaning forwards to get a better look. "Only, he has no face. How strange. You're conflicted."

Jolie braced for the words she knew would come tumbling out of her mouth like a roaring waterfall. "I want to avenge my mother. She was murdered." She looked at the space where her feet might have been; now they were encircled at the ankles by an asteroid belt—a pair of shackles. "Poisoned. I used to think it was Peter Pan. Or, on his orders at least."

"And now?"

"Now I don't know what to believe."

"I bet you know," Wendy answered. "You seem like a strong girl. And there is nothing weaker than uncertainty."

Jo blinked at her words and suddenly they were back in Wendy's room. *The Poisoner's Hand* card on the table was sliced cleanly in two and Wendy picked up the pieces and set them aside.

"I'm sorry about your mother," the ghost added quietly. "I don't think my mother is alive anymore either."

Jo nodded, slipping momentarily back into the sad thoughts of what could have been. How would her life have ended up? Where would she be now? She could barely remember her. The wisps she had were stitched together into a blanket that she wore over her heart, but even that was full of holes.

Full of missing pieces.

"For what it's worth," Wendy added, "Peter lost his mother too, a long time ago. I don't think he'd take that away from anyone...even someone who considers him an enemy."

Jolie cleared her throat at the same time as she cleared the cobwebs from her mind. "Let's keep going. Or should I even bother, I don't think I'm good at this game," she said, picking a card at random and throwing it down.

"No, not face up!" Wendy hissed, scrambling for the card. Before she could rip it off the table, the world twisted around them. Jo tumbled out of her body and smashed hard into the world of the card.

It was a room of only mirrors. On the floor, the walls, the ceiling. She turned around in awe. In them she was reflected as she normally saw herself: Jolie Hook, dark hair, dark eyes with a fiery glint. Muscled arms from sword training, fingers twitching and ready for her enemies.

When she looked down at her legs, though, they were still starry. The mirrors reflected something that wasn't actually there.

"Oh dear," Wendy muttered, looking around. "Well, this has never happened before." She tutted at Jolie, "You've nearly broken the game."

"We're not stuck in here, are we?"

"Until you give the mirror your truth we are. *The Broken Mirror* card is an interesting one," she mused. "It can reflect so many things. But the one I want to know about..." she turned to Jo, "is what you're most afraid of."

The temperature in the mirror room spiraled downwards. A chilled breeze blew through Jo's body even though there were no windows, nowhere for the wind to hide and whistle.

But nothing happened. No magic fingers pulled the truth from Jo's mouth. No buzzing light emerged from her chest.

She looked from mirror to mirror. "Is something going to happen?" she asked Wendy.

Except Wendy was no longer there.

And no sound came from Jo's mouth.

She tried again, but again her tongue moved and her lips turned and there was nothing.

Her heart began to jump over itself. What was this new dust forsaken magic?

What she was most afraid of.

She honestly had no idea what her truthful answer was to that question, but she was confident it wasn't losing her ability to speak. That was scary, yes, but there were far worse things in life.

Things like...

The mirror nearest to her lit up, her reflection dissolving away. In its place, the massive, toothy grin of the croc. Jolie's eyes widened and then narrowed. It was just a reflection. It couldn't hurt her. And yet when it snapped its jaws at her she couldn't help but move away.

"Come on, you've fought that beasty before. And this time it's not even real." Jo spun, eyes skipping over the rows of mirrors in search of the voice. A young woman's voice, but not Wendy's. Still, it sounded familiar, like when you've been searching for just the right word and finally find it.

If she had her voice she would have called out, would have demanded the person show themself.

"Psst, over here!"

She turned again, but all she could see were hundreds of her own reflections staring back at her. Jolie Hook, dark hair, dark eyes with a fiery gl–

That one has no eyes.

It looked like her. It was her. But there were dark holes for eyes, and instead of hands…hooks. Her mirror twin smiled even though no such thing graced Jo's own lips, and then she raised one hook and waved.

"Hello," she said.

What are you?, Jolie wanted to ask, but of course when she opened her mouth nothing came out but soft pants.

In the space of a blink the mirror—and the girl—were just inches in front of her. But who had moved? Jolie? Or the mirror?

The reflection tsked gently. "Look at you. Pathetic." The flash of disappointment on her face…Jolie sucked in a breath. She looked like her father. It was Jolie's face to be sure, but everything else about her screamed: Hook.

The mirror image shifted and Jo saw that her fake-self had her lost sword strapped to her hip. She really needed to ask Peter to give that back.

"Don't have anything to say?" mirror Jolie asked, voice a coy poison. "Oh, that's right, I have your voice, don't I? Now, maybe you should've fought harder to keep it. With this voice I can command armies. And you'd give it away so fast?" She shook her head, black waves spilling across her shoulders. "Why are you so scared to use your voice? A Hook is never afraid, have you forgotten?"

Jolie glared. *What do you want?*

"Quit playing with her, darling girl." Jo jumped at the new voice, flinching hard into herself as another body entered the mirror. A new reflection, drawing her own in close, hand curled tight around her shoulder. *Intimately.* Mirror Jolie tilted her head up, eyes slit, mouth drawing wide.

The real Jolie could only watch, without a voice to protest, as in the mirror, Jo Hook and Peter Pan kissed.

Peter pulled back and she noticed that, like her own reflection, this one was off. His eyes, normally green but sometimes tinged gray or black, were now hollow pits. There was no iris, no pupil, no whites.

It was like he looked out at her from the heart of darkness itself.

His gaze was just as cold as he looked her up and down. Whatever he saw in her eyes he must have found lacking, because he shrugged and quickly turned away. "Take what's yours and be done with it. Leave the fearful darling girl to her nightmares and hauntings. She'll never be more than her legacy, no matter how hard she tries."

Jolie flushed. His tone was so dismissive. Detached. He truly didn't care for her at all in that moment.

He's not real. She reminded herself. *It's the magic. He's not real.*

"Fine," her fake-self sighed. She held up her hands—both hooks, one silver and one gold. "It's not the hooks themselves that scare you. It's not even what they represent." She smirked. "It's what it means for you to cast them aside. What a version of you untethered by them looks like." Her voice went so low that Jolie caught herself leaning forwards to hear it. "Did I get that right?"

There was a sudden searing pain in Jolie's hands, like someone was taking a serrated knife to her bones. She held them to her chest as she cried out, only air, while hot tears splashed from her eyes. Her legs gave out and she hit the floor, the cool tile doing little against her burning skin.

It hurt it hurt it hurt.

And then it stopped. Her hands were no longer on fire, they were just heavy. Jolie dragged her eyes up towards the mirror, towards the girl who looked like her but couldn't be her because–

She sucked in a breath. Not-Jolie had her hands on Peter's face, caressing his cheeks.

That hurt.

But it was the fact that she had hands that hurt the most. When before...she'd had hooks.

Momentarily stuck between needing to know and needing to never find out, Jolie's brain stuttered on the image in front of her. Her and Peter, as they could never be.

She untucked her hands from her chest.

Not hands.

Hooks.

Shining, curved, wicked blades that had helped her father build his pirate empire. For while he had always been smart and savvy, it was when the rumors of a hook-handed bandit began to circulate through Neverland that his legacy was truly born.

His legacy.

Now hers.

Her chest heaved in tune with her heart. It was beating too fast and her breaths fell too short. It was like after her fight with Tinkerbell, when the world had pressed in on her so tightly that she was sure she'd never be able to squeeze back out again.

"I think you broke her," Peter mused, his voice far away, like he was underwater.

Peter Pan could never break me, she thought.

Only vaguely did Jolie startle when the two of them stepped out of the frame together, hands intertwined. Not-Jolie rested her head against Peter's shoulder. "I have everything you ever wanted. I am everything you will never be." She crouched down and trailed her hand along Jolie's wet cheek. "It's okay, Jolie. Don't be scared."

But she couldn't will her heart to slow down nor her ears to stop ringing. She also couldn't move, save for the shaking of her arms as they held her up.

The reflection's hand moved from her cheek to her brow, and then hovered over her eyes. "Our mother's eyes," she said softly. "I'll be needing these the most."

And then her fingertips turned to claws and there was a great roar and pain at her head, pain behind her eyes, pain where her eyes used to be as the reflection tore them out and fitted them into her own hollow slots. Then Jolie she couldn't see a thing and it was pure black and smoke and–

Don't be afraid. The darkness comes for everyone.

Her mouth opened but there was nothing left to scream.

Jolie fell back into Wendy's room as a whirlwind of terror and tears. For a moment she couldn't focus on anything except the sound of her own breathing, catching on itself like a pebble stuck in a rolling tide.

She lifted her hands.

Not hooks.

Her fingers lifted up to her eyes, as though expecting to find nothing there but a blank canvas.

She tested her voice. "I don't understand." It was a whisper, paper thin and frail, but it was her voice. She looked at Wendy. "What just happened to me?"

The ghost's face was sympathetic as she pet the top of Nana's head, the dreadwolf looking between the duo with more understanding than one might expect from an animal. "That's what happens if you don't play the game right." She looked at the card Jo had set down. *The Broken Mirror.* It was singed, the edges burnt back and scorched like it had been held to a torch. "You're meant to put it facedown. Always face down."

"You never told me the rules," Jo snapped back, rubbing her arm over her eyes, demanding them to dry up, to stop the flow of tears. "This is your fault!"

"They're your fears Jolie, not mine."

Jo was stunned. "Whatever that was...that wasn't my fear. I don't even know what it meant." Why had Peter been there? The hooked hands...?

"It seems simple to me," Wendy said, looking at her like she was three steps behind. "You saw yourself. Or a version of yourself. A version you're afraid of."

"Why would I be afraid of myself?"

"Of who you could become."

"I. Don't. Get. It," she gritted out, failing to find the meaning in Wendy's words. "She took my voice. She took my hands. She took m-my eyes. And she stood with...I don't understand."

"She took your hands to be free of the hooks."

A future me where I'm not chained to my father's legacy.

"She took your eyes because they're your mothers."

A future me that sees the world as she did. A peaceful world.

"She took your voice because right now you're too afraid to speak your truths."

Jolie blinked back tears. "I'm not afraid of any words."

"Then tell me why she had Peter Pan?" Wendy asked simply, as if that was the key, the answer to all the rest.

"I–I don't know," Jo admitted.

"You do know, you're just afraid to say it. You're afraid to speak that future into truth. You're afraid to *want* that future because it goes against everything you've ever known, everything you've been preparing for. You're afraid of yourself and who you could become–"

"Enough!" she interrupted, the word as sharp as her sword point.

Wendy drew back, her waters rippling with uncertainty. Jo knew her future.

She knew where she belonged: on her ship as captain, with Peter Pan nowhere in sight. "I've had enough of *you* and *magic* and this *castle*. I'm leaving." She stood, knocking the teacup to the floor with a clatter. The dredges of amber liquid spilled out across her slippers and she pulled back with disgust.

"No!" screeched Wendy, following her up. "You can't leave! We're not done!" She nearly stamped her feet as she spoke, as she *demanded*. Jolie realized then that Wendy had never grown up. That act had been taken from her. There was, and always would be, a petulant child simmering beneath her watery surface.

And that made her sad. A ghost who was nothing more than a girl.

"I'm sorry," Jo said, shaking her head. "I need to leave now."

Wendy's eyes sparked dark waves. "I said no–!" She stepped towards Jolie and her foot sunk into the spilled tea. At once her entire body went rigid, the water ceasing to even tremble along her arms.

Her head snapped back, mouth jerking open as if someone was prying it apart with claws.

"Alone, here forever," Wendy whispered. "He won't let me rest. Won't let me leave. Dark magic gets darker. Broken hearts mend and break again. I'm trapped, I want to go home, I wan–" she cut herself off, whipping her head to the side as if listening for something. Her body seized violently, liquid bones somehow screeching against each other, and then she relaxed.

Jo stood stunned, wavering between wanting to run away and wanting to try and soothe the shaken ghost. She looked down at the tea again—the tea that revealed truths.

Dark magic indeed.

"Sorry," Wendy said after a moment, gathering her arms around her like a life preserver. "That wasn't very ladylike."

"Are you alright?"

"That's a silly question to ask of someone who's dead."

Jolie frowned. She tried again. "Who has you trapped here? Is it Peter?"

"The shadows." Her voice was a thin strand of fear. "They have teeth and claws, they hide but they're always watching. Always hoping you'll set them free. Never set them free." Two scared eyes snapped up to meet Jolie's, and a watery hand crushed against her forearm. "Never."

"O-okay," Jo stuttered out, shivering at the impossibly cold touch.

Wendy looked at her like she was searching for something tangible in her words. Jolie wasn't sure if she found what she was looking for, but the girl finally nodded. "Thank you for playing with me. It's been so long since I had someone proper to talk to."

There was such a desperate, longing to her voice that Jo bit back any further questions. "I will try to help you, if I can."

"Oh, sweet friend. I don't think there's help coming for either of us. Once the darkness has you it's too late."

She flicked her wrist and the world turned inwards on itself, a vortex of blank black nothing spreading around Jolie.

"Wait!" Jo cried. "I still need to know his weakness! Wendy! What is Peter's weakness?" She squeezed her eyes shut and tamped down on the nausea bubbling up in her until the constricting feeling stopped and she popped back into reality.

She was back in the castle—a hallway she vaguely recognized by the intricate painting of the Neverwoods hanging on the wall. At her side, Nana licked her knuckles, and Jo realized that she was holding something in her hand. She peeled her fingers apart and stared at the crumpled card—

The Heart.

—and the words penned across them in gold ink—

*His weakness has always
been his heart, you see. It
crushes him. He just wants
love, after all.*

Chapter 37

Jo was dazed as she wandered the halls, trying to retrace any semblance of steps back to her room. It had been a whirlwind of a day, and while she'd woken up with a clear mind it was now muddied as ever.

That girl, the ghost, who was she? What had happened to her?

His weakness has always been his heart, you see. It crushes him. He just wants love, after all.

Questions on top of questions battered her brain, and underneath it all the grumble from the depths of her stomach reminded her that she still hadn't eaten. The dreadwolf who had gotten her into the entire mess had bounded off the minute they'd been whisked back to reality, no doubt to go get the dinner that eluded Jolie.

She was lost and tired and hungry and homesick. And, above all else, she still hadn't been able to shake loose the blanket of fear covering her shoulders like a shroud.

The Broken Mirror card had done its job.

It had scared her.

Her mirror twin, what she'd said, who'd she been with…Wendy had said it was a vision of the person Jolie was afraid to become, and she felt the truth in that burrowing deep into herself.

Suddenly she blinked, recognizing the hallway that opened up in front of her. She had finally found her way back to her room, the mahogany door a beacon for her weary feet. She shuffled over and nudged it open. Using what strength she had left, she collapsed face first onto the duvet

The duvet groaned underneath her in return.

Jolie screamed and leapt from the bed, reaching for whatever she could find as a makeshift weapon. The pot of flowers would do. She lifted the porcelain handle and swung it towards the lump shifting out from under her bedspread and–

Peter caught her wrist before it made contact.

With a stuttering heart, Jolie stared up at her captor. His eyebrows were raised in clear amusement. "My weakness is not a pot of sunflowers, Jolie Hook."

Her mouth went dry. She was half leaning over the bed, her upper body pressed far too intimately against Peter's chest, mind reeling at the energy crackling between them. Was that his magic's doing? Sometimes it was so strong around him that he seemed like human lightning.

"Why are you in my room?" she whispered, before catching herself and clearing her throat. "What are you doing here?" she said again, voice stronger. She pulled back against his grip and there was a moment where his gaze flickered as he drank in her face before letting go.

She clutched the pot to herself protectively, waiting for his answer.

"I wanted to see how your day was."

"You wanted to see how my day was," she repeated flatly.

He grinned. "Is that so hard to believe?"

She squinted at him. His freckled cheeks, his sparkling eyes—green like forest beetles—the way she could see a sliver of chest peeking out from an unbuttoned shirt.

"My day was fine," she answered, pulling herself away from her treacherous thoughts.

She turned her face, hoping he couldn't see its rosy tint, and set to righting the flower pot back in its place. She wouldn't tell him about Wendy. Their time together felt private. Secret. And if it brought her closer to his weakness then she didn't want him to have forewarning.

"I thought up twelve different ways to murder you, hid your favorite pair of socks, and stuffed your cellar full of stinksap."

"You *what*?"

She couldn't hide her smile. "That was a joke."

"...so you're saying you only came up with eleven different ways to murder me?"

"Ten now, since my flower pot idea clearly didn't work."

Peter barked a laugh, finally pushing himself up and out of her bed. "You haven't figured out my weaknesses yet, I take it?"

"Maybe I have and I just enjoy your company so much I haven't told you," she said, rolling her eyes.

He smiled, but it was strained. "Try not to get a man's hopes up too high, darling girl."

Leave the fearful darling girl to her nightmares and hauntings. She'll never be more than her legacy, no matter how hard she tries.

Jolie flinched back, the memory of Peter—mirror Peter—so vivid, so raw that for a moment she thought she was back in the cursed magical world.

In an instant he was at her side, one hand cupped around her elbow to steady her. Had she been shaking? "Are you okay?" he asked, green eyes searching her face.

Warm.

His hand was warm.

Nothing like the icy touch of the mirror's illusions. She closed her eyes and centered herself on that feeling. It was so gentle, and yet there was a strength behind it that balanced her, kept her in the present, kept her from falling fully back into that moment where she had been mute, blind, and without touch.

"Jolie? Jo? Look at me, hey." He lifted his hand to her chin, tilting it upwards so that their eyes met. Pool of forest green. They nearly looked worried. About her?

"I'm fine," she said. *Dust forsake me,* she swore, internally chastising the shake in her voice. "I don't need your help."

His look told her he didn't believe her liar's words. His mouth flattened and, while he let her chin go, his hand slid instead to tuck a lock of hair behind her ear. "I think you're hiding something, Jolie," he murmured.

"I think you're hiding a lot of things," she answered, words unsticking from her throat.

His throat bobbed. Behind his eyes, Jo saw Peter searching for his response. Finally, slowly, he replied, "There are things better left to the shadows."

"Shadows don't scare me."

His face tightened and all at once he looked tired.

"Maybe they should." Without another word he exited, clicking the door shut behind him.

Jolie shivered, her body craving his quickly evaporating warmth. Just when she thought she had Peter figured out, he kept surprising her. Who was he really? What was he gaining from this friendship? Is that what he wanted?

She knew her choices were either to stay up and over analyze her day or succumb into the willing arms of sleep. She easily chose the latter.

Her dreams weren't tangible. They were feelings, rather than images. Curiosity, wonder, fear, sadness, love.

She woke up all too soon, feeling no less tired than she had the night before.

She pulled a dress from the closet—short and simple in gray fabric—and tossed it on without care, thankful for the lack of buttons or straps. She didn't have the brain capacity to deal with those, not running on such little sleep.

She only allowed herself one brief moment to think about her encounter with Wendy before shoving it from her mind. Wendy had said that those who didn't want to see her wouldn't, and Jo kept that idea resolutely in mind.

She'd had enough games and magical beings to last a lifetime.

Still, her fingers clutched at the card stuffed into her pocket. *The Heart*. Wendy had left her with one clue, though Jo couldn't imagine a less helpful one.

Peter's weakness was his heart?

It couldn't be his literal heart, that would be too easy. Everyone's weakness was their heart if you stabbed them hard enough. So a metaphorical heart. Something he held dear, maybe? Something he loved?

Someone he loved?

That thought made her pause. Did Peter Pan have it in him to love? Or had so many years of being unable to grow up stunt him of that? She vividly recalled the dream they'd shared; Peter's childhood was not one filled with love.

Surely he must care for his Lost Boys. At the very least he didn't want to see them harmed.

Wendy had said that she'd had a relationship of some sort with him once, but clearly that had dissolved into nothingness over time.

Her feet dragged as she shuffled down the hallway towards the room she and Peter had shared together the other morning. Her mind hurt, but coffee and sugar might be the salve she needed.

When she stopped in front of the sun room the spread was there, but no Peter. Still, she nabbed a pastry, stuffing another in her pocket, and nibbled on it as she made her way out into the gardens.

The castle, as beautiful and elegant as it was, was too stuffy. It was why she always preferred the top deck of the Jolly Roger to the rooms beneath: Jolie needed to be able to see the sky.

Today it was pale blue, with clouds so puffy it was as if they were painted with a sponge. A gentle breeze played with the ends of her hair and she found a spot overlooking the ocean.

The ornate metal bench seemed to hum in delight as she sank down on it, happy to have a visitor for once. The smell of salt and sea was so strong that Jolie could almost imagine she was back home.

That Damien was resting his chin on her shoulder, that Smee was bustling about with the daily orders, that her father was watching her with a look in his eye that so often wavered between glee and disappointment.

She sighed, looking out across the water. Could the Jolly Roger pull right up to this cliffside? Dock along its rocky shore and climb up the face? Would she want them to?

Though she was a captive she didn't feel like she needed rescue. And being forced to leave Peter's side by anything other than her own volition stirred a restless anger in her chest.

If you leave now you'll never learn his weakness, she thought, pulling at that thread like a lifeline to explain her feelings. Coming home to her father with Peter's defeat at her own hands would undoubtedly be the push he needed to hand over the ship.

So why did it feel like the wrong thing to do?

"You're a hard girl to track down, Hook."

Jolie frowned at the intrusion, her eyes flicking over to the blonde fairy as she settled down on the bench next to her, arms flung open, one leg resting on the other. The picture of confidence.

Could Tink be Peter's heart?

"What do you want?" she huffed, brushing the last remaining crumbs of her breakfast onto the grass.

"Just your delightful company."

Jo rolled her eyes. Tinkerbell knew how to get under her skin, how to writhe under it like a slug. "I wasn't aware your life was so lonely, Tink."

The other girl scowled, before pulling a tightly bound scroll out of her pocket. She waved it in front of the pirate's face. "Be nicer, little Hook, or I won't give you this."

"Your diary?" she said, unimpressed. "Dear diary, today I squished a bug, sharpened my knives, and helped an innocent old lady cross the Neverwoods."

Jo heard the paper crunch slightly under Tinkerbell's grip. "You know what? I don't know why I bother. If you want to stay in the dark as to who poisoned your mother then be my guest, brat." She made to rise but Jo's hand shot out against her arm, eyes wide.

"What?"

Tink sat back down. "Have I got your attention now?"

Jo stared at the scroll. "What–" she cleared her throat. "What does that say?"

Tink hummed, stretching languidly overhead. "Say please."

"Just–"

"Say. Please."

Jo squashed her ire, biting back the curses on her tongue. "*Please*."

For a moment she thought the fairy would still get up and leave, taking whatever dangling carrot she had and hide it away. But instead she held it out and let Jolie snatch it, unfurling it immediately.

"I don't understand," she admitted, eyes roaming the page. It was numbers and letters, dates and names. What did this have to do with her mother?

"Judging from everything I know, your mother was poisoned with the Nightmare's Kiss," Tink said. "It's incredibly rare and nearly impossible to get your hands on. It grows once a year, in the blood of a sacrificial lamb, and only under a full moon sky."

"Morbid," Jo muttered.

"And deadly," Tink countered. "As poison's go, it's one of the worst. Which is good for you."

"How," she gritted, "is the fact that my mother was killed with one of the worst poisons good for me exactly?"

She sighed. "*Because*," she stressed, as if talking with a child, "it's so rare and deadly that only one fairy in all of Neverland sold it."

"Let me guess, you?"

Tink snorted. "Dust no, do I look like a merchant? I don't quite have that customer service personality."

"Who then?"

Tink's eyes dimmed a fraction. "Doesn't matter. She's dead now. Your father saw to that." The anger in her voice was palpable, nearly tangible. "But after her death—all of their deaths—their belongings passed on to me." She nodded at the parchment. "The person who bought your mother's poison will be on that list."

Jo hadn't realized before that moment, or maybe hadn't wanted to realize—still trying to ignore her father's shameful atrocities—that Tinkerbell was the last fairy left in Neverland. If it had been anyone except the assassin she might have asked if she was lonely because of it, but she knew that Tink would rather stab herself than open up to an enemy.

"Say I believe you...why would you give this to me?"

"Maybe I have a bleeding freaking heart," she said. "Or maybe I don't like being made out to be the bad guy in your sordid tale. Read it. Or don't, I don't care. But believe me when I say that you won't find my name on that list." She stood, wings flaring out from her broad shoulders. "I might be an assassin, but even I'm not that evil."

She left a glittering trail of fairy dust in her wake, the silver shower of sparks falling onto the grass like rain.

Jolie swallowed the thick tangle of emotions in her throat and glanced at the paper once more. Her mother's murderer's name was somewhere on the list.

The problem was, it could have been any of them, because they were all foreign to her. She deflated, unsure what she had been expecting. A name she knew? A big red arrow pointing to the correct one?

The list trailed back decades. Each line was dated, with a name and quantity purchased. She read through it once, twice, then paused on a specific day. A month before her mother had died.

Heir Apparent. 10mg. Second day of the Second month.

"Heir Apparent?" she muttered, flipping over the paper as if the answer would be on the back. The words—a name?—meant nothing. The date only tangentially related to her mother. The murderer could have bought it further in advance, or Tink was wrong and there was another way to access to the poison, or–

She drew her knees up to her chest and rested her head on them, her skin prickling at the sea breeze. Not for the first time, and not for the last, Jolie Hook wished she could talk to her mother.

Chapter 38

*"A great number of Neverland's art pieces were painted
by the late great Abdulahi Mezore, whose affinity for
using crushed up precious stones and metals in his paint
always leant an ethereal quality to his work. You can
find a stunning collection of them at [REDACTED]."*
- THE MOSTLY ACCURATE TRAVELER'S
GUIDE TO THE ANCIENT WORLD OF NEV-
ERLAND

Peter found her two hours later.

Whatever moment they had shared in her room the night
before was gone. In fact, he was almost as insufferable as ever.

"I'm bored," he whined, drawing out the last word like taffy. His
head was resting in his palm as he lounged, floating midair beside her.

She would have been impressed by the magic had her temples not been pounding.

A roaring headache had seized her, and he was merely stoking the flames. Plus, she just wasn't sure how to act around him right then. They had shared...something. Some tender tendril of a moment between them in those twilight hours.

If she was honest with herself, they had shared more than a few *somethings* over the last week. But thinking on that just made her head hurt even more.

"Go play with your Lost Boys," she snipped, brushing past him. "I'm busy."

"Ouch, she's a feisty one today," he said. "But Jolie," he tried to catch her arm as she slid from his grip. "You're meant to be my entertainment, otherwise why have you around?"

"Then go play with Nana. I saw her chasing a rat outside." She decided it was much easier to go back to yelling at Peter than to try and untangle the mess of emotions threaded through her heart.

His nose wrinkled as he righted himself, settling back onto the floor with a thunk of boot against wood. "What are you doing anyways?" he asked, peering over her shoulder to where she was fiddling with the edge of a painting. It was a beautiful oil masterpiece of sunshine streaming onto a lake, but that wasn't why Jolie was sliding it off its hook.

"Looking for something."

"What?"

"Anything! A secret passage, a secret treasure box, I don't know." She hung the painting back up, content but disappointed that there was nothing hiding behind it. "Your weakness has to be around here somewhere."

She'd been at Peter's castle for over a week and had made frustratingly little progress in their game.

Peter's weakness was his heart.

Whatever that meant.

There was a pause as Jolie stepped over to another painting—this one of a toastfly—and then Peter descended into mad, unceremonious laughter. She spun towards him, hands on her hips. "What is so funny?"

He straightened, calming his breaths. "Oh darling girl, you do amuse me. My weakness is not hidden behind a painting," he laughed. "Or under the carpet," he called as she started to lift one up by its gold tasseled edge.

"Well give me a hint then, you annoying prat."

He feigned shock. "Annoying? I'll have you know I pride myself on my charm."

"Oh really–?" she started, but was cut off with a tumultuous flip and roar of her stomach. Her ears burned at the sound and Peter chuckled again.

"Hungry?"

She twisted her lips, raising her nose in what she hoped was indignation. "Well, it's past lunch time isn't it? Or does the great Peter Pan not eat sandwiches? You definitely didn't eat breakfast today."

Peter smiled. "Did you miss me then, darling girl?"

She sniffed. "Hardly. I just like keeping a close eye on my enemies and you make that hard when you go sneaking off."

Her stomach then made a smaller, pitiful mewl and she clapped her hands over it. "Shut up," she hissed down at herself, cursing her traitorous body.

He gave a fake bow. "What my lady wants, my lady gets. Two sandwiches, coming right up." He disappeared before she could protest that she was only joking and that she could feed herself. She smiled. It was moments like these that reminded Jolie that Peter Pan was just a boy. And that she was, after all, just a girl.

"Well, there's no clues behind the painting and nothing under the rug," she mused, determined to find something of use before Peter came back. Her gaze snagged on a door down the hall. The castle had at least a hundred rooms, she might as well start with that one.

She gave a tug on the handle and it popped open. Peter didn't believe in locked doors, apparently. Her breath stole out of her as she entered.

It put her father's treasure horde to shame.

Rows and rows of pedestals, each with a plaque and an object, stretched down the length of the room. Even along the walls there were mounted art pieces, embroidered blankets hung along ropes, pieces of decorated armor placed on mannequins.

It could have been chaotic had everything not been so neatly arranged into a particular place. No dust tickled her nose, nor did any dirt appear to be accumulating underfoot. It was an exquisitely kept collection, one that Peter clearly had the pride to maintain.

She moved over to the closest pedestal.

Feather from the last farshad bird. Bartered from the Fairies.

It was a gold plume with a striking red pattern across the ends. Jolie had never heard of such a bird, but judging from the feather it must have been quite the sight.

She looked at the next pedestal.

Jewel from unknown world. Found on beach.

The dark oval nestled on the white cushion seemed to attract all light to it, so eager to gobble it up within its own mirrored shine. She resisted the urge to run her fingers across its smooth surface, content to hungrily commit it to memory instead.

She was almost giddy as she took in as many objects as she could, the pirate thirst for treasure and knowledge at the forefront of her mind.

So much of what laid in the room was from eons before her birth, some even from other worlds, and not for the first time she wished that Neverland hadn't been cut off from the portals in the sky. The things she might have seen! As it was, she would live vicariously through this collection.

A pen that *bore witness to the birth of a nation.*

A stack of red beads along a looping string that apparently once belonged to a god.

A picture, mostly burned around the edges, of a beautiful straw house.

A finger—*from my first enemy*—that she initially drew back from but soon came in close with morbid curiosity.

Row after row—Peter Pan had quite the collection.

"Do you like it?"

She jumped at the voice, taking the time to gather her words into cohesion as Peter set down a plate—with two sandwiches, she noted with a smile. "Where did you get all of these things?"

He hummed, wandering over to the center of the room to meet her. With all the objects around them they had to stand quite close together. "Here and there," he offered. "Immortality comes with its perks."

"Do you have a favorite?"

"Hm?"

"A favorite piece of the collection," she said, her gaze sweeping across the trove she'd only begun to dive into. "Something in here that's more precious than the others?" It was partially strategy—maybe his heart was there—but mostly curiosity that prompted her question.

A soft smile played on his lips, the kind that sent that warm pool of ocean water inside of Jolie into a flurry. He took her hand and gently led her over to a pedestal.

Within, a simple card, handmade on thick blue paper, with a drawing of a flower on the front.

The plaque read: *Birthday card. A gift.*

"Of all things? A birthday card?"

"It was the only thing in the entire room that was gifted to me," he admitted, dimples popping. "Consider me sentimental."

"Who would have thought," she mused, trailing her fingers closer to the card but not quite touching it. She had a whole stash of cards like it from Damien, wrinkled and torn from years of being in her trunk but treasured nonetheless.

She clasped her hands behind her back and continued moving on through the room. Peter trailed behind, watching her intently.

"Were you expecting something different?" he asked, watching her reactions to his horde.

"A torture chamber maybe," she said. "Or rows of heads on spikes. A pile of fingers still clutching their swords. A burnt up leg–"

"Alright, I get it," he said. His footsteps followed her as she wound between the rows. "But have some more imagination, hm? Of all the treasures in all the worlds, you expect me to keep something so common as a head on a spike?"

Something caught her eye and Jolie paused. "What's this one?"

It looked like a music box made from a seashell, and she was reminded of one her mother had that looked nearly alike, only that one had been cracked into a million pieces and thrown into the ocean. Jo would know, she did it herself in anger after her mother's death.

She reached out her hand, looking at Peter. "Can I...?"

He nodded and she gingerly picked it up. "Have you ever played its song? Siren songs are beautiful, when they aren't trying to kill you," she said, rotating the windup key until she heard the click. A beautifully haunting melody sprung forth, and Jo almost had to laugh.

"*My Jolly Sailor Bold?* Fitting that you'd own such a song."

Peter frowned for a moment, reaching for the shell. "Actually, I don't quite remember where I got this–"

"Do you know," she continued, closing her eyes to the melody, "that us pirates don't dance to music much? It's not really in our nature. But there is one thing we do when we hear a beautiful tune..."

"Oh?"

A wicked red rose smile bloomed as she pulled two crossed sabers from a pedestal to her left. She tossed one at Peter then dropped her stance and readied her sword, pointing it towards his chest. "We fight."

She lunged before he had a chance to react to her words, her weapon aimed for a shoulder that tilted out of the way at the last moment. Her playful eyes met his shocked ones, though they quickly melted into gleeful competition as he parried her next blow.

"If you break any of my things," he said, shifting on his back foot, "I will not be kind."

"Is the big bad monster going to get me?" she mocked, tossing her hair over one shoulder. She drew back a step behind a pedestal. Something darkly dangerous had taken hold of her and she wasn't willing to douse the thrill in her veins now. "If you want me, Peter Pan, come and claim me."

He barked a laugh and the dance began.

Her steps methodical, slow, strategic.

His quick, antsy, full of electric energy.

Their swords clashed to the tune of the siren's song, punctuated by stuttered breaths and the movement of feet on carpet. Unlike any other time she had crossed swords with an enemy—though that word was losing much of its gusto lately—it had been with the orders to injure.

Now, it was about the beauty of it all, the way she could command her sword to twirl in her palm, to soar through the air.

She relished the fact that Peter was an equal match for her. Heat on heat. Sword on sword. They were holding back from real bloodshed but not from trying to disarm the other, and some of Peter's flourishes were positively oozing with his ego. She could see him in the positioning of his feet, in the light in his eye.

The only thing Peter Pan loved to do more than play games was to play with fire, and Jolie could feel herself burning.

She gasped as she backed into a large glass cabinet, dropping her sword to reach out and steady it with both hands. She breathed out a sigh of relief when none of the brightly colored vials within toppled from their places.

"So careless," Peter tsked from behind her, resting his weapon gently on her neck. Jo glared as she turned back to face him. He was dripping with smug satisfaction.

"I dropped my own sword, this hardly counts as a victory for you," she sniffed, crossing her arms.

With a wave of his hand both weapons disappeared—no doubt vanished back to their pedestal. From somewhere nearby, the music shell continued its haunting song.

He moved closer until the tips of their feet were touching, just a whisper of a connection. One of his hands lifted up to her cheek, but he hesitated and dropped it down again before he touched her.

"Do you know what Lost Boys do when we hear music?" he asked.

Jo racked her brain but found nothing.

He smiled and grabbed her hand in his, pulling her close. Rough lips brushed against the shell of her ear, his words filling up their hollow and she allowed a shiver to roll across her body. "We dance."

She blinked, surprised at how she enjoyed the feeling of her hand in his. Her other fingers found his shoulder easily, the soft tunic smooth. "We're not really about to–"

"Oh yes we are."

"There's no room to dance!" she replied, though laughter easily wormed its way into her words.

"A sway, then," he replied. "And I will take my waltz another time."

She pursed her lips but let him shift her around, as much as the rows between treasures would allow for, at least. "You think there will be another time?"

"I know it," he winked.

"Is that before or after I kill you?"

His reply was only in the fractional tightening of his smile, the brush of fingers against the sensitive part of her spine, the thin exhale of air. After a moment: "Am I truly so awful that you actually want to kill me?"

Jo scoffed, meaning to tear her hand out of his grip but he held fast. "I think that you kidnapped my father, have kept me locked up in here, have waged war on us for decades–"

"A war you started."

"Even if that was true," she said, "does it matter? You're my enemy. A Hook's enemy."

"You father didn't think so. He wanted peace, remember?"

"Yes, right before you kidnapped him!" Her voice was halfway between a shriek and a seethe.

"Only for a bit of fun," he shrugged. "It had all gotten so boring. I just wanted to see what would happen, how hard he would fight to get free."

"I don't believe you."

Peter raised an eyebrow. Throughout the entire argument they still danced. A sway for a room full of empty treasures.

She continued on. "I think you covet things. You hoard them." Her mind went back to the orphanage where he had been abandoned. No clothing, no toys, no family. It was clear why he guarded his things so well. "You wanted to trap my father in here just to add him to your collection."

"You agree that I wouldn't have actually hurt him, then."

Her cheeks flared. "No! That's not–no!" Both her tongue and her feet stumbled, but Peter's strong grip caught her. He steadied her stance, though her heart kept up its wailing thump against her chest.

"I may have shadows behind me, Jolie, but I'm not so evil as that. He would not have come to real harm."

"You dropped me in front of a croc."

His eyes flashed his guilt. "An unfortunate accident. One that I saved you from, though. That's got to count for something."

Jolie cursed that she found his grin so disarming. That something about his words seemed so genuine. What kind of easily affected maiden had she become? Dancing with the enemy, in his treasure room of all places?

But maybe he was right. Her father had wanted peace. Could she reach for that too? Should she? She believed that Peter had nothing to do with her mother. She believed it now, after so much evidence. But did that excuse everything else?

"And," he said, softer, "I'm sorry."

She looked up at him in surprise. "Sorry?"

"I like games. I like playing with things...and people," he admitted. "But I don't want to hurt anyone."

"That makes you better than me," she admitted after a pause. "I've dreamed every night about how I will hurt the person who murdered my mother." She looked up at him. "That person used to wear your face."

His throat bobbed. "And now?"

"And now it's just darkness inside of me, and nowhere for me to put it. And I wonder..." she faltered, taking a breath. "I wonder if I'll ever be rid of it, or if I'm cursed to be suffocated by it forever."

At some point they had stopped dancing, though the music played on. Now they were just holding each other, so close that it made Jo's head spin off course.

"Everyone has darkness," he said. "But they all die in the face of one thing."

"What thing?"

His eyes were sad when he answered. "The thing that I would covet the most, if only I was worthy to have it." His fingers pressed tighter on her shoulder. "Love."

"Love?" she echoed. The word itself held such weight that she wanted to cup it in her palms instead of letting it fade away from her lips. It was a great and terrible word to throw around.

"I think a mother's love can be the purest of all, under the right circumstances. What would your mother say?" Peter asked.

Her grip tightened in his. "What do you mean?"

"About taking revenge. About holding on to that anger. What would she say?"

Jolie about her mother's bright eyes, how she so often wove the best bedtime stories. How she could make the perfect cup of tea to cure any illness.

"She..." The weight of tears pressing against her eyes was immense, but Jolie refused to let even one fall. Her mother was, above all things, the strongest person Jolie had ever known. And she wouldn't want Jo to waste her tears on the past.

"I can help you find who did it, if you want," he offered, honesty and truth in his voice. "If it will help mend your torn heart. I can help."

"Thank you," she replied softly. Suddenly everything around them felt so still, like one move would shatter the illusion and ricochet her back into a reality she didn't want to face.

It was just her and Peter, and the comfort she found in his arms was rivaled only by the comfort she had always found in the stars above.

Somehow she had felt more alive in the last week than her entire life before, and she knew it was because of him. His stupid games, his stupid smile. Her heart thumped.

"If I don't win this last game are you going to keep me in here too? With the rest of your prizes?" she breathed.

"If I'm lucky." He stared at her, eyes ablaze. His face was so close that even the slope of his nose had vanished, and all she could focus on were his forest eyes and his mouth. A mouth she wondered if tasted like sugared lemons. "I would worship you like the night worships its stars—just happy for whatever moments of brilliance it's given. Hoping it can capture their attention enough to persuade them to remain forever in its sky."

Her breath hitched at the same time as his hand found the small of her back, as she closed those final few millimeters between them. Her brain was fuzzy with anticipation and magic and the heady swell of the moment.

"I would work the rest of my life to try and deserve you, if you would allow it," Peter murmured, cupping her jaw.

The music shell wound down its final notes and shut off with a click.

And the room around them exploded.

Chapter 39

Before it happened, Peter had been thinking about Jolie Hook.

About how soft her hand was in his, despite the years of sword training and ship rigging. About how her face had lit up with such wonder while looking through his treasures—really, mere trinkets in comparison to her. About how close they were, how easily she fit into him, how right it felt to be holding her.

Jolie Hook was a rare, beautiful, feisty thing.

And now Peter was holding her hand again, this time praying to a God who wasn't part of his world and whose name he had forgotten that she would fight through this too.

Her face was pale, the usual tan and sun freckles washed away in the grips of pain and healing. Her brow was sweat slicked, causing her hair to cling to her neck and drench the pillow being used to prop her up. What once was a bed of such luxury had devolved into nothing more than a hospital mattress and, if his magic couldn't do its work, maybe a coffin.

No. He thought viciously. *Not again.*

There was a faint knock, a patter of feet, and the tickle of fairy dust in his nose.

"Tell me, Tinkerbell."

She cleared her throat. "I traced it back to the underwater city. It came from a home for those who have lost people in the war."

"Revenge."

"Yes."

Peter sighed and screwed his eyes up in disgust. Would rivalries never cease between them? Would they keep haunting him, his past dogging his every footstep?

At the back of his mind, a shadow tingled, whispering for him to take revenge, to pull out his sword and his magic and–

"Peter!" Tink barked, shaking him.

His eyes snapped open in time to see a shadowed claw sink back into himself, his dark magic slipping his control for just a moment until he pulled it back. He breathed out a rattling sound. "Sorry Tink, sorry, I just–"

"I know."

Beneath his hand, Jolie's small fingers didn't even stir, barely even pulsed.

When his treasure room exploded, the shell box a hidden firestorm, it had knocked them both off their feet, hands ripped from each other's embrace. He ended up crashing into a pedestal that had once held a map of the star portals—and now was burnt ruin.

And she...

"Jolie!" he yelled, voice hoarse from the gray churning smoke. "Jolie!" He coughed, covering his mouth with the bottom of his tunic.

Everything was on fire, utter destruction. But he didn't care about the broken treasures or trinkets. He cared about the girl.

His head whipped back and forth as his panic grew. Where was she?

Finally: a sliver of an arm, barely visible underneath a collapsed table. He raced towards her, hand flung out wide in a magical arc as he sent the furniture crashing into the wall away from them.

His breath stalled in his throat at how still she was, the pool of blood running from her crown, the way her hand was out, almost pleading, begging to be found.

Jolie Hook was about to die.

He stooped down, hands fluttering, and gently lifted her head into his lap. "Jolie, Jolie, please say something. Please."

Tink had found them not moments later, Nana yapping at her heels.

Together they put out the flames and she'd pried Jolie from his grip. The fairy would have bruises from how hard he tried to fight her, but Tink's snap of "She needs a healer!" shook him loose.

A healer. He was the only one around, their Lost Boy medicine men and women too far. So Peter had sat by her side and poured all of himself into her, all of the light and goodness he still had hidden away went into saving her. Her skin knit back together, her breathing evened out.

That was hours ago.

"She's still not awake," he muttered, running his finger over her knuckles.

"Magic takes time," Tink supplied uselessly. "Maybe you should get some rest too. You look exhausted."

Peter shot up, anger licking at his face. "Rest? While we're getting attacked in our own home? While things like this slip through our fingers? While–" he cut himself off with a vicious exhale. "No. There is no time for rest." He sneered at the word. "This is the time for retaliation. For war."

"For war?" Tink replied, features twisting. "Do you not remember the last war? Or have your petty skirmishes with Hook and his daughter addled your mind."

"Watch your tone," he said flatly, eyeing his second in command. "You are part of my army, remember?"

"I remember," she snapped. "I remember decades of fighting, of death, or seeing things that Neverland wasn't made for. I remember the last time we went to war over some girl, and look how that ended up!"

"I-"

"With her in a coffin and you in your cups. With blood on all of our hands, blood that we've only just recently washed out. None of us wanted to go to war with the Merfolk, and yet we did it anyway. Because you were heartbroken. So heartbroken that-"

"Enough!" he roared, darkness dimming his vision for a moment before he collected himself. "Enough," he repeated, quiet and small. "What would you have me do, then?"

Tink's features softened. "We can tighten up our borders and run security on the entire castle. We'll send a note to the Merkingdom that we will not take this lightly, and we will let them deal with their own private citizens. Is that not part of the treaty that was agreed upon at the end of the war?"

"Maybe, but-"

"And we will send Jolie Hook back home."

His nostrils flared. "What?"

"She doesn't belong here, and now she's getting hurt." Tink's voice was hard, determined. "Unless you want a repeat of what happened last time, it's best for her to go home."

Peter grasped for something to say in response.

She was right, of course she was right, Jolie didn't deserve to be caught in his own tangled past of mistakes. But sending her home opened an unending pit in his stomach. Not one from losing something he coveted.

But rather from the thought of losing someone that he had grown to care for.

"What about my game?" he responded, nearly cringing at the weakness in his voice.

"Screw your game. This is her life we're talking about."

"I didn't know you gave a damn about her."

Tink sighed. "It's not about her, Peter."

The vortex in his stomach widened and he was thrown back to that day, so long ago. If he had been just a little faster, his fingers a little longer, he would have caught her, she wouldn't have–

"Okay." He turned to look back at the sleeping Jolie Hook. His steps were heavy on the floor as he walked to the head of the bed and brushed the hair from her forehead. "Okay. But she won't want to go. No one tells Jolie Hook what to do."

Tink sighed. "Then make her think it's her idea. Make her want to leave. Make her storm out. As long as she's far away from here, she'll be safe."

He squeezed the unconscious pirate's hand one last time. "Gather the Lost Boys, they need to be briefed and be on the lookout for other attacks. That, at least, you can begrudge me."

Tink nodded. "I'll have them here within the hour."

Chapter 40

"To keep milk from spoiling, an old Neverland mother's tale says to mix it with wild honey and thyme."
- THE MOSTLY ACCURATE TRAVELER'S GUIDE TO THE ANCIENT WORLD OF NEVERLAND

J olie was dreaming about honey and trees and sugared lemons when something wet slicked up her cheek.

"Go away," she grumbled, trying to swipe at whatever was interrupting her dream. There was a sniff and then a bark and she was shooting upwards, fully awake.

"Nana!" she exclaimed, trying and failing to push the dreadwolf off. She groaned at the sudden movements, her body feeling stiff, disused. Her mouth, too, was parched. "Nana, what in dust's name happened?"

All at once it came back to her. The treasure room. Dancing with Peter. The explosion.

The last thing she saw was Peter's frightened eyes as she was blasted away.

The last thing she felt was her body breaking and crumbling as she laid there, wheezing what she thought was her last breath.

She fingered her temple, almost expecting to pull her hand away bloody, but there was no wound. She slowly checked over her arms. Nothing. Had she really come away from the ordeal so unscathed?

And...someone had changed her clothes. Out of a dress, she was now in a simple white tunic and black trousers. She supposed her old outfit might have burned away.

"Or was it magic," she muttered, giving in to Nana's begging and scratching her behind the ears. "Was it Peter? Is he okay?"

She sighed when the dreadwolf said nothing more. For some reason the thought of him hurt made her feel uneasy.

"Shall we go find him then?" She swung her feet over the edge of the bed, and stood on shaky legs, waiting a moment for her strength to come back. For her part, Nana merely spun in circles on the bed and flopped over, content to enjoy her slumber.

"Lazy beast," Jo scoffed, finally confident enough in her steps to head towards the door.

Before she could reach for it, though, it swung open on its own.

"Peter!"

The shock on his face was clear, though he quickly steeled it back into a mask. Jolie assessed him. Dark smudges under his dark green eyes. A scratch across his cheek—had he not healed himself?—and rumpled clothes hanging limp from his body. He looked tired. And she told him as much.

He laughed at her words. "It's been...well, an attack in one's own home demands a lot of action. Are you–?"

"I'm okay," she responded, moving back into the bedroom to let him enter. "Did you heal me?"

He nodded mechanically, pausing his gaze at Nana on the bed before turning towards Jo. "It was the only way to–well your injuries I just–"

"Hey," she took his hand in hers, pressing it up against her chest where a steady heart was beating in tune. "I'm okay. I'm alive."

His mouth was a thin line as his fingers tapped on her skin, a sliver over her collar where the tunic fell open.

"I'm fine, Peter."

His eyes snapped up to hers. "Fine? For now. They will never let me forget my past."

Jolie's eyebrows knit together. "They? Who?"

"The Mer," he muttered, removing his hand. Jolie shivered at the lack of warmth. "The trap was a remnant from that conflict, I'm sure of it. They've never forgiven me for...I didn't mean for you to get caught in the crosshairs." He paused. "Do you know the history of the Merfolk war?"

Jo leaned against the edge of the bed, confused as to where this conversation was going. "I know more than most, I suppose."

"Tell me."

She frowned. "You declared war on the Mer. It lasted decades; it turned the sea red and the Neverwoods barren. It only ended when..." she looked up at Peter, biting her lip. "When my father got involved. He sided with the Mer and sent you back into the woods. The Merfolk accords followed soon after."

Peter slumped into a chair tucked into the corner of the room. "Half right. But you're missing the most important part." His head was down, his body language desperate and defeated. "The why."

Jolie blinked. Truly she had never bothered to consider the why. Peter Pan was maniacal. Peter Pan was the villain. Peter Pan didn't need a reason. That's how the stories went.

He kept speaking, lost in a world she wasn't even a part of. "It was for revenge. There was a girl, a friend–" he stumbled on the word, Jolie recognizing it for a lie. *Wendy*. By her own admission they were much more than just friends. "She wasn't from Neverland and there was so much she wanted to see, wanted to experience. I took her to the Mountain in the Sea."

His eyes slipped up to Jo's, ensuring she knew exactly where he was speaking of.

She'd lived her life in the sea, of course she knew. The Mountain in the Sea was massive, sublime, dangerous. Below the waves, a giant formation of rock and coral, the bottom of which only the Mer had ever seen. Above the waves were piercing tips, like the tops of mountains.

Slippery and dangerous, the beauty of the darkened opal slopes enticed many travelers.

Her father had always forbidden her from going, his hushed warnings that the mountain devoured those who came too close echoing in her mind.

Jolie swallowed hard. "Why?" Peter must have known how dangerous the Mountain in the Sea was. If Wendy had meant so much to him, why had he put her in harm's way?

He sighed. "Because my will turned to ash around her. I could never refuse her anything and I regret it to this day. The wind was high, that should have been my first clue. But she was determined to press on, nothing could stop her. Even her brothers had declined to journey with us, their survival instincts better than her own...than my own. We went out onto the rocks, she was just a bit ahead of me the entire time. Her eyes were so bright, her smile so wide, that I didn't even notice the crack in the rock, the crevice that tripped her. And I wasn't close enough. I was too far I–" he closed his eyes, breathed in. "The last thing I felt were the tips of her fingers as she tumbled into the sea below."

Jolie's heart clenched for him. For the guilt that he must have carried for so many years, the darkness that must have rested, *still* rested, on his shoulders.

"It wasn't your fault," she said, reaching for his hand. He jerked himself away, standing from his chair and pacing the length of the room. "Peter there was nothing you could have done."

"I should have refused her! I should have used my head! I should have remembered that she was flesh and blood and light and that of course the world would seek to snuff her away! I should have used my magic instead of keeping it locked away like I did then, I should have–" he cut himself off. "It doesn't matter. There are many things I should have done, and many more I shouldn't have."

His entire body was wound tightly on itself, tense and furious. Under his surface, Jolie could see his frustrations boiling and rising like a world-ending tide. On his face, shame and rage spiraled like intertwined lovers.

"I don't understand," Jo murmured, wrapping her arms around herself. "I'm sorry for your loss Peter I truly am. But why go to war with the Mer?"

His eyes were glassy as he looked at her. "They were there. Merfolk, swimming just below the surface, watching our every move. They saw her fall. They heard my anguish. They..." He spun away from her, hiding his face again. "They did nothing as I watched her drown. They did not help her. They did *nothing*. They didn't care about one human soul, an innocent soul."

All the cracks in her understanding of the world were shifting into place with Peter's revelation. He blamed himself for Wendy's death, but he couldn't go to war on his own soul—or maybe he tried and found it lacking.

Instead he went to war on those who swam idly by and did nothing while his heart drifted down into the depths.

That had to be it. Wendy was his heart. But she was already dead. How could she be Peter's weakness?

Jo could only imagine how she would feel if it had been her father, or her mother, or Damien who'd been embraced by the Mountain in the Sea. How she would have screamed and begged and pleaded with the Mer to save them.

Jolie couldn't stop herself from walking over and placing a hand on his shoulder, wanting him to feel that he was not alone. "I'm sorry, Peter. I understand."

He slowly turned. "Do you? You have lost some, yes, your mother...but it wasn't your fault. You don't have to live with her scream in your mind every night when you close your eyes. Didn't have to bathe in blood just to help yourself believe that you were avenging her. I don't think you know that, Jolie Hook."

Jo's anger spiked. He thought she didn't know pain? "I know that her spirit lingers here and you refuse to let her pass on, refuse to even look at her!" she snapped.

His face slackened, horrified. "What?"

She opened and shut her mouth with a click.

Dust, she swore. *Mistake mistake mistake.*

Wendy had warned her not to mention their dalliance. "No, I mean I–"

"You–" For once Peter seemed too shocked to speak, but then the weight of it all slammed across his face. "You've met her?"

"She appeared to me, in the castle," Jo stumbled her words out, suddenly afraid of the hole she'd found herself in. "I talked to her once, we played a game."

Peter paused one long terrible moment, then let out a low, sinister chuckle. "Ah, I see. So now you think you know everything about me, is that it? You see into the dark past of Peter Pan and think you know me? How long have you been diving into my secrets? Laughing about what you find there?"

"No I–"

"What did she tell you?"

"Nothing." Her voice was barely more than a whisper.

"I don't believe you." He shrugged off her hand. "And I think you should leave."

She stumbled. "Are you serious?"

"Darling girl, I'm never serious," he answered, words dark, eyes black flames. "I killed her, and unless you want to follow into whatever damnable fate she's found, I suggest you leave."

Confusion threaded through her anger. Was he sending her away to punish her...or protect her? His fingers twitched at his sides, and she wondered if he was going to pull her close or push her away.

All she knew for certain was that there was a flicker of fear lacing through his words, and she just wanted to hold him and make it go away.

Her gaze steeled. "I'm not leaving."

His hand snaked for her forearm, leaving in so close she could feel his heat. "It's not a question."

She seethed under his grip. "So you have darkness in your past, so what? We've all done things, made mistakes. Life is about moving forward from those, it's about learning and growing up."

His arms fell uselessly to his sides. "Then it's a terrible thing that I can't grow up. You need to leave."

Jolie growled. "I'm not going just because you're afraid!"

"Don't talk to me about fear, Hook," he sneered. "Who would you be without fear holding you up? Everything you do is to try and convince yourself that you're not afraid, that you're worthy of your father's precious legacy, even as you're afraid to become him." His lips peeled back in disgust. "It blinds you. I see through that paper-thin facade of yours, darling girl. Underneath the pirate talk and the sword fights...you're just a scared little girl."

Her skin prickled hot shame. "Don't presume to know anything about me," she lashed, tongue itching to spear him through. "When all you do is sit in your high castle and think up clever ways to ruin other people's lives. A Hook is never afraid. I am not afraid!"

"And I don't deserve forgiveness!" he roared the candles in the room flickering with his rage. His eyes, *dark dark eyes*, were stuck against her gaze.

Flames sprung into his hands, blue and dizzying. Some monster from the recesses of Peter's mind had taken over, one that didn't recognize her. He took a step forwards, and Jolie cursed her cowardly feet when they slid back an inch.

She couldn't help but think that the Peter from the last few days—the Peter she had confided in, who had confided in her and soothed her anxieties and was honest with her.

That Peter had been devoured.

Only a shadow that wore his skin remained.

"I am the monster you always thought I was, Jolie Hook," he said, voice pitched low. "It is the blood that I spill that turns the sea red, that paints the sunset auburn. I am the dark magic that lurks in the Neverwoods, and I am the thing that nightmares fear. So you'd better run, and you'd better run fast."

Jo turned on her heels and fled.

Chapter 41

"Take only pictures (for those who come from worlds where you can do such a thing). Leave only footprints (for those who come from worlds with feet)."
- THE MOSTLY ACCURATE TRAVELER'S GUIDE TO THE ANCIENT WORLD OF NEVERLAND

She saw nothing of the blurred landscape around her as she ran, only focusing on getting as far away from Peter Pan as she could.

Jolie had thought he was proving all the stories about him wrong, that under his villainous facade was a boy just desperate for companionship.

She had been wrong. The darkness in his eyes and the flames at his palms so readily turned towards her proved that. Perhaps he hadn't been the villain in her mother's story, but he was a villain nonetheless.

He wants me to go? Fine. I'll go and forget every good thing I might have discovered about him. I'll forget his breakfasts. I'll forget his healing touch. I'll forget the way we shared our pasts. I'll forget the heat in my belly when he got close. I'll–

Jolie's feet slowed to a halt. She had made it into the Neverwoods. Looking behind her, she couldn't even see the castle anymore.

"Good riddance," she grumbled, kicking at a wayward shrub. Dimly she realized she shouldn't clunk around the woods so loudly, having no idea what manner of beasts lurked about.

Whatever they were, though, she'd take them over Peter bloody Pan.

"He's the one who makes me jump through all these hoops, get accosted by a ghost girl, get nearly blown up!" Her voice was veering on hysterics now. "And then he kicks me out! Because–because–" She fumbled for the end of the sentence.

Why had he thrown her out? She retraced his words, the fear in his eyes, the acid on his tongue.

He was an enigma.

Nothing he did made any logical sense to her. His actions, the way he was with her—gentle, funny, charming—didn't match up with his words—those biting, vicious things so easily thrown at her.

She let out a deep groan. Had she walked right into his hand?

He said leave and she fled? Should she have stayed? Fought? Shown him that he can't just dangle her about like a puppet on a string? That his beastly exterior didn't scare her, despite what he thought?

"You're a fool, Jolie Hook," she sighed. She needed to figure out where she was, then she could find her way home. Her heart clenched. *Home.* Back to the Jolly Roger. Her crew must have so many questions for her; they'd also be expecting her to divulge all of Peter's secrets.

"Joke's on them, I never found out his weakness in the end," she huffed. "Or I did but it's useless. Wendy is his heart. Wendy is already dead. What use is she against someone living? And…I'm talking to myself. Great. I've been around fairy dust too long."

The canopy of leaves overhead was too thick to see the position of the sun to direct her. Which way was the northeast coast? In fact, was her ship even still where it had been anchored?

"Father wouldn't have abandoned me," she whispered, pushing a bramble of branches away and slipping past a tree. "He'll be waiting for me, I'm sure of it."

Sweat started to slick down the small of her back. Though she had no injuries to speak of from the incident, her body was still tired, her muscles cramping and begging for respite. She needed food, and more sleep, and the calming ocean waters to drift away in.

Suddenly, there was a rustle from behind her.

On instinct, she reached for a sword that wasn't there, cursing as she realized that Pan would probably have her sword for the end of time now. *Dust forsaken thief.* It would probably end up in his treasure room, amongst his other stolen things.

"Hello?" she called out. "You'd better show yourself, I am highly pissed off and would love a good fight!" The woods were silent. She cocked her head, listening for the sound of footsteps.

"Ahh!" she yelled when something small and blue shot out from the trees, heading straight towards her. Before she could move, it slammed into her sternum, falling back against the forest floor in a daze.

Jolie didn't know if she wanted to laugh or cry. "John? Michael?" The two headed bird shook its feathers, righting itself and shooting back up into the air so that they were at eye level. Both sets of beady pupils were blown wide, and the beaks were squawking over each other in a cacophonous chorus of cries.

"Calm down! Quit shouting!" she interjected, making placating motions with her hands to try and sooth the magical aviators. "What has gotten into you two?"

And how do we keep running into each other? The forest was too big for so many coincidences, but then again Jolie knew that her life has been rather upside down lately. Meeting her two-headed bird friend at every corner was the least weird of what had been going on.

Finally, with a gulp of air, John got his words out, his wings flapping erratically. "There's been an a-t-t-t–"

"An attack!" his brother finished for him, voice high and sharp, pure panic. "On the castle!"

Jolie rolled her eyes. "Pan can take care of himself. I thought you hated him anyways." She turned to leave, content that with his magic and his Lost Boys, there was nothing that could break down Pan's walls.

He didn't need her help, he'd made that abundantly clear.

"The front door was left open—and they got in!" Michael continued. "The Lost Boys are there but they're losing!" the duo cried together, pecking at Jolie's hands. "You have to help him!"

Her heart sunk for a moment. The door? She racked her brain. She had been so busy storming out that she hadn't bothered to close the door at all. "Who's there?"

Adrenaline roared in her ears at their answer. "The pirates! Captain Hook has stormed Peter's castle!"

Chapter 42

"There is something to be said about the determination of pirates. This author has never found a single sailor willing to back down from a challenge."
- THE MOSTLY ACCURATE TRAVELER'S GUIDE TO THE ANCIENT WORLD OF NEVERLAND

For the second time that day, Jolie found herself racing through the Neverwoods.

Only this time she was following the cries of a two-headed bird who she could barely hear over the roaring of her own heart.

Her father was storming Peter's castle. Why?

To get you back. The answer was obvious.

Peter had said she would never understand the guilt that came with someone you cared for getting hurt because of you—but if her father dipped his sword red then she would.

The terror gripping her chest spurred her legs on faster and faster until she was tumbling out of the woods and onto the castle's front lawn.

The birds had been right: the drawbridge was down, the front door open. Off in the distance, just beyond where the land turned into ocean waves she could see the tip of a familiar mast.

For a moment her heart swelled. Her father had come for her, and he'd brought the entire crew. He hadn't abandoned her to some unknown fate.

Then she heard a terrible crash from inside the castle and raced towards the entrance without a second thought. She turned to the birds: "Try and find help!" They nodded, flapping upwards and away.

Help? Who would come to help? There were no mediating parties left in Neverland. Once the fairies died out it was everyone for themselves.

Her father had seen to that. Was he now regretting it?

She skidded to a halt in the front foyer, nearly tripping on the uprooted carpet. Everything around her was painted in the thick red brushstrokes of pure pandemonium.

Lost Boys were everywhere: jousting on the stairwell, fighting back-to-back along the window ledges, waving spears and swords and shields and yelling things about Peter and their home.

Pirates were everywhere: teeth gritted and swords clashing, they had no qualms about dropping their weapons and using their fists, ramming shoulders into ribs when the opportunity arose.

"Stop!" she cried, pulling on the arm of the nearest pirate; a crew-mate named Stan who'd always saved the best dregs of coffee for her in the morning. "What are you doing?!"

He spared her a glance, then another, with shock in his eyes. "Jo! We're–" He parried a thrust of a spear by a Lost Boy. "We came to save you! Where's the captain?"

"You tell me!" she said, angling to be heard over the din. "I need to find him before–"

A roar and a crash was their only warning before the chandelier above them came tumbling down. Only Jolie's instincts, polished to shine after years of training, saved her from being crushed as she rolled out of the way just in time.

"Stan!" she called, not able to see him through the muck.

"Go find yer father! He ran after Pan!" he yelled from across the wreckage. "Or ain't no one gonna stop until there's nothing left!"

"Dust it all," she muttered, tripping a Lost Boy running in her direction. It was the pig faced boy from the Lost City, his face tightened up into a sneer.

"You!" he shouted.

"Me?"

The boy swung for her with meaty fists, his weapon apparently lost in the fray. Jolie ducked, then kicked out at his knees, smirking in satisfaction when he went down. "Where's Peter?"

He glared up at her. "None of your business, pirate witch."

"Witch?" she scoffed. "That's a new one." Swallowing down the urge to give him a boot to the stomach for good measure, Jolie shot away, weaving through moving bodies and broken furniture.

Peter's castle is huge, there's no way I'll be able to find him in time.

A howl louder than the cannon fire of her ship echoed through the foyer, the vibrations throwing Jolie into the closest wall.

"Nana," she realized, rubbing her shoulder. It would no doubt be bruised come morning, but it didn't matter. All that mattered was finding Peter.

But why? The little voice in her head asked. *To save your father from him? Or to save him from your father?*

She pushed the annoying thought to the recesses of her mind. She would find Peter first and deal with her decisions later.

The howl had come from somewhere to her right, and that's where Jolie's feet took her. The fighting was lessened there, a few unconscious pirates, one Lost Boy who was trying to unstick his spear from the wall, and two battling women who paid Jo no mind as she jogged by.

Out of the few rooms she knew laid in her direction, she raced for the one that came immediately to mind, praying to the second star to the left that she was right.

Her feet skidded under her as she came to a stop. The door to the dining room was blown wide open—the mahogany woodwork dangling only by a single hinge on either side. The carpet leading into the room—one which Jolie knew should have been green with gold fairies—was stained deep ochre.

The stench of iron, cloying and syrupy, filled the air.

Blood had been shed.

But the question was, whose?

She felt detached from her feet as she inched forwards. Was it her father's blood? Would the fearsome Captain Hook have gone down so quickly?

Was it Peter's? Did his blood even run red at all?

The whirling anxiety in the pit of her stomach raged forward, growing bigger and bigger inside of her, swallowing her in fear—*Hooks don't feel fear*—and tension until-

"Peter?" she called out.

He was alone except for Nana, dutiful, loyal Nana, who sat at his side, licking his palm. Peter's face was turned down, golden brown curls hiding him from view, shoulders tensed, like he was expecting an attack at any moment.

And he was covered, dripping, *bathing* in blood. Splashed across his chest, puddled under his feet, drawn along the skin that showed through a rip in his trousers.

Jolie's breath hitched, but her feet didn't stop until she was right in front of him. Belatedly, she realized that the entire dining table had vanished. The chairs too. Even the candelabras were gone. Dark, massive scratch marks scorched the walls in inky black.

Nana growled, low and in warning as she approached. Jolie paused, pleading with her eyes: *she was not the enemy.*

After a moment, the wolf lowered her head.

Jo turned back to Peter. He had yet to move. Hadn't even acknowledged her presence.

"Peter?" Her voice was soft, she didn't want to spook him. "Whose blood is that?"

His? Her father's? She didn't see any bodies, but that meant nothing when magic was your weapon of choice. She took his hand lightly and felt him quiver in response. He was shaking.

"Peter?"

A too long moment of silence stretched between them, taut and unending, until finally his lips moved, just barely, just a fraction.

"I don't know." His voice was hoarse, like he had been screaming.

"What happened here?"

"I don't know."

"Peter. *Peter*, look at me." She took his cheeks in both hands and tilted his face up so that her eyes met his. Jolie sucked in a sharp breath.

Twin pools of dark black abyss, much like the shadowy marks on the wall, darker than she'd ever seen them, like his eyes didn't even exist at all. Not just pupils, but the whites were gone too, and black tears leaked from the corners in streams.

He looked like the vision in the *Broken Mirror* card.

"Dust," she swore, breathless. "Peter, who did this to you? Was it my father?" She knew he was nearly immortal, but something was *wrong*.

"No," he mumbled. "I did this to myself. A long time ago."

Her eyebrows knit together. She had no idea what he was talking about, but she had to snap him out of it fast. The fighting was still raging on and it would only be a matter of time before her father found him. He needed to leave, to hide, just until she could set the crew of the Jolly Roger straight.

"Listen to me, it'll be okay," she said. There was no response beyond the glassy-eyed look of a man not altogether there. "Peter Pan!" she snapped, jerking his head forwards. "I'm not asking, I'm telling. We're running out of time and people are getting hurt. Snap out of it right now or you'll have me to deal with."

Slowly, far more slowly than Jolie would have liked, the dark of Peter's eyes receded, fading back into startling forest green. He blinked, clarity returning to him.

"Jolie?" he muttered, his hands—bloody, red hands—moving up to cup her own, still pressed against his cheek. "You came back."

She huffed a laugh of surprise. "Of course I did. You didn't think some angry villain could really tell me what to do, did you?"

His smile was rueful. "I should never attempt to figure you out, darling girl."

She grinned in response, but it quickly faded when Nana stiffened from beside them, her hackles suddenly raised, a growl dripping from between her canines. Someone was coming.

Jolie dropped her hands. "You need to leave. My father is here, and he's out for blood."

"Peter Pan doesn't run away from a fight," he answered, settling his hand on her shoulder. "And neither do my Lost Boys. Tell your crew to stand down and we'll let them go."

"What? This isn't some pissing contest! People are dying–"

"I won't let anything happen to you," he murmured. Gently, slowly, his hand went to her face, tucking a wayward curl behind her ear. His words seemed like a brush of hot oil against her skin, at once burning her to the core and sending a thrill of shivers down her spine. He wanted to protect her?

All her life Jolie had been forged to be the point of her own blade, the curve of her own shield. She'd always been her own protector, and the protector of others...her crew...her father...

Part of her was mad he thought she needed protection at all. But the other part lifted the edges of her lip into a smile and painted a thin trail of roses across her cheeks.

She realized then that she would let him protect her. That she would trust him with her life.

And, more startling, in a way that made her head spin, was the knowledge that she'd do the same for him.

When had she decided that Peter Pan was part of her crew?

In small pieces, the voice in her head offered. *In those times when you saw beneath the rogue mask, when you dove below the charade of villain to swim in his waters. You realized that the enemy you'd thought him to be was more than that—that he leaned into it as a way to guard himself, to wrap his heart in thorns and wire. Just like you.*

She swallowed. "I–"

Nana barked, ears flattened against her head as a group entered the room, a fivesome of pirates, led at the helm by the fiercest of them all.

"Unhand my daughter, Pan."

Chapter 43

"Neverland is as much a living, breathing entity as you are, dear reader. Please remember to treat it with respect if you hope to be invited back."
- THE MOSTLY ACCURATE TRAVELER'S GUIDE TO THE ANCIENT WORLD OF NEV-ERLAND

"Father!" she cried out, alarmed, as Peter grabbed her and crushed her into his side. "You're alive!"

He looked eons better than when she'd last seen him: shriveled, shaking, and dirty in Peter's dungeon. And, just like Peter had said, it looked like there's been no lasting damage done. Not a scratch on his face—glowing in anger—not a speckled on his clothes—covered in dark blood—nor a tooth missing from his mouth—not even the gold one he liked to keep polished.

He looked every bit the formidable Captain Hook that Neverland had always known. Except she'd never quite seen him so enraged.

Not even when he had told her that her mother had died. That had been the quiet ice of detachment. *This* was lava; hot and bubbling, it threatened to spill onto the carpet and burn the entire castle down.

When his eyes moved to hers, she saw the briefest flicker of relief, but that was quickly banished behind his rage as he turned once more to Peter.

"My crew has infiltrated your castle like an infection in your blood, Pan. At this very moment they're cutting down your precious Lost Boys, and they'll continue cutting until they are nothing more than a footnote in Neverland's history books." His voice was as eloquent as ever, like the cut of a perfectly forged dagger as it sang across her skin. "Or you can hand my daughter over, and we might leave a few of you intact. To tell the tale."

"Father," she tried. "It's not like that. This is all some misunderstanding, if you'd just lay down your weapons."

"His villainous magic must have poisoned your mind some, daughter, or have you forgotten that you are here against your will?"

She wriggled in Peter's tight grip, still flushed against the heat of his side. "He let me go!" she snapped. "I was heading to you when this fighting drew me back!"

Her father narrowed his eyes. "Some ploy of his then. You were right when you said not to trust him. He's proven his past actions aren't mistakes, they're a pattern. They're who he is. And he is the *villain*."

"You're not listening," she bit. "What about peace?"

"Peace is no longer an option," Hook spat, tilting his sword in hand.

Jolie's face fell flat. "Is that what you said before you murdered all of the fairies? Is history about to repeat, only with new players?"

He drew back, mouth parting in surprise. Beside him, the sailors shifted on uncertain feet, but their faces didn't show any shock. *They already knew.* "How did you find out?"

Jolie clenched and unclenched her fists. When Peter had first told her—first shown her—that fateful night when her father had crept into the fairy village she hadn't believed it. Hadn't wanted to believe it. The legacy that she had always fought for, always reached for, nothing more than a bloodstain to be covered up? A body to be sunk to sea?

"Why?" she croaked out, the pitiful word all that she could muster.

Why did he do it? Why did he keep it a secret?

"Now isn't the time, Jolie. I did what I had to do to protect our family."

"Mom dying doesn't justify what you did!"

"It sent a message!" he roared back, taking a step forward. "If someone goes against our legacy then it's *their entire legacy that burns.*"

She reeled back, lifting her hand to her mouth in horror. Her skin was clammy and, at her side, she felt Peter's grip tighten in reassurance. "You don't believe that."

She watched for any twitch of the brow, any waver in the eyes that might show remorse. But Captain Hook was, as always, unflappable. Unmovable. The great, ferocious Captain Hook.

"If you do then you're no captain of mine." Her words were chips of ice chiseled straight from her heart. She tried to close the gap between them but the strong hand at her arm stopped her. "You need to leave—Peter get off of me for a second!" She snapped her head up to glare at the boy who was refusing to let her go, refusing to let her plead for his safety, and her face fell.

His eyes were back to ichor and now, even more frightening, tendrils of shadowy magic were spiraling outwards from his body. "I won't let you hurt her," he said, a whisper that somehow echoed throughout the room.

"Hurt her?" her father sputtered. "You truly are mad with magic." At his side, two men raised short bows, arrows knocked taut and aimed for them both. "She's my daughter, you're the one who's using her as a human shield! Let her go so we can fight like real men!"

Peter frowned. He looked down to where his strong hands were gripping Jolie against him, molding her to his side, palm splayed across her back.

A curled shadowy finger reached out to caress her jaw.

She shivered when it made contact, the feeling like cold smoke. This did not feel like the honeyed sugared lemon healing magic he'd used on her three times now. This magic did not feel like Peter Pan at all. Her breath hitched in tune with the beat of her heart. It was dizzying, being so close to his power.

Suddenly, there was a twang of a loosened bow string, a curse as one of her father's men accidentally let an arrow fly. She barely had time for her eyes to widen, to turn her body into Peter's, before the arrow was on them—but no pain ever came.

She looked up, startled.

In front of them was a massive shadowy fist, bursting from the center of Peter's chest. It gripped the arrow not inches in front of his own heart.

"You imbecile! You could have hit her!" her father roared, elbowing his man out of the way.

For his part, Peter merely stared at the arrow.

"It was an accident," Jolie whispered, pulling away slightly, sensing the rising tension of chaos about to be unleashed. "Let it go."

He turned to her, eyes sparks as he made sure she was unharmed. "Accidents are the most deadly of all," he said, monotone, detached once again. In his palm the arrow crumbled to dust. In its place, a dozen shadowy counterparts sprung up before them, each aimed at her father and his men.

"Peter no!" she hissed, finally finding the strength to pull completely away from his side. She tugged on his arm. "Don't do this! We can still stop this!"

"This is the way of the world, Jolie. Hook versus Pan. How it was always meant to be." He bent down then, lowering himself to Nana's height. The wolf had been so still, so watching, that Jolie had nearly forgotten she was there at all.

He whispered something in the dreadwolf's ear and ran his hand along her fur. Where he touched, black fume pooled, until the dreadwolf was covered in it, and then she grew, taller and taller, until she was three times her usual size. Black flames covered her paws and red venom dripped from sharp twin fangs.

Jolie gaped at the display of magic. It was six to one. But that one now had a massive shadowhound—a beast Jolie had never thought she'd lay eyes on. Her heart fell into her feet. This was...this was a full declaration of war. Of intent to let no pirate leave this castle alive.

"Please," she tried, one last beg. "Please don't do this."

Peter stood again and gently took her cheek in his hand. "If I ask you to choose a side, would you?"

Her throat closed up at the question. All she could do was breathe out a whoosh of stale breath. *Choose a side?*

She looked at her father. His crew—*her* crew—so ready to save her, defend her, bring her home.

She looked at Peter Pan. Enemy turned something else. Willing to risk it all to keep her, not as a prisoner, but as a partner.

Her Captain was her blood.

But Peter might very well have been her heart.

She could not survive without them both.

"I–"

"Shhh," he interrupted, thumb caressing her trembling lips. "Don't answer. I don't think I want to know. And..." He faltered, staring at her as if committing her to memory. "And don't hate me for this."

"For wh–?"

She didn't get the chance to answer before a whirling stream of shadows spun up around her like she was the eye of a hurricane.

Her hands flew to her face to shield herself but the shadows never touched her. They merely encased her, a sphere with her as the center, even under her feet, which rested on the fog like it was thick glass.

"Peter!" she howled in frustration. He had trapped her away from the fighting, away from trying to talk them all down, trying to save the situation. She pressed her hands against the fog but it was thick and hard like cement. She banged on it with two fists. "Can anyone hear me!"

She threw her entire weight against it but bounced off uselessly. She began to hyperventilate. What if she was trapped there forever? What if Peter died and never let her out? Was the air thinning? Was her skin heating? She tugged at her hair in desperation. She needed to get out. She couldn't just stand there while the people she cared about got hurt.

Are you talking about Peter, or your father?

"Both," she gritted. "History be damned, I want them both to live."

With the last of her willpower, Jolie banged once more against the dome. "Please," she whispered. "Someone help me here. Pirate. Lost Boy. Fairy. I believe someone will come. I believe."

Pop!

The dome around her broke, dissolving into a scintillating sparkle of silver dust. Without it to prop her up, Jo tumbled forward, catching herself at the last second. Or, rather, something caught her.

Someone.

"Tink!" she cried, for once blissfully happy to see the fairy. "Where is he? Please, tell me he's okay!"

She raised an eyebrow, a splash of blood staining her striking blonde hair. "Your father? Or Peter? They're both destroying this castle as we speak."

"We have to stop them, they're going to kill each other. Or Peter is going to kill my father, and then I'm afraid the darkness is going to get him too."

Tinkerbell pushed Jolie out of her arms, standing her straight. "You know, I could be really pissed off at you right now. I could be gutting you like a fish because it's your fault these pirates are here, and it's your fault we're all fighting for our lives."

Jo swallowed. "But?"

"But," Tink sighed, "it's not the time. I'll kick your ass when it's all over."

"If you help me save them I'll even let you," Jo nodded fervently. "But my father is enraged, Peter is dark, I don't know–"

A roar—Nana?—shook the castle. The panes of glass on the outer wall cracked and shattered, the few paintings that remained tumbled from their hooks.

"Dust, we're running out of time," Tink swore, her teeth gnashing together in frustration. "Peter won't stop. He's too far gone right now, the dark magic in him has completely taken over."

"What do you mean?"

Tink grabbed Jo's arm and dragged her out of the dining room. "When Peter first came to Neverland, he made a deal with a dark entity. A shadow being. In return, it gave Peter power, and lots of it. Peter tries to use it for good but dark entities are like parasites. They attach onto you and feed, and they grow and grow until–"

A shadow, thick as a tree trunk, burst through the wall in front of them and straight through the other side, a poor person trapped in its clutches. Pirate or Lost Boy Jolie couldn't say.

"Peter…" she whispered in horror. The sheer destruction of it all was startling.

"It's not Peter," Tink snapped. "Haven't you been listening? This isn't him. He's tried to fight it off. For decades he's battled it down, only letting it out in small doses to keep it content." Her eyes slid to Jo's. "But now he has something he wants to protect, and he's willing to call on the darkness. Only it was all too eager to take control of the reins."

They jumped over a vicious crack in the flooring that revealed a dark hollow of earth beneath. Tink pulled her into a small alcove.

"What do we do?" Jo asked.

"Did you ever figure out his weakness?"

Jolie stopped. "No, I got close but–"

"If we can weaken Peter, maybe the darkness will recede."

"It was something about his heart," she admitted. "His weakness is his heart. I think it used to be Wendy."

"Wendy?" Tink's eyebrows rose. She shook her head. "Blasted boy. Well Wendy's gone."

"I know that!" she snapped. "So what, or who, is his heart now?"

Tinkerbell gave her an incredulous look. "It's you, daft girl."

Another roar, and this time there was a rallying cry and a stampede of feet that followed. The fighting was getting worse.

"I don't understand what I'm supposed to do!" Jo cried in frustration. "Why me? What is that supposed to mean?"

"It means you're the only chance we've got to make this right," Tink said. Then, softer, "And, for what it's worth, it's pretty obvious how you feel about each other."

Down the hall, a door burst open and a dozen small creatures made of shadows spilled out, racing towards the duo. "The darkness doesn't even know friend from foe at this point," she said, moving to stand in front of Jolie. "You'd better hurry. Think about your heartbeat, about every moment you've ever spent with Peter." She clapped Jo on the shoulder. "You can do this." The last fairy in Neverland roared and rammed her sword into the first shadow beast, which disappeared in a puff of gray smoke.

Jolie nodded, emboldened by her words. She was the daughter of Captain Hook. She had fought through the Neverwoods. She had survived an explosion. She had stood against a Neverbeast and lived to tell the tale.

She could do this.

"And Hook!" barked Tink as Jo turned away. She unclipped something from her belt and tossed it towards her. Jo caught it with practiced fingers, fingers that had ached to hold this exact thing for days.

Her sword.

"Don't let us down."

Chapter 44

"Knowing how to wield a sword is an invaluable skill in many worlds, with Neverland topping the list. In fact, if you don't know how, this author suggests you brush up on some classes prior to your journey. If your journey has already begun, I do hope you know how to run fast."
- THE MOSTLY ACCURATE TRAVELER'S GUIDE TO THE ANCIENT WORLD OF NEVERLAND

J olie's sword trilled with the song of one who had been silenced for too long as she sliced through a rolling tide of black and gray shadow monsters.

She had never seen anything like them, more animal than not, but thoroughly made of pure magic. They didn't bleed, they didn't speak, they just went for the kill. Some looked like wolves, others like wylde-beast. Some she didn't recognize at all, except for the fact that they had sharp tipped claws and teeth.

As she moved through the castle she noticed groupings of pirates and Lost Boys, no longer fighting each other, but rather fighting this new, strange enemy together.

She grunted as she slashed another aside.

As long as they keep coming, that must mean Peter's still alive, she thought. *And her father too, hopefully.*

Her mind was reeling through all of her conversations with Peter. Wendy had said his weakness was his heart. And Tink said...she said Jo was Peter's heart.

Even as she stepped over blood and dust and dirt the thought brought a hint of a smile to her face. A warmth to her belly.

Think about it later! she chided.

She was moving without a sense of direction until she spotted the gilded library doors and skidded to a halt. The library. She had poured over the tomes often enough and nothing had jumped out, but for some reason she couldn't ignore the tug in her navel that assured her that the line of thinking was the right one.

A book, then. What did that have to do with her? With his heart?

Unbidden, a memory rose to her mind.

*And who could play it well
enough*

*If deaf and dumb and
blind with love?*

*He that made this knows all
the cost,*

*For he gave all his heart
and lost.*

A scrap of paper clearly torn from a book, found in Peter's room in the Lost City.

For he gave all his heart and lost.

She'd paid it no mind then, but had it been a clue all along? She needed to find the book it came from.

She stormed towards the door. Out of thin air, a figure melted into view. Jo raised her sword, ready to run another shadow monster through, when she pulled back with a start. "Wendy?"

"Peter's heading to a dark place he won't be able to get back from," she whispered. The girl's eyes were teary pools of ocean blue—like the ocean that had claimed her life. "Will you help him?'

"Yes, yes I'm helping him but you're standing in the way!"

"What you seek isn't in there."

"You know what I am looking for?"

Wendy nodded, "Of course I do. It used to belong to me, after all."

The heart? Or the book? Jolie's mind whirled. Or were they one in the same? Was the book merely a representation of that which Peter loved?

Loved.

The word stuck in her ribs.

"Where?"

Wendy tilted her head up towards the staircase. A giant hole had been blown through it at some point by some beast. "In his room. You saw it before, you just didn't know to look."

"Of course I did," Jo muttered. Her legs had started to burn from running and her chest felt like there were needles pricking at her lungs, but Jolie knew she couldn't stop. She was on a precipice, and the longer she took the closer to the edge she got. Everyone she ever knew and loved might die. "Peter's room, Peter's room," she repeated, racing up the stairs.

Where in dust's name was his room again? She tried to mentally retrace her footsteps but she had been sleepwalking there and had been in a daze on the way back.

Left. No, right? Dust!

There was a clamoring sound and a high-pitched screech of terror as she rounded what felt to be a familiar corner. Someone was in trouble. Her side? Peter's? It didn't matter anymore. She'd save who she could.

She tore towards the sounds, harsh, discordant noises that she knew would soon haunt her nightmares.

Four shadow beasts were stalking around a pirate who was attempting to keep them at bay with a candlestick that did little more than push them back a few inches. In a few moments, they'd cease playing with their prey and they'd lunge.

"I swear to the stars I will end you!" the captive growled, his shaking words hidden behind a very thin veneer of confidence. One Jolie immediately recognized.

"Damien!" she cried, both in relief to see him, alive, unharmed, and in annoyance that after years of training he thought a candlestick was an appropriate weapon.

"Jo!" His reply was followed by the slight sag in his shoulders, a tired smile on his lips. "Oh, now you're all screwed," he sniffed at the shadows. Jolie rolled her eyes—Damien, forever a fan of the theatrics—and quickly sliced down the beasts, stepping through the dark fog residue of where they once stood to pull her friend into a hug.

"Jo! You're alive, you're okay! I mean—obviously Pan couldn't hurt you, you're Jolie Hook, dust it's good to see you–" His words cut off when Jo put a quieting finger to his lips.

"Damien." She smiled. "I never thought I'd see the day when you'd break your pacifist vows."

He puffed out his chest. "That's what best friends are for."

"That's what best friends are for," she echoed. Then, with a smart flick to his forehead: "Friends are also for calling you an idiot if you go charging into danger with a bloody candlestick."

He laughed and dropped the twisted iron piece. "Figured this way I could just knock some people out, maybe keep my vows to the stars after all."

"Speaking of...*I swear to the stars I will end you*? We need to get you a new catchphrase," she snorted. "But later. I need to go."

He caught her arm. "*We.* You think I'm letting you out of my sight again? I know I'm a jolly giant of a man, but I need you to take this as your first and only warning that I will not accept you sneaking off and getting kidnapped any more. You gave me a right scare, idiot." His voice was stern, and it brought a tinge of shameful color to Jo's cheeks.

"I'm sorry. I didn't mean for this all to spiral so out of control. I didn't think–"

"No, you didn't think!" he snapped. "Here I am, waiting for you on the ship, lo and behold you've gone gallivanting off! Do you know how worried I was?"

Jolie withered. She had never heard Damien yell at anyone except for the cook when he wanted an extra helping of pudding. But the redness in his eyes, the dark circles underneath them…he looked like a wreck. "I'm sorry, I really am. I promise I won't do it again."

"Dust is right you won't!" he said, looking as shocked as she felt that she'd folded so fast. But if there was one thing Jolie had learned over the course of this all, it was that there was only so much time you had with those you loved, and it wasn't worth wasting on frivolous things. "Now come on," he continued. "We need to find your father and kick these Lost Boys back to Neverland. And if I see Pan…well I probably won't do much but I'll glare at him!"

Jolie smiled. "I appreciate the gesture. But Damien, this is all a misunderstanding. And I need your help."

As quick as she could, Jolie recapped all the terrible things that had been happening. How Peter didn't deserve to die, how peace could maybe, finally be in their grasp after all. By the time she'd finished her retelling, not stopping at any point to catch her breath, his mouth had fallen wide open.

"I need you to get to my father. Get to Peter. Make sure they don't kill each other until I find what I need to find!" she finished, panicked. How much time had she wasted explaining this to him? Would she be too late in the end, all of this for nothing?

Outside the nearest window, Jolie watched as a streak of red—her father—tore after a darkened orb of green—Peter. They were heading for the cliffside. "We're almost out of time." She grabbed his hand. "Will you do this?"

He closed his mouth with a snap, a fire lighting up in his eyes. "I won't even pretend to understand half of what you just told me, but if it means a chance for peace, I'll do it." He ran a hand through his short hair. "But if I get magically turned into anything unnatural while trying to protect your boyfriend from your father, I'm haunting you until the end of time."

"He's not my boyf–"

"Ah, shut it Hook. You always were a bad liar."

"Here." She scooped someone's fallen knife off the ground and handed it to him. "Just in case."

Damien looked green, but nodded nonetheless, gripping the weapon tight and placing a quick kiss to her brow. "Be safe."

While she still wasn't sure that the amount of wasted time was worth it, it had provided her mind with enough space to remember something.

She knew where Peter's room was, and it was close.

Her legs screamed at her as she urged them along—*just a little further, keep going*—until his gray bedroom door lit up ahead of her like a beacon in the night.

"Yes!" she cried, nearly slamming into it in her desperation. She tugged on the handle.

It only rattled.

She pulled again. Then pushed. Nothing. Locked. Jo's eyes went upwards towards a small golden plaque.

Will only open for named invited guests.

"Jolie Hook," she demanded, pulling on the knob. Nothing happened. "Jolie Hook!" she barked again, louder. Still, the door gave nothing away. She kicked at the bottom in frustration. "Jolie. Jo. Jo Hook." She kept trying combinations of the words but nothing made the door spring open under her touch. "Dust you Peter Pan you always said I was a guest in your home!" she barked. She lifted her fist as if to punch clean through the wood, then stopped, her knuckles hovering mere inches away as her mind stuttered on a thought.

Will only open for named invited guests.

Peter never did love using her name, did he?

Jolie cleared her throat. "Darling Girl."

The latch clicked and the door swung open.

She hovered over the threshold for a moment, peering into Peter's room. Why did it feel so irreverent to be there? She had been inside once before. And yet the room felt still. Like thick magic was spread over it like a blanket.

She shook the thought out of her head. People were counting on her. As she stepped into the room, the spell broke.

It was just a bedroom. A bedroom that held the secret to Peter's weakness.

She spun in place until she saw it: the small, sloping bookshelf. Jolie crouched, running her fingers over the spines. These books were special to Peter in some way. Special enough to live up here instead of in his library.

Her fingers paused and pulled out a tome labelled Poetry Anthology IV. It was thick, bound in leather, with gold buckles keeping the weathered parchment together.

And who could play it well
enough

If deaf and dumb and
blind with love?

He that made this knows all
the cost,

For he gave all his heart
and lost.

She knew, somewhere inside of herself that relied on heartstrings instead of logic, that the poem she'd found was torn from this book. And that it, in turn, would hold Peter's weakness.

With shaking hands she popped the buckle on the front and the book fell open, split in half to reveal a secret space: a hole had been carved through the pages, a final resting place for–

"Not what you expected?" Wendy's voice whispered. Jo turned her confused eyes to the specter standing at her shoulder.

"I don't understand," she admitted, looking furtively back at the book. At the secret within.

"It's his weakness, exactly as I told you," she chided. "You can use it to help him, to banish the dark magic. Everything it has ever tainted will disappear." She paused. "Or you can kill him. The choice is yours."

"Why are you giving me a choice at all? Don't you want me to save him?"

"I do, more than anything. But I'm just a ghost, Jolie Hook. You still have a long life left to live. Just make sure you *can* live with whatever you choose."

Chapter 45

"Neverland will often bless you with something you didn't know that you needed. Make sure to pack an empty suitcase to bring this blessing home."
\- THE MOSTLY ACCURATE TRAVELER'S GUIDE TO THE ANCIENT WORLD OF NEVERLAND

When Jolie burst out into the backyard, the book magicked into pocket size and stuffed into her trousers thanks to Wendy, she nearly cried out in disbelief.

The garden was in ruin.

Flowers trampled. Trees set ablaze, the smoldering ash and smoke filling the sky. Scorched earth and spidery cracks in the dirt. Something terrible had devastated this once beautiful oasis.

"But where is everyone?" she murmured, tightening her grip on the sword. There were no pirates, no Lost Boys. No shadow beings. No Hook, no Peter, no Tink, no Damien.

There weren't any bodies either, which seemed a momentary marvel.

Her steps quickened as a fierce, unending feeling of running out of time crushed her chest. The last she had seen, her father had been chasing Peter towards the cliffs, and so that's where she rushed, begging to the stars to let her find them still alive.

As she scrambled around a crop of cherry trees—cleaved in two and fruits squashed underfoot—she saw them.

Everyone.

To the left: pirates, trapped in a smoky gray box of shadow magic. Pounding on the walls uselessly.

To her right: Lost Boys, in a similar situation, but waiting, barely even moving except to track their eyes across the field.

And before her: the rest.

Her father, Damien, Smee. On their knees, arms outstretched at their sides and attached to thick shadowy chains.

Peter stood in front of them all with that malignant blankness back on his face. He had no sword, no spear, but Jo knew he didn't need them. His magic was calling the shots.

By his side was Tinkerbell. She looked weary and bloody but still she stood tall, ready as ever to be his lieutenant no matter the costs.

Jolie would not suffer the farce any longer.

"Peter!" she called, turning the entire field's attention her way. Her steps didn't waver as she stomped up to them, putting herself between him and his captives. She turned to look back at her father, her best friend, her crew. "Are you okay?"

"Jolie! Get out of here, get back to the–" her father cried as thick tendril of shadow slithered up to his throat, cutting off his airway.

She spun to Peter. "Peter! Stop it."

He smiled at her and held out his hand. "Darling girl. You're back. I should have known you were too strong to stay in that barrier for long." He chuckled. "You never cease to surprise me."

She stared at his hand, stunned. "You...Peter, you need to stop this." She slid her sword back into her belt loop and gestured around. "This is madness! Let everyone go. Let my father go."

"Let him go?" he echoed, voice laced with confusion. His dark eyes flickered. "Why would I do that? Not when I have the chance to best my enemies once and for all? Not when they'd try to steal you away? No, no," he tutted. "That wouldn't do."

"This isn't you," she replied, mouth pressed into a line. "I know what darkness lives in you and feeds from you. I know you try to keep it at bay, but it doesn't always work. Let me help you."

"Help me?" He laughed. And it sounded so much like the laughter she'd come to know from him that she almost broke in two hearing it. "Ah...you've been talking to dear old Wendy again, haven't you?"

She swallowed but said nothing. This wasn't Peter. This was a shadow walking in his skin. But her Peter was in there somewhere, she knew he was. All she needed to do was to coax him out.

And if you can't?

She stomped on the thought.

"This isn't about Wendy. This is about you. Us. Peter, I came back for you. Not whatever version of you this is. This is not the Peter Pan I came to know. Came to..." She couldn't get the rest of the words out. Not with the entirety of her life standing around them, listening.

Coward.

"This is the real me," he crooned, tucking a loose curl behind her ear. The act was so frustratingly familiar. "And you know what I think?"

"What?" she whispered.

"I think the real you is hiding somewhere too, just waiting to take over." His eyes burned black fire as he gripped her shoulders and slowly turned her around to face the three captives on their knees.

Her father looked angry, pulling furiously against his smoky bonds.

Damien was resigned. His eyes glistened with tears of failure.

Smee looked like he was about to vomit onto the grass. He never was good at confrontation.

"I think," Peter said, slowly, words curving like a knife, "that there is a darkness in you too, darling girl."

"I don't know what you're talking about."

His breath tickled the hollow of her ear. "What if I told you that one of these prisoners is the person who murdered your mother?"

She nearly reared back in shock, but Peter's firm presence at her back meant she had nowhere to go. It couldn't be her father, not after the lengths he went to avenge her death.

Damien?

She looked at him, but the tears tracking down his cheeks were honest. And what would he have had to gain from her mother's death?

Her gaze moved again.

"You," she breathed, the thickness catching in her throat. "You did it?"

Peter snapped his fingers and the smokey gag around Smee's throat lifted. "Jolie! Don't listen to this scoundrel, to whatever poison he's honeying in your ears!"

"Poison?" Peter hummed. "Yes, poison is exactly what you bought from the fairies all these years ago. What you slipped into that poor woman's wine, wasn't it?"

There was a crashing noise against Jolie's ears. An entire ocean was raging against her, throwing her thoughts around in the fray.

Smee?

Her father's second in command? The one who'd always seemed so loyal?

She looked at Hook, but his eyes were only on Smee. Flitting between rage and confusion and betrayal.

Smee.

"The Heir Apparent..." she realized with a gasp. "Your name was on the ledger. You–" Her face crumpled. "Why Smee?" Nothing in her memories was reconciling with this news, with this complete and utter travesty.

He glared at Peter, beady eyes under bushy brows. "He's lying! Nothing he says is the truth Jolie! Nothing!"

"I don't lie," Peter snapped, hands tightening on her shoulders.

He was right. He didn't lie.

He'd tricked her, played with her, even skirted around the truth. But not once had he ever lied to her face.

"Why did you do it?" she asked, words broken by emotion.

"I didn't–"

"Why!" she roared, making to lunge forward but quickly held back by Peter. She took comfort in his fingers, in his steadying grip on her. Even if he was a shadow, even if there was blackness taking over him, she still leaned into his touch for safety. "She was good! And innocent, and she was my mother, why did you take her away from me! Why did you kill her!"

"The poison wasn't meant for her!"

Silence.

Thick, pressing silence.

"Oh this should be fun," Peter chuckled, flicking a wrist and removing the gags from both other prisoners.

"Smee." Her father's words were laced with ice. "I advise you to speak plainly now, for it might be your last chance with your tongue still attached."

"Dad?" That was Damien. His face was shattered. Jolie longed to hug him, to shield him from the fact that his father was–that he had–

"The poison was meant for you," Smee sneered, admitting the truth that they had all figured out in the last few moments.

Briefly, Jolie wondered if the pirates and Lost Boys could hear any of their words, or if the smoke was a guard against that.

Smee tugged at his chains and glared. "The great Captain Hook! Scourge of the Dead Man's Sea! You would have never seen it coming."

"Why?" Her father was hiding his sadness under rage, a facade she knew well.

"Because it was time for a new Captain. Because I had sailed under you for too long, done your slave duty for too many years, and what do I get to show for it? I get the knowledge that the ship I've loved more than anything won't even go to me in the end." His hateful eyes turned to Jolie. "It would go to her. A child. A brat. Not fit to sail a rowboat."

The smoke crept up their throats and cut off further conversation. Peter tutted, pulling Jo in close. "All that rage, all that planning...and still he messed it up." He took Jolie's chin in his hand, tilting it away from the murderer and into his own dark eyes. "You probably feel so betrayed. So disappointed. Someone you thought was a friend, was family, he's the cause for all your pain. For so much of your fear." He swiped a thumb over Jo's lips. "I know how to take that fear away."

"How?" she asked. Nearly begged. Her heart was in tatters. She could feel it peeling away inch by inch as she replayed nearly two decades of memories. Not once had she ever thought Smee held such a hatred for her. For her father.

Gently, Peter lifted her hand, lifted her sword from her belt, and fused the two together. "Embrace it, Jolie Hook. Embrace your desire for revenge. Help your mother's spirit find rest, after all these years." He nudged the small of her back and she went to stand in front of Smee. In front of her mother's murderer.

Her sword was loose in her hand. Her thoughts adrift somewhere else.

Was Peter right? Was this what her mother wanted? She looked towards her father, eyes steeled.

Her father would do it.

She looked at Damien, who shook his head desperately. His cheeks were ruddy and stained with tear tracks. This was Damien's father. She couldn't take that away from him.

Then she looked at Smee.

There was no remorse in his eyes. There was a proudness in the tilt of his chin. He did not regret what he did. Perhaps he only regretted that it didn't actually work. Perhaps he was running through a million different ways he could have taken control.

Perhaps his life was flashing before his eyes.

She lifted the sword and set it lightly where his shoulder met his neck.

"Let him speak," she said to Peter.

The smoke vanished.

"Do you have anything to say?" She tilted the sword delicately, carefully not to cut him. Not before she was ready. "My mother probably didn't get the chance for last words. But I'll be nice. For Damien's sake."

"You'd take your best friend's dad away?" He scoffed. "You're just as selfish as your father."

Jo kicked him in the stomach, relishing the pained oof that tore from his throat.

She did it again, just for the feeling of it.

"That's my darling girl," Peter cooed from behind her. She looked back. Peter had a wicked smile, a smile dripping with glee. She looked beyond him to Tinkerbell. She blinked. Tink was...frowning? She caught Jolie's eye and shook her head ever so slightly. Don't do it, she mouthed.

That was rich, coming from an ex-assassin. She had probably killed dozens, hundreds, thousands. And all Jolie wanted to do was kill once. One person. One murderer. It would tilt the balance back. It was only fair.

She turned back to Smee.

Simpering, slithering Smee.

She put the sword against his throat.

His lips peeled back, a row of cracked teeth glinting at her. "This is the moment, Jolie." She reared the sword back. "This is the moment you've been waiting for your entire life." She slashed it down, hard and unstoppable. "You've finally become exactly like your father."

The weapon hit the grass with barely a sound. Or, if there was, she didn't hear it.

All her life she'd tried to be like him. To emulate him. To be forged in his own image.

But that wasn't true.

There was a time, before her mother had died, when she'd wanted nothing more than to be exactly like *her*. Kind. Open. Giving.

Where had that Jolie gone? Miles below a cracked marble surface, was she still there? Crying out for her mother?

Smee said something that she ignored. She turned in place.

"This isn't what my mother would have wanted," she said finally, looking at Peter from tear twisted lashes. "And it's not what Peter Pan would have wanted either. Peter Pan once told me that peace was always an option, it had just taken him a while to see it. He told me that everyone's darkness is different, but they all die in the face of one thing."

He quirked an eyebrow. "What's that?"

"Love," she said. "And I'm giving mine to you. To the real Peter Pan. If he's only brave enough to come out and take it."

His eyes widened, and then they changed. Small at first, just a smudge of color like a thumb against wet paint, and then a bright green ring around his pupil. He dropped his arms, unclenched his fists. He opened his mouth to speak, then flinched and held a hand to his chest.

"Come back, Peter. Find your way out of the darkness, and I'll be here."

Around them, she noticed the smoke barriers keeping the armies at bay flicker, like a strong wind was pushing aside black curtains. It was working.

"*And who could play it well enough, if deaf and dumb and blind with love?*" she said, hand fisted in her pocket where the shrunken book was hiding. Peter stepped closer, eyes full forest green again.

"*He that made this knows all the cost, for he gave all his heart and lost,*" he finished, breathless. "Jolie."

A roar came from behind and Jo was tugged backwards by her hair. She cried at the tearing sensation, the fire in her scalp, before she was pulled against a sweaty, dirty chest, her own sword against her throat.

"Don't make another move or I'll slice her ear to ear," Smee barked. He had slipped his chains when Peter's magic wavered, she realized.

She resisted the urge to wiggle, a bead of blood already marking the column of her neck. In front of her, Tink drew her weapon and Peter raised his hand, fingers ready to unleash an attack. Jolie swallowed a cry as she saw the black veil fall across his eyes again.

"No Peter!" she yelled. "Fight it! Don't give in to the darkness!"

He raised a shaky hand to his head. He was in pain, which meant that he was fighting.

"Peter!" she called again, hoping her voice could lead him back to them, lead him back to her.

With a tremendous scream, Peter clawed at his own skin, fingers tipped in black claws, Black smoke sprung from the ground, enveloped him, and then–

BANG!

Two bodies came flying out of the smoke.

One, Peter. Whole but unconscious, tumbling to a heap too close to the cliff.

The other...

She gasped, heart clenching.

Also Peter. But Peter as a shadow. Pure, inky onyx, with two blazing eyes like rubies set in his face.

"Who are you?" she whispered. At her back, she felt Smee stiffen.

He turned to her, cracking his neck. "I am Peter Pan as he should have been. All of the power. None of the..." he paused, tapping a clawed hand to his chin, "attachments." The word was a hiss between his peeled lips. "I think it's time for a clean slate in Neverland, don't you agree?"

He lifted both arms and then sent them crashing down. As he did, the world turned dark, like he'd covered everything in black silk. Only...no, Jolie realized. It wasn't silk.

It was birds.

Hundreds of huge birds, wingspans as large as she was with heads of ebony flame. They angled towards the cliffside.

The smoke barriers around the Lost Boys and pirates fell. The chains around her father and Damien fell.

And then the beasts were upon them.

Chapter 46

The first thing Jolie did was to smash her head into Smee's nose.

Though she had decided to give him clemency, she still savored the crack as the bone shattered under her hit. He dropped her sword in panic and she scooped it up, twisting around to backhand him to the ground in a single hit.

"Stay down," she spat, moving to help Damien and her father up. The former was shaking, his hands clammy and stiff. "Get back to the castle, Damien. Hide."

He nodded and sent Smee one last fleeting, desperate look before his feet caught the wind and he was gone.

Her father seemed mostly alright. There was just a thin scratch down his cheek, and his hook had at some point twisted backwards. "I'm fine," he said, answering her unspoken question. "Are you–?"

"Fine," she echoed.

There was a moment of tense, awkward, oppressive silence. The world was descending into ruin around them, but in that instance it was just the two of them and the fierce knot of family that bound them together, for better or for worse.

"I want to let you know..." he started, then cleared his throat. "Sparing Smee and wishing for peace..." His eyes were kind as he took his human hand and gently brushed her hair from her face. "Your mother would have been so proud of you."

Jolie's breath hitched as his words filled up the hollow spaces in her bones.

"And because I know I don't say it enough, I'm proud of you too."

She almost wanted to laugh. She had been waiting to hear those words her entire life, and it had only taken a kidnapping and a dark magical demon to make it happen.

"Thanks, captain."

He smiled, then cast his eyes down. "And..."

"And?" she asked, quirking a brow. What other parts of him did he have to lay bare?

"There is not a single day when I don't feel ashamed for what I've done."

The fairies.

Somewhere further down the battlefield she locked eyes with Tinkerbell, fighting off a duo of smoke monsters. "It's not my apology to take," she said softly. "But she might listen." She nodded towards Neverland's last remaining fairy. "One day, if you're ready to try. I've found her to be surprisingly willing to make things right."

He nodded. "When the time is right." He put his hand on her shoulder. "Until then, I sure as dust need something to kill, and we can't keep standing here."

She shoved her sword into his open hand right as a flying beast zoned in, diving and snapping at them with its flaming beak. Her father roared as he cleanly sliced a wing off, spattering the ground with thick, black tar blood.

"Kill as many of these things as you can—stay away from the darkness." She twisted around but she couldn't see the shadow Peter anywhere. That wasn't a good sign. "I can fix this. I can fix this." Her hand went into her pants, pulling out the shrunken book, which immediately swirled back into size. She clutched it to her chest.

"A book?"

"Not the book," she shook her head. "What's inside–dust!" She pushed him out of the way as another beast swooped. Around them, pirates and Lost Boys were fighting once again side by side against the fell beasts. She spotted Tinkerbell taking on four by herself. "Go! Help Tink!" she cried over the din, pointing out the struggling fairy. She turned and ran before he could say another word, peeling off in the direction she had last seen Peter.

Where was he? She moved between pockets of fighting but no one bore his face. "Peter, Peter, Peter," she chanted his name. "Please be here."

Finally, she spotted him, crumpled to the ground like a broken doll. For once he seemed so small. She ran towards him, book outstretched. She could save him, could save them all, she knew it.

The ground shook, tossing her off-balance as the book slipped from her grasp.

She clambered to her feet, tripping over herself as she dove towards the poetry anthology. Her hands grasped the edges and she tugged at the same time as a dark boot slammed across her fingers.

She cried out in pain and the foot lifted slightly but didn't let go. She looked upwards.

"Now, you weren't going to use this to try and kill me, were you Jolie Hook?" the dark Peter said, almost with a mirth, like this whole situation was amusing to him.

Up close now she could truly see the cracks, places where he could never measure up to the real Peter Pan. Ripples of red lines scratched down his face, wrinkles of chaos and flimsy scabs of darkness. Where should have been freckles were deep pock marks. And his smell: fire and suffocating ash.

Her lungs burned for the smell of sugared lemons.

"Give it to me!" she snapped, tugging at the book again. Then, like being caught in an unseen fist, Jolie was lifted by magic until she was at eye level with the being, her feet no longer touching the ground.

"Let me go," she seethed.

"I can see why Peter liked you. Feisty. Too bad that love story will end without a happily ever after." He shrugged. "I no longer need him as a vessel, and you are a mere nuisance."

She shot her fist out to hit him but it went straight through—a hand grasping at smoke.

He frowned. "Not nice." The shadow drew back a fist and punched her across the jaw. Jo's head snapped to the side as pain shot like a steel arrow through her skull.

She was trapped. Her bleary eyes scanned what she could see of the battlefield as her ringing ears strained for what sounds she could make out.

They were losing.

The beasts kept falling from the sky like unwanted black raindrops. As soon as a pirate cut one down, two more sprung up in its place. The moment she heard a Lost Boy cry out in triumph, she shuddered at the follow up squelching sound of claws through flesh.

There was no way out, this was the end—

Clarity struck her the moment before shadowy, fire tipped fingers found her chest. She tasted blood in her mouth as she sealed her fate: "I want to make a deal."

Chapter 47

"This author hopes that you found this Traveler's Guide informative and entertaining. As we have reached the last chapter, I only hope that your visit to Neverland is magical. Please remember to review this book on whichever book platform is most popular in your world, this humble independent author does so appreciate it."
- THE MOSTLY ACCURATE TRAVELER'S GUIDE TO THE ANCIENT WORLD OF NEVERLAND

S he felt time slow.

She could feel the beads of sweat on her brow stop their race down her forehead, could sense the shift in the air as the wind trickled to nothing more than a slow bubbling stream.

And around her, around *them*, no one moved.

Her eyes flicked back to the shadow. She could find nothing behind his orange eyes, but there was a twist to his mouth that proved the truth: he was curious. He leaned forwards, their noses almost touching.

"What kind of deal?"

She shivered at the chill of his breath, so different from the heat of his skin. "A game. My life for yours."

He laughed, waving his hand so that his magical grip on her dissipated and she crumbled to a heap at his feet. "You misconstrue your importance in all of this. Your life is hardly an equivalent exchange."

"It's worth more than my death," she gritted. "I have a ship. A crew. Our deaths wouldn't help you, what's more bodies at your feet?" She wondered if her eyes were as flaming as his own right then. "If you win we will turn ourselves over to you."

For a moment there was no reply. Her heart quickened. Could she pull this off? She had no choice.

The shadow hummed. "The eagerness to throw your own life away doesn't surprise me. I have been watching you on your trek to save your father, after all." He gave her a small mock round of applause. "Bravo, by the way. Quite the show, best I've seen in centuries."

"It wasn't for you," she snapped. Finally finding her strength, Jo pushed herself off of the ground and stood, hands clenched.

He shrugged. "No, it was for love wasn't it? The same kind of love that now brings you on your knees before me, begging for a plea deal."

"I'm not on my—" she started, but a set of harsh, invisible fingers gripped her shoulders and shoved her to the ground once more. Her nostrils flared as she tried to keep her vitriol in. If she made him too mad he'd just kill her for her insolence and be done with it.

She needed him to accept the deal. To trust in his own ego that nothing a mere human did would ever match up to his own power.

For her crew.

Her father.

Peter.

"Do we have a deal or not?" Jolie said, holding out her hand.

"You won't win, you know."

"I know."

He huffed a laugh. "Then, Jolie Hook, I daresay we have a deal." He took her hand in his. Jo held back a scream as fire licked its way up her wrist, but she didn't pull back. She wouldn't pull back.

Finally, he dropped her fingers. "Name your game."

Her knees ached and her legs shook but she forced herself to stand again. "If there's one thing I've learned from Peter Pan," she started, "it's that sometimes the simplest games can be the hardest. A riddle."

The shadow looked unimpressed. "I have lived eons, before even the first stars made their appearances. I have eaten worlds, devoured civilizations. I have seen more than you can ever imagine...and you stake your life, your crew's lives, on a riddle?"

Her fingers itched for the sword she had left with her father. If only she could slice his tongue and be done with his patronizing words. She ignored his jeers. "*I am a drum. I am a star. I am a flame. I am not a drum. I am not a star. I am not a flame. What am I?*"

His mouth opened and her blood turned icy, but Jo soon settled when he closed it again without answering.

"How many guesses do I get?"

"One."

The flames on his fingertips turned blue in frustration and he advanced a step towards her.

"You should've asked for the rules before we started," she said, eyes slits. "You've already agreed to play my game, and there it is. Answer the riddle correctly and you have a new army. Answer it wrong..." She smiled. "Answer it wrong and you're mine. Mortal. I'll kill you, and no one will ever think on you again."

"Be quiet and let me think," he growled. The shadow left a burning patch of grass in his wake as he paced back and forth. "There is some witch's spell on your words no doubt, rattling my mind."

Finally feeling like she had the upper hand, Jolie couldn't help but to prod the monster further. "You're overthinking it. It's so simple, even a human could figure it out. Or perhaps you're not as all-knowing as you claim?"

Her words were light but the retribution was swift. Flames burned through her vision once more as the shadow grabbed her by the front of her shirt, dragging her so close she could feel her eyebrows singing.

"I would have this entire world on its knees before I listen to the lies of a doomed pirate girl."

Smoking tendrils of chaos swirled from his chest and wrapped themselves around her throat. "Make your guess," she coughed out. "Seal your fate."

"It's simple," he replied, but she saw the doubt on his face. "*I am a drum. I am a star. I am a flame.* The answer is victory."

Jolie breath caught. It was over.

Shaking fingers reached into her pockets and pulled out a crumpled, but intact, playing card. Unlike the last time she'd played a game with it, though, the picture had changed.

She held it up between them. On one side, the side facing her, was a drawing of a pirate queen manning the wheel of the Jolly Roger. On the other, she knew, was the image of an ocean soaked girl with a sad smile and a pool of blood at her feet.

Across the top of each side: *The Heart.*

"The heart," she whispered, the smoke at her neck tightening once more. "It beats as loud as a drum. It shines as bright as a star. It—"

She grunted as the shadow twisted around her. "It's ever-burning like a flame."

The shadow sneered. "I should have known. You humans are so pathetic, so weak, especially in the face of something so foolish as love."

"You lost," she croaked, trying to slap his magic away.

"And yet I am the one about to snuff your life out. Ironic, isn't it?"

"You're mad." She spat, a red tinged glob hitting him on the cheek before sliding underneath his black smokey skin.

"Mad? Maybe. But I am also power. I am endless. I am fire."

"You know what puts out fire?" she asked, as the card in her hand shimmered. A column of light burst free, blinding them both as the smell of sea water slapped them across the face. As the light dissolved, a lone figure stood in its wake. It was Wendy, the ghost girl a swirling vortex of angry waves. "Water," she finished.

Wendy launched herself at the darkness, who dropped his hold on Jolie in surprise as the duo went tumbling to the ground. The world around them become to move at normal speed again as she scratched at him, water dripping from her body and sizzling as it hit his own.

"Hurry!" the ghost girl called. "He may be mortal now but his magic is still stronger than mine, I can't hold him for long!"

Jolie scooped the book back up and nodded, thankful for whatever time she might have just been bought. Her heart beat like a wild bird as she slid down onto the grass next to the real Peter, her Peter. He still hadn't moved. She set the book down, rolling him onto his back and gently fluttering her hands around, unsure what to do.

"Peter, Peter, wake up," she urged, leaning her body over his, trying to protect him from the onslaught around them. She brushed his hair from his brow and smoothed his sweat-stained skin. Was he dead? Were the shadows capable of killing him?

Slowly, he groaned and cracked a single eye open. "Jolie?"

"Yes!" she cried, "Yes, it's me. Peter, are you alright?"

"Feel like death," he muttered.

"It's okay, I'm here. I can fix this." She tugged the book into view.

He laughed, wincing at the movement. "You figured it out. I knew you would. My darling girl." He raised his hand to grab hers. "Did you mean what you said before? About love?"

Her smile was cracked but pure as she nodded.

Peter's green eyes shone, and for a moment all was still and quiet and good. And she imagined that somewhere in the stars was a world where Jolie Hook was just a girl, and Peter Pan was just a boy, and nothing else mattered.

But this was not that world.

"Use it," he said finally. "Use my weakness and kill me."

Jolie reared back as if slapped. "What?"

He swallowed, looking behind her to where pirate and Lost Boy fought side by side. "If the darkness kills me, and believe me, he can, he becomes me. But if I die any other way, the darkness dies *with me*. All of this will stop." He smiled. "Peace. At last."

"He's mortal now Peter, we can finish this another way!"

"Mortal, maybe, but still stronger than us. All of us."

"No!" she said fiercely, crushing his hand against hers. "I'm not killing you!"

"Then why did you find it? Why bring this to me? What's the reason you came to this castle at all? To kill me."

"No. There's another way, there must be."

"Jo–"

"I hate you," she said. She could feel herself fracturing. "I hate you so much. I hate that after all this time, you weren't the nightmare I thought you'd be. That you are funny, and charming, and good. I hate that you know me, the deepest parts of me, the parts I've tried to hide, tried to destroy. I hate that I'm trying to hate you, trying to convince myself to hate you, because if I did this would be so much easier. But I can't. I can't hate you, Peter. And that's your fault."

She set her forehead against his, urging herself not to crack, to keep it together. Now was not the time to break.

"I love you," he said, and it shook loose a part of herself that had started gathering dust. A desperately longing part. "I love you so much. I love that after all this time, you weren't just the daughter of a misbegotten enemy. That you are strong, and fierce, and good. I love that you know me, the deepest parts of me, the parts I thought were dead for years. I love that the universe allowed me to love you, at least for a moment, at least for an instant. Even though it has made everything so much harder. I love you, Jolie Hook. And that's your fault."

And then his hand was at her neck, pulling her down into a kiss. His lips, soft, tender, moved against hers, desperate, longing. Jolie poured all of herself into him and took all of himself that he was offering in return. She tasted tears on her lips—hers? His? It didn't matter. This was a moment that was stretching into a lifetime, that was exploding in her mind like a universe of stars, twinkling, dazzling, blinding. She would live in that moment if she could.

But as she pulled back, she understood the kiss for what it really was.

A goodbye.

"Do it Jolie," he whispered, pulling open the cover of the book, exposing the secret place to the world. "It'll be okay. Death is just another adventure."

Jolie couldn't staunch the tears, nor could she quell the shaking of her hands as she dipped into the book and pulled Peter's weakness out.

"There's only one way to kill me, and I'll give you one free chance."

"His weakness has always been his heart, you see. It crushes him. He just wants love, after all."

"I have never imagined myself as your enemy, Jolie Hook."

She held it in her hands with reverence. The still beating heart of Peter Pan. Carved from his chest by his own magic after Wendy died. A missing heart that had allowed the darkness inside of him to flourish.

It was slick in her palms and all too warm.

Peter closed her hands over it. "It's okay. Let me do something good, for once." He smiled, soft. "I only wish we'd had more time."

Crush Peter's heart. Kill him. Banish his magic.

Crush her own heart in the process.

It was the only way.

Jolie closed her eyes and thought of her mother. For once, her image was clear; it wasn't tainted by sadness or revenge. It was simply her mother. The first person Jolie had ever loved. Peter would have adored her.

You can have anything in life if you're willing to sacrifice everything else for it. Her mother's words from long long ago echoed in her ears.

In her hand, the heart thumped.

In her chest, her heart thumped.

Something shot by her vision across the sky. A shooting star.

She pressed the heart against Peter's chest, where she now knew was just a hollow space between ribs.

"What are you–?"

"Give it back to him," she whispered, her wish floating from her lips up towards the star. If anyone could hear her, it would be the second star to the left. Her father had always told her that she had star stuff in her veins, and now was the time to unlock it. If she just believed hard enough, if she just wanted it hard enough.

"Jo–"

"Give it back to him!" she cried, shoulders shaking from a heady mix of adrenaline and exhaustion. She needed the stars to understand. She needed them to help her. "He's good, he deserves love. Take anything you want from me, I'll give you anything, but GIVE IT BACK TO HIM!"

All at once the heart began to shine, a golden bright light that blinded everything across the field. It was warm, borderline uncomfortable against her shaking fingers, and pressing against every fiber of her being. And then, slowly, it melted through Peter's chest. A heart back in its proper place.

Peter's mouth fell open. He traced a finger across his sternum. "You...what did you do?"

A sound halfway between a laugh and a sob bubbled up from Jolie's chest. "This is absolutely worth the 17-years of unfulfilled wishes."

Around them there was a screech of surprise as hundreds of flaming flying beasts burst into ashes and the remaining shadows in the castle disappeared. A roaring yell as the darkness—laying prone at Wendy's feet—curled up in on itself, twisting, thrashing, and then it too was gone.

The trees knit themselves back together. The blood siphoned away from everyone's skin. It revived those whose injuries were near death.

Jolie couldn't believe her eyes. *Good* magic, pure and light and smelling like sugared lemons, was fixing everything.

And Peter himself was glowing. Hair shining like gold, freckles like the starry sky, eyes clear, so clear they almost weren't green anymore. She helped him stand.

"You did it, Jolie," said Wendy, dissolving into view. "You saved him."

"Hi Wendy," Peter whispered, hushed, like he didn't want to break a spell.

"Hi Peter." She smiled. "You're lucky to have her, you know."

He swallowed and grabbed Jolie's hand. "I know."

Wendy's head turned northwards, her ears cocked as if she heard something. "I think I'm finally being called."

"By who?"

"Not who," she corrected lightly. "Where. The other side. It's finally ready for me."

There was a squawk and Jolie flinched, expecting a fell beast, but it was only a colorful forest bird.

"John? Michael?" Instead of answering, they landed on the ground next to Wendy before dissolving into shimmering sparks. In the place of the animal were now two boys. Young. One wearing glasses.

"You found her!" they said in unison, grabbing for Wendy's hands. "You found our sister!"

The ghost placed a kiss on the tops of both of their heads. "It's been too long. Are you both okay?"

"We're okay," they echoed.

"Are you ready to go home?"

The boys looked at Jolie, then next to her at Peter. "He turned us into birds. After you disappeared," John said.

"No," Michael interrupted, "Not him. The other one. The dark one."

John hummed, nodding. "You're right. Let's go home."

The trio stepped forwards and in the next blink they vanished.

"Where did they go?" Jolie murmured. "Wendy is a ghost. I...I'm not sure what they are."

"They went to find peace," Peter said.

Jolie looked around and found her father's face as he picked his way over to them. He looked at her, then at Peter. At the way their hands intertwined, at how their shoulders leaned against each other. His face softened. He nodded.

"Peace sounds lovely," she replied.

Epilogue

T he Jolly Roger was preparing for a feast.

The crew themselves were also helping, of course, but the majority of the planning came from the ship itself.

The downstairs dining room had widened to incredible proportions. Red banners and streamers sprung up on nearly every surface overnight and a gold threaded version of the ship's flag had mysteriously been strung up in place of the traditional black and white skull.

The cook had been creating a storm of foods: lacquered pigs with crisp apples stuffed into their mouths; sweet berries with fresh whipped cream; rainbow hued deep ocean fish; even the good wine, the wine from off-world that her father had been saving ever since the star portals had closed.

Nothing less than the best for Captain Hook's retirement party.

The energy was palpable as Jolie tightened the laces on her boots one final time and made her way above deck. The sun was graciously pouring warm rays over them that afternoon, making the wood of the freshly polished deck shine.

"Jo!" Damien called, catching her by the arm. "Thought you might be worrying yourself sick down there."

"I'm not worried," she said, smoothing down her tan trousers.

"Really? So that wasn't you I heard throwing up over the side of the bow this morning?"

She elbowed him in the side, making her way towards the banister. Below, the sea lapped at the ship as if it too was eager for the festivities to begin. She breathed in deep, the salt in the air centering her, calming the restlessness in her veins.

"You don't think this is a mistake?"

"What's a mistake?"

"This." She gestured around to where crewmates were rolling kegs, hoisting colorful celebration sails, polishing buttons and every bit of brass they could find. "All of this. You don't think it's too soon?"

Damien's friendly hand found her shoulder. "I think it's the perfect time."

Her smile was tight, one wrong move and it would snap and cut her in two, but she nodded.

They'd been back on the Jolly Roger for a month, trying to find normalcy after everything.

The pirates had picked themselves back up like nothing had changed after Jolie returned Peter's heart to him. They were a practical bunch and, truthfully, most of them told her in secret that they were glad for peace. That it eased the weights from their backs for a few moments.

Her father had declared his retirement not soon after his boots hit the deck, citing that his job as the mighty Captain Hook was complete but that he expected a raucous festivity in his honor.

The Lost Boys split in two. Half went back to the Neverwoods to make sure that all traces of dark magic had been banished from

Neverland for good. So far she hadn't heard anything otherwise, but she was always wary of any prickle at her neck, any dark shadow in the corner of her vision.

The other half stayed behind to clean up the castle. Many things knit themselves back together but the castle itself was a mess of dust and broken wood. Tinkerbell was overseeing that.

For his part, Peter had gone on a diplomatic mission to the Merfolk.

He had been insistent on making things right, as best he could. She could still remember the power behind the explosion that had knocked his treasure room into pieces.

The Mer had long memories and they seldom forgot anything, but maybe news that the pirates and the Lost Boy army had settled their differences might sway the court of public opinion.

She sighed, thinking on Peter. She missed him.

Their time together after the battle had been far too brief, especially with her father hovering around them with his knowing smile and glinting eyes. She longed to be with him again. She'd even invited him to the party, though she knew he'd be busy.

She knew that Damien still had nightmares about the battle.

She'd woken him from the throes of fear more than a few times, clutching at him knowingly to try and sooth his wild heart. Smee was a prisoner in the bowels of the ship, for now, until they could come up with a more permanent solution. Damien visited him, but he never said anything. He just stared at his father the whole time.

And Jolie...

She no longer felt held together by revenge and her father's legacy. She had her own legacy to uphold now. She felt more whole, more herself, than she had since before her mother had died, and the feeling was light as air. Freeing. There were no more vengeful words disquieting her thoughts. No more enemies to slay.

Peace. For as long as that would last.

"Come, Jo," Damien said, reaching her hand. "I think they're ready now."

"I just need a minute. I'll meet you down there, okay?" She smiled and hoped that it reached her eyes.

"Don't be late for your own father's party," he winked, slapping her playfully on the shoulder before heading the opposite direction.

When she was sure that he was out of earshot—him and the rest of the crew—she let herself feel it.

The rotting feeling that had been tearing at her since the battle. Thick branches of wrongness that were feasting their way through her body.

It bubbled up between her lips and she coughed into her hand, glaring at the black blood staining her fingers. Jolie clenched the evidence into a fist and shoved it into her trousers.

No one needed to know.

***

"For decades I have served as captain of this ship. The mighty Captain Hook, fiercest pirate in all of Neverland."

A roar of agreement went up, followed by the clanking of ale tankards against wood tables.

Jolie smiled from her spot at the table with him. Her father did love his dramatic speeches. It was just the two of them at the head, and from there she could see every single face of the crew. The crew who had barreled into the dangers of Peter's castle just to save her, and then fought against dark monsters to save all of Neverland.

She was so proud of them.

"We have fought, looted, and made more coin than we'll ever rightly need—and it's been a pleasure. In this new era, an age of peace, I know that this crew, this ship, will continue to find prosperity. And it is with an open heart that I gladly step down my post as Captain, knowing that she will be in good hands." He raised his ale. "So raise your drinks, raise 'em up high like only pirates can! Three cheers for my legacy!"

Whoops went up across the crowd.

"Three cheers for the Roger, and the best crew she's ever had!"

More yells, and stomps this time for good measure.

"And three cheers for her new captain, Jolie Hook!"

Her breath caught in her throat at the words. She'd known he was going to say that, he had told her as much last week, but to hear the words from his mouth, after so long, didn't feel real.

The cheer that clambered up like monkeys on a vine was deafening. Even the ship itself seemed to shout her name. Her ears reddened as she rose. She held her hand out for her father, but he surprised her by crushing her into a bruising hug instead, sweeping her clean off her feet for a moment.

When he set her back down, he did so with care, his eyes gentle.

"It was always going to be you, Jolie. I know you'll take care of them."

"Like you always taught me."

"Like you always taught yourself," he amended. He grabbed her hand and raised it high. "Captain Hook!"

"Captain Hook!" came back the echoing call. Jolie laughed again, breathless. Her crew. Her people. Her ship. No longer her father's legacy, but her own. The girl who had helped broker peace in Neverland.

Her heart clenched, knowing that she didn't do it alone. Peace wouldn't have been possible without Peter Pan. Idealistically, roguish, villainous Peter Pan.

"Speech!"

The voice was a familiar pull of a drawstring, sending her gaze like an arrow to the back corner of the room where two people lounged against a pillar.

Tinkerbell, a massive mug of ale in one hand, a turkey leg in the other, smiling—no, grinning—and looking at ease for once.

And next to her, of course, was Peter Pan.

Wild curly hair. A smattering of freckles. A smile to dazzle even the stars. Her mouth went dry looking at him, and for a moment all she could do was hold herself back from running straight into his arms. But there was a room full of people waiting for her to say something. So she said the only thing she possibly *could* say in that moment: "To peace!"

***

Peter found her later, when dusk had settled over the horizon and the lanterns of the Jolly Roger were lit. Her attention had been captured by pirate after pirate, until she finally shooed them away, telling them to speak further with her second-in-command. Damien was always better at conversations than her.

She was leaning against the railing at the front of the ship, watching as a school of glowing fish passed underneath. Her mother had always said that was a sign of good luck. Warm hands slid around her, pulling her close. She breathed in sugared lemons as she relaxed into his chest, finally letting the anticipation of the day seep out from the bottom of her feet.

"You came," she said. "I thought you'd be busy politicking with the Mer."

"The Mer can wait. I wouldn't have missed it for the world." He set his head atop hers, until she twisted in his arms so that they were face to face. She drank him in, like a lost man finally reaching water. Jolie ran her hand lightly over his brow, down his cheek, across his jaw.

He quirked an eyebrow at her.

"Just making sure you're not really an apparition," she said, smiling.

He laughed, his dimples popping free. "No more apparitions, I promise."

"Good," she murmured, "because then I wouldn't be able to do this." She pulled him closer, brushing her lips against his at first tenderly, then with gusto. He wrapped his arms so firmly around her she was worried they'd never come apart again as she melted into his solid warmth. He tasted sugared lemons.

"Not to break up this little love-fest, but can I get a word in before he kisses your lips off?"

Jolie leaned past Peter's shoulders, grinning. "Hello Tink."

"Hello, pirate girl." She crossed her arms, shifting, "Or, Pirate Captain, I guess. Congrats."

"Be nice or I'll throw you off my ship," she warned, but there was no malice in her voice, not even a hint of animosity. Tinkerbell, and any Lost Boy, was welcome on the Jolly Roger for as long as she was behind its wheel. After setting the score straight on some of Neverland's history, the crew were all too willing to mend that bridge.

There was no more room for silly wars in her and Peter's version of Neverland, a version they had fought for and would *keep* fighting for.

"I'd like to see you try," she snorted.

Jo untangled herself from Peter's embrace, immediately shivering at the chilly night air. "You asked for a word and I'll give you two. Be quick because I think my presence is about to be missed." She spotted Damien's head poking out the door, waving her back inside, down to where the party was swelling louder and drunker as the night progressed.

The fairy held up a finger, "Star," then another, "Portals".

Jolie blinked confused.

Star Portals used to be, in the days before the Mer War, the gateway into other worlds. Wendy had come through on one, and so had Peter, a long time ago. Neverland used to host a rolling tide of visitors, and you could visit other worlds in turn, trade with them, even move there. Jolie had been too young to use the portals before they'd sealed up for good after the fairies had been wiped out.

Peter groaned. "Straight into business Tink? I was hoping for a little more alone time before..."

"Before what?" Jolie prompted, looking between the duo.

"We've been cleaning up the castle ever since, well, you know. The library got hit hard. Books and pages everywhere. It's taken us weeks to just see the floor again."

"The point?" Jo prompted, annoyed that her alone time with Peter was being hijacked.

"The point," she stressed, "is that we had to read a lot of torn pages, match them to books. Peter was a stickler about the whole thing, and since his magic is gone–"

"Your magic is gone?" Jolie interrupted, spinning around. "You didn't tell me that!"

He scratched his head awkwardly. "I was going to, it just never seemed like the right time."

"Well do you–"

"Anyways!" Tink interrupted, tapping her foot. "We found something interesting. Something old. Didn't even know we had a book on the Star Portals, but leave it to Peter to covet weird old things."

"What did you find?"

Tink's eyes flared with light as a slow smile spread to her lips. She looked to Peter, who in turn looked down at Jolie. He took her hand and ran his fingers over her knuckles.

"We found a way to open them again. We can open the Star Portals."

A note from the author

T hank you so much, dear reader, for making it this far with me. If at least one person reads this page, it will have meant the world to a debut indie author.

I would be so appreciative if you would leave a rating or review of "The Legacy of Villains" on your platform of choice! It truly helps independent authors survive, and I'd love to know what from this book resonated with you.

I'd also love to chat with you on socials. You can find me at @JulietLockwood_Writes on Instagram, and Juliet Lockwood on Goodreads.

From the bottom of my heart, thank you for reading.

- Juliet Lockwood

Acknowledgement

This book wouldn't have been able to exist without so many amazing people.

My family, who have always encouraged me to keep on writing, even when I wanted to stuff all of my work in a closet and never pick up a keyboard again. You've never had any doubts, even when I was full of them.

My husband, my number one fan for the rest of my life.

My cats, lizards, and dog, for providing much needed cuddle breaks when I had writer's block.

The fine folks of my TWS writing cohort. Probably the single best group of people to have at your back while you try to navigate the muddied waters of being a writer. Thank you for all those late-night workshop sessions and being the first set of eyes on so many of my plots and characters. Also, for sending glorious memes and inspiration.

All of my friends who have stood at my side for so many years, cheering me on to follow my passions.

Ms. Emily Darby, teacher of grade 12 Writer's Craft at Glebe Collegiate Institute. She probably won't remember me, but her words to keep going have been at the front of my mind every time I write.

To all of my readers (ARC and otherwise), people who preordered, or anyone who follows me on social media: I do this for you. I can only hope that you enjoyed the journey.

Until next time,

Juliet Lockwood

About the author

Juliet Lockwood is an author based out of Ottawa, Ontario. Like any good Canadian, she believes that the fix for writer's block is a bag of all dressed chips, a butter tart (raisins, please), and listening to The Tragically Hip.

When not writing, she devours books, gets sucked into video games, and explores the city with her husband and son.

You can find her online here:

@JulietLockwood_Writes (Instagram)

@Juliet.Lockwood (TikTok)

www.JulietLockwoodAuthor.com